JOSEF

BERLIN, GERMANY—1938

CRACK! BANG!

Josef Landau shot straight up in bed, his heart racing. That sound—it was like someone had kicked the front door in. Or had he dreamed it?

Josef listened, straining his ears in the dark. He wasn't used to the sounds of this new flat, the smaller one he and his family had been forced to move into. They couldn't afford their old place, not since the Nazis told Josef's father he wasn't allowed to practice law anymore because he was Jewish.

Across the room, Josef's little sister, Ruth, was still asleep. Josef tried to relax. Maybe he'd just been having a nightmare.

Something in the darkness outside his room moved with a grunt and a scuffle.

Someone was in the house!

Josef scrambled backward on his bed, his eyes wide. There was a shattering sound in the next room—*crisssh!* Ruth woke up and screamed. Screamed in sheer blind terror. She was only six years old.

"Mama!" Josef cried. "Papa!"

Towering shadows burst into the room. The air seemed to crackle around them like static from a radio. Josef tried to hide in the corner of his bed, but shadowy hands snatched at him. Grabbed for him. He screamed even louder than his little sister, drowning her out. He kicked and flailed in a panic, but one of the shadows caught his ankle and dragged him face-first across his bed. Josef clawed at his sheets, but the hands were too strong. Josef was so scared he wet himself, the warm liquid spreading through his nightclothes.

"No!" Josef screamed. *"No!"*

The shadows threw him to the floor. Another shadow picked up Ruth by the hair and slapped her.

"Be quiet!" the shadow yelled, and it tossed Ruth down on the floor beside Josef. The shock shut Ruth up, but only for a moment. Then she wailed even harder and louder.

"Hush, Ruthie. Hush," Josef begged her. He took her in his arms and wrapped her in a protective hug. "Hush now."

They cowered together on the floor as the shadows picked up Ruth's bed and threw it against the wall. *Crash!* The bed broke into pieces. The shadows tore down pictures, pulled drawers from their bureaus, and flung clothing everywhere. They broke lamps and lightbulbs. Josef and Ruth clung to each other, terrified and wet-faced with tears.

The shadows grabbed them again and dragged them into the living room. They threw Josef and Ruth on the floor once more and flicked on the overhead light. As Josef's eyes adjusted, he saw the seven strangers who had invaded his home. Some of them wore regular clothes: white shirts with the sleeves rolled up, gray slacks, brown wool caps, leather work boots. More of them wore the brown shirts and red swastika armbands of the *Sturmabteilung*, Adolf Hitler's "storm troopers."

Josef's mother and father were there too, lying on the floor at the feet of the Brownshirts.

"Josef! Ruth!" Mama cried when she saw them. She lunged for her children, but one of the Nazis grabbed her nightgown and pulled her back.

"Aaron Landau," one of the Brownshirts said to Josef's father, "you have continued to practice law despite the fact that Jews are forbidden to do so under the Civil Service Restoration Act of 1933. For this crime against the German people, you will be taken into protective custody."

Josef looked at his father, panicked.

"This is all a misunderstanding," Papa said. "If you'd just give me a chance to explain—"

The Brownshirt ignored Papa and nodded at the other men. Two of the Nazis yanked Josef's father to his feet and dragged him toward the door.

"No!" Josef cried. He had to do something. He leaped to his feet, grabbed the arm of one of the men carrying his father, and tried to pull him off. Two more of the men jerked Josef away and held him as he fought against them.

The Brownshirt in charge laughed. "Look at this one!" he said, pointing to the wet spot on Josef's nightclothes. "The boy's pissed himself!"

The Nazis laughed, and Josef's face burned hot with shame. He struggled in the men's arms, trying to break free. "I'll be a man soon enough," Josef told them. "I'll be a man in six months and eleven days."

The Nazis laughed again. "Six months and eleven days!" the Brownshirt said. "Not that he's counting." The Brownshirt suddenly turned serious. "Perhaps you're close enough that we should take you to a concentration camp too, like your father."

"No!" Mama cried. "No, my son is just twelve. He's just a boy. Please—don't."

Ruth wrapped herself around Josef's leg and wailed. "Don't take him! Don't take him!"

The Brownshirt scowled at the noise and gave the men carrying Aaron Landau a dismissive wave. Josef watched as they dragged Papa away to the sounds of Mama's sobs and Ruth's wails.

"Don't be so quick to grow up, boy," the Brownshirt told Josef. "We'll come for you soon enough."

The Nazis trashed the rest of Josef's house, breaking furniture and smashing plates and tearing curtains. They left as suddenly as they had come, and Josef and his sister and mother huddled together on their knees in the middle of the room. At last, when they had cried all the tears they could cry, Rachel Landau led her children to her room, put her bed back together, and hugged Josef and Ruth close until morning.

....

In the days to come, Josef learned that his family wasn't the only one the Nazis had attacked that night. Other Jewish homes and businesses and synagogues were destroyed all over Germany, and tens of thousands of Jewish men were arrested and sent to concentration camps. They called it *Kristallnacht*, the Night of Broken Glass.

The Nazis hadn't said it with words, but the message was clear: Josef and his family weren't wanted in Germany anymore. But Josef and his mother and sister weren't going anywhere. Not yet. Not without Josef's father.

Mama spent weeks going from one government office to another, trying to find out where her husband was and how to get him back. Nobody would tell her anything, and Josef began to despair that he would never see his father again.

And then, six months after he'd been taken away, they got a telegram. A telegram from Papa! He'd been released from a concentration camp called Dachau, but only on condition that he leave the country within fourteen days.

Josef didn't want to leave. Germany was his home. Where would they go? How would they live? But the Nazis had told them to get out of Germany twice now, and the Landau family wasn't going to wait around to see what the Nazis would do next.

ISABEL

IT TOOK ONLY TWO TRIES TO GET THE SCRAWNY calico kitten to come out from under the pink cinder-block house and eat from Isabel Fernandez's hand. The cat was hungry, just like everyone else in Cuba, and its belly quickly won out over its fear.

The cat was so tiny it could only nibble at the beans. Its tummy purred like an outboard motor, and it butted its head against Isabel's hand in between bites.

"You're not much to look at, are you, kitty?" Isabel said. Its fur was scraggly and dull, and Isabel could feel the cat's bones through its skin. The kitten wasn't too different from her, Isabel realized: thin, hungry, and in need of a bath. Isabel was eleven years old, and all lanky arms and legs. Her brown face was splotchy with freckles, and her thick black hair was cut short for summer and pulled back behind her ears. She was barefoot like always, and wore a tank top and shorts.

The kitten gobbled up the last of the beans and mewed pitifully. Isabel wished she had something else to give it, but this food was already more than she could spare. Her lunch hadn't been much bigger than the cat's—just a few beans and a small pile of white rice. There had been rationing and food coupon books back when Isabel was little. But a few years ago, in 1989, the Soviet Union had fallen, and Cuba had hit rock bottom. Cuba was a communist country, like Russia had been, and for decades the Soviets had been buying Cuba's sugar for eleven times the price and sending the little island food and gasoline and medicine for free.

But when the Soviet Union went away, so did all their support. Most of the farms in Cuba grew only sugarcane. With no one to overpay for it, the cane fields dried up, the sugar refineries closed, and people lost their jobs. Without Russia's gas, they couldn't run the tractors to change the fields over to food, and without the extra food, the Cuban people began to starve. All the cows and pigs and sheep had been slaughtered and eaten. People had even broken into the Havana Zoo and eaten the animals, and cats like this little kitten had ended up on dinner tables.

But nobody was going to eat *this* cat. "You'll just be our little secret," Isabel whispered.

"Hey, Isabel!" Iván said, making her jump. The cat skittered away underneath the house.

Iván was a year older than Isabel and lived next door. He and Isabel had been friends as long as she could remember. Iván was lighter skinned than Isabel, with curly dark hair. He wore sandals, shorts, a short-sleeved, button-down shirt, and a cap with a fancy letter *I* on

REFUGEE

For John Gratz

Library of Congress Cataloging-in-Publication Data available

ISBN 978-0-545-88083-1

201918171615141312   18 19 20 21

Printed in the U.S.A   23
First edition, August 2017
Book design by Nina Goffi
Map art by Jim McMahon

ALAN GRATZ

REFUGEE

SCHOLASTIC PRESS / NEW YORK

Also by Alan Gratz

Grenade
Projekt 1065
Prisoner B-3087
Code of Honor
The Brooklyn Nine
Samurai Shortstop

More Praise for REFUGEE

A *New York Times* Notable Book
An Amazon Best Book of the Year
A *Kirkus Reviews* Best Book of the Year
A *Publishers Weekly* Best Book of the Year
A Junior Library Guild Selection

"This heart-stopping novel is not only compelling—it is *necessary*."
—Judy Blundell, National Book Award-winning author of *What I Saw and How I Lied*

"With urgent, clear-eyed storytelling, *Refugee* compellingly
explores the desperation and strength that unites those struggling
for a place to call home." —Eliot Schrefer, *New York Times* bestselling author
and two-time National Book Award finalist for *Threatened* and *Endangered*

"Powerful. *Refugee* is more than a story about children fleeing their
homelands, it is a story about what unites us all: love, family,
and perseverance." —Christina Diaz Gonzalez, award-winning author of *Moving Target*

"A gripping, visceral, and hold-your-breath intense story
of three young refugees." —John Green, #1 *New York Times* bestselling author
of *Turtles All the Way Down*

"An intelligent, human, harrowing read." —Ellen Silva, *NPR*

eant to be read, discussed, and shared widely." —*School Library Journal*

A haunting fictional treatment of historic events." —*Booklist* it—the logo of the Havana baseball team the *Industriales.* He wanted to be a professional baseball player when he grew up, and he was good enough that it wasn't a crazy dream.

Iván plopped to the dusty ground beside Isabel. "Look! I found a bit of dead fish on the beach for the cat."

Isabel recoiled at the smell, but the kitten came running back, eating greedily from Iván's hand.

"She needs a name," Iván said. Iván gave names to everything—the stray dogs who wandered the town, his bicycle, even his baseball glove. "How about Jorge? Or Javier? Or Lázaro?"

"Those are all boy names!" Isabel said.

"Yes, but they are all players for the Lions, and she's a little lion!" The Lions was the nickname of the *Industriales.*

"Iván!" his father called from next door. "I need your help in the shed."

Iván climbed to his feet. "I have to go. We're building . . . a doghouse," he said, before sprinting away.

Isabel shook her head. Iván thought he was being sneaky, but Isabel knew exactly what he and his father were building in their shed, and it wasn't a doghouse. It was a boat. A boat to sail to the United States.

Isabel was worried the Castillos were going to get caught. Fidel Castro, the man who ruled Cuba as president and prime minister, wouldn't allow anyone to leave the country—especially not to go to the United States—*el norte*, as Cubans called it. *The north.* If you were caught trying to leave for *el norte* by boat, Castro would throw you in jail.

Isabel knew that, because her own father had tried and had been thrown in jail for a year.

Isabel noticed her father and grandfather heading down the road toward the city to stand in line for food. She put the little kitten back under her house and ran inside for her trumpet. Isabel loved tagging along on trips into Havana to stand on a street corner and play her trumpet for pesos. She never did make much. Not because she wasn't good. As her mother liked to say, Isabel could play the storm clouds from the sky. People often stopped to listen to her and clap and tap their feet. But the only people who could afford to give her pesos were the tourists—visitors from Canada or Europe or Mexico. Ever since the Soviet Union had collapsed, the only currency most Cubans had were the booklets you got stamped when you went to pick up your food rations from the store. And food ration booklets were pretty worthless anyway—there wasn't enough food to go around, whether you had a booklet or not.

Isabel caught up with her father and grandfather, then parted ways with them on the Malecón, the broad road that curved along the seawall on Havana Harbor. On one side of the road were blocks of green and yellow and pink and baby blue homes and shops. The paint was peeling, and the buildings were old and weathered, but they still looked grand to Isabel. She stood on the wide promenade, where it seemed all of Havana was on display. Mothers carried babies in slings. Couples kissed under palm trees. Buskers played rumbas on guitars and drums. Boys took turns diving into the sea. Tourists took pictures. It was Isabel's favorite place in the whole city.

Isabel tossed an old ball cap on the ground, on the off chance that one of the tourists actually had a peso to spare. She lifted the trumpet to her lips. As she blew, her fingers tapped out the notes she knew by heart. It was a salsa tune she liked to play, but this time she listened past the music. Past the noise of the cars and trucks on the Malecón, past the people talking as they walked by, past the crash of the waves against the seawall behind her.

Isabel was listening for the *clave* underneath the music, the mysterious hidden beat inside Cuban music that everybody seemed to hear except her. An irregular rhythm that lay over the top of the regular beat, like a heartbeat beneath the skin. Try as she might, she had never heard it, never felt it. She listened now, intently, trying to hear the heartbeat of Cuba in her own music.

What she heard instead was the sound of breaking glass.

MAHMOUD

ALEPPO, SYRIA—2015

MAHMOUD BISHARA WAS INVISIBLE, AND that's exactly how he wanted it. Being invisible was how he survived.

He wasn't literally invisible. If you really looked at Mahmoud, got a glimpse under the hoodie he kept pulled down over his face, you would see a twelve-year-old boy with a long, strong nose, thick black eyebrows, and short-cropped black hair. He was stocky, his shoulders wide and muscular despite the food shortages. But Mahmoud did everything he could to hide his size and his face, to stay under the radar. Random death from a fighter jet's missile or a soldier's rocket launcher might come at any moment, when you least expected it. To walk around getting noticed by the Syrian army or the rebels fighting them was just inviting trouble.

Mahmoud sat in the middle row of desks in his classroom, where the teacher wouldn't call on him. The desks were wide enough for three students at each, and Mahmoud sat between two other boys named Ahmed and Nedhal.

Ahmed and Nedhal weren't his friends. Mahmoud didn't have any friends.

It was easier to stay invisible that way.

One of the teachers walked up and down the hall ringing a handbell, and Mahmoud collected his backpack and went to find his little brother, Waleed.

Waleed was ten years old and two grades below Mahmoud in school. He too wore his black hair cropped short, but he looked more like their mother, with narrower shoulders, thinner eyebrows, a flatter nose, and bigger ears. His teeth looked too big for his head, and when he smiled he looked like a cartoon squirrel. Not that Waleed smiled much anymore. Mahmoud couldn't remember the last time he'd seen his brother laugh, or cry, or show any emotion whatsoever.

The war had made Mahmoud nervous. Twitchy. Paranoid. It had made his little brother a robot.

Even though their apartment wasn't far away, Mahmoud led Waleed on a different route home every day. Sometimes it was the back alleys; there could be fighters in the streets, who were always targets for the opposition. Bombed-out buildings were good too. Mahmoud and Waleed could disappear among the heaps of twisted metal and broken cement, and there were no walls to fall on them if an artillery shell went whizzing overhead. If a plane dropped a barrel bomb, though, you needed walls. Barrel bombs were filled with nails and scrap metal, and if you didn't have a wall to duck behind you'd be shredded to pieces.

It hadn't always been this way. Just four years ago, their home city of Aleppo had been the biggest, brightest, most modern city in Syria. A crown jewel of the Middle East. Mahmoud remembered neon malls, glittering skyscrapers, soccer stadiums, movie theaters, museums. Aleppo had history too—a long history. The Old City, at the heart of Aleppo, was built in the 12th century, and people had lived in the area as early as 8,000 years ago. Aleppo had been an amazing city to grow up in.

Until 2011, when the Arab Spring came to Syria.

They didn't call it that then. Nobody knew a wave of revolutions would sweep through the Middle East, toppling governments and overthrowing dictators and starting civil wars. All they knew from images on TV and posts on Facebook and Twitter was that people in Tunisia and Libya and Yemen were rioting in the streets, and as each country stood up and said "Enough!" so did the next one, and the next one, until at last the Arab Spring came to Syria.

But Syrians knew protesting in the streets was dangerous. Syria was ruled by Bashar al-Assad, who had twice been "elected" president when no one was allowed to run against him. Assad made people who didn't like him disappear. Forever. Everyone was afraid of what he would do if the Arab Spring swept through Syria. There was an old Arabic proverb that said, "Close the door that brings the wind and relax," and that's exactly what they did;

while the rest of the Middle East was rioting, Syrians stayed inside and locked their doors and waited to see what would happen.

But they hadn't closed the door tight enough. A man in Damascus, the capital of Syria, was imprisoned for speaking out against Assad. Some kids in Daraa, a city in southern Syria, were arrested and abused by the police for writing anti-Assad slogans on walls. And then the whole country seemed to go crazy all at once. Tens of thousands of people poured into the streets, demanding the release of political prisoners and more freedom for everyone. Within a month, Assad had turned his tanks and soldiers and bombers on the protestors—on his own *people*—and ever since then, all Mahmoud and Waleed and anyone else in Syria had known was war.

Mahmoud and Waleed turned down a different rubble-strewn alley than the day before and stopped dead. Just ahead of them, two boys had another boy up against what was left of a wall, about to take the bag of bread he carried.

Mahmoud pulled Waleed behind a burned-out car, his heart racing. Incidents like this were common in Aleppo lately. It was getting harder and harder to get food in the city. But for Mahmoud, the scene brought back memories of another time, just after the war had begun.

Mahmoud had been going to meet his best friend, Khalid. Down a side street just like this one, Mahmoud found Khalid getting beaten up by two older boys. Khalid was a Shia Muslim in a country of mostly Sunni Muslims. Khalid was clever. Smart. Always quick to raise his hand in class, and always with the right answer. He and Mahmoud had known each other for years, and even though Mahmoud was Sunni and Khalid was Shia, that had never mattered to them. They liked to spend their afternoons and weekends reading comic books and watching superhero movies and playing video games.

But right then, Khalid had been curled into a ball on the ground, his hands around his head while the older boys kicked him.

"Not so smart now, are you, pig?" one of them had said.

"Shia should know their place! This is Syria, not Iran!"

Mahmoud had bristled. The differences between Sunnis and Shiites was an excuse. These boys had just wanted to beat someone up.

With a battle cry that would have made Wolverine proud, Mahmoud had launched himself at Khalid's attackers.

And he had been beaten up as badly as Khalid.

From that day forward, Mahmoud and Khalid were marked. The two older boys became Mahmoud's and Khalid's own personal bullies, delivering repeated beat-downs between classes and after school.

That's when Mahmoud and Khalid had learned

how valuable it was to be invisible. Mahmoud stayed in the classroom all day, never going to the bathroom or the playground. Khalid never answered another question in class, not even when the teacher called on him directly. If the bullies didn't notice you, they didn't hit you. That's when Mahmoud had realized that together, he and Khalid were bigger targets; alone, it was easier to be invisible. It was nothing they ever said to each other, just something they each came to understand, and within a year they had drifted apart, not even speaking to each other as they passed in the hall.

A year after that, Khalid had died in an airstrike anyway.

It was better not to have friends in Syria in 2015.

Mahmoud watched as these two boys attacked the boy with the bread, a boy he didn't even know. He felt the stirrings of indignation, of anger, of sympathy. His breath came quick and deep, and his hands clenched into fists. "I should do something," he whispered. But he knew better.

Head down, hoodie up, eyes on the ground. The trick was to be invisible. Blend in. Disappear.

Mahmoud took his younger brother by the hand, turned around, and found a different way home.

JOSEF

1 day from home

IT WAS LIKE THEY WERE INVISIBLE.

Josef and his sister followed their mother through the crowd at the Lehrter Bahnhof, Berlin's main railway station. Josef and Ruth each carried a suitcase, and their mother carried two more—one for herself, and one for Josef's father. No porters rushed to help them with their bags. No station agents stopped to ask if they needed help finding their train. The bright yellow Star of David armbands the Landaus wore were like magical talismans that made them disappear. Yet no one bumped into them, Josef noticed. All the station attendants and other passengers gave them a wide berth, flowing around them like water around a stone.

The people chose not to see them.

On the train, Josef and his family sat in a compartment labeled *J*, for *Jew*, so no "real" Germans would sit there by accident. They were headed for Hamburg, on the north coast, where his father would meet them to board their ship. The day they had gotten Papa's telegram, Josef's mother booked tickets for all four of them to the only place that would take them: an island half a world away called Cuba.

Ever since the Nazis had taken over six years ago, Jews were fleeing Germany. By now, May of 1939, most countries had stopped admitting Jewish refugees, or had lots of official applications you had to fill out and file and pay for before they would let you in. Josef and his family hoped to one day make it to America, but you couldn't just sail into New York Harbor. The United States only let in a certain number of Jews every year, so Josef's family planned to live in Cuba while they waited.

"I'm hot," Ruthie said, pulling at her coat.

"No, no," her mother said. "You must leave your coat on and never go anywhere without it, do you understand? Not until we reach Cuba."

"I don't want to go to Cuba," Ruth whined as the train got under way.

Mama pulled Ruth into her lap. "I know, dear. But we have to go so all of us will be safe. It will be an adventure."

Ruthie would have started kindergarten that year if Jews were still allowed to go to school. She had bright eyes, wild brown hair cut in a bob and parted on the side, and a little gap between her two front teeth that made her look like a chipmunk. She wore a dark blue wool dress with a white sailor's collar and carried her white corduroy stuffed rabbit, Bitsy, everywhere she went.

Ruthie had been born the year Adolf Hitler was elected chancellor of Germany. She'd never known any other life except this one. But Josef remembered how it used to be. Back when people saw them. Back when they were Germans.

They had gotten up early and it had been a stressful day, and soon Ruthie was asleep in Mama's lap, and Mama dozed with her. As he watched them sleep, Josef wondered if anyone would really be able to tell they were Jews if they weren't in a Jewish compartment, wearing armbands with the Star of David on them.

Josef remembered a time in class, back when he was allowed to go to school. His teacher, Herr Meier, had called him to the front of the room. At first Josef thought the teacher was going to ask him to do a math problem on the board. Instead, Herr Meier lowered a screen with the faces and profiles of Jewish men and women on it and proceeded to use Josef as an example of how to tell a real German from a Jew. He turned Josef this way and that, pointing out the curve of his nose, the slant of his chin. Josef felt the heat of that embarrassment all over again, the humiliation of being talked about like he was an animal. A specimen. Something subhuman.

Without these stupid armbands, without the letter *J* stamped on his passport, would anyone know he was Jewish?

Josef decided to find out.

He left the compartment quietly and walked along the corridor past the other Jewish families in their compartments. Beyond the next door was the "German" part of the train.

Heart in his throat, skin tingling with goose bumps, Josef took the paper armband with the Star of David off his arm, slid it into the inside pocket of his jacket, and stepped through the door.

Josef tiptoed down the corridor. The "German" train car didn't feel any different than the Jewish car. German families talked and laughed and argued in their compartments, just like Jews. They ate and slept and read books like Jews.

Josef caught his reflection in one of the windows. Straight brown hair slicked back from his pale white forehead, brown eyes behind wire-frame glasses that sat on a short nose, ears that stuck out maybe a little too far. He was about average height for his age, and he wore a gray double-breasted pin-stripe jacket, brown trousers, and a white shirt and blue tie. Nothing about him actually matched the pictures on Herr Meier's presentation on how to identify a Jew. Josef couldn't think of any Jewish people he knew who *did* look like those pictures.

The next car was the dining car. People sat at little tables, smoking, eating, and drinking as they chatted or read the newspaper or played cards. The man at the concession stand sold newspapers, and Josef took one and put a coin on the counter.

The concession stand man smiled. "Buying a paper for your father?" he asked Josef.

No, thought Josef. *My father just got out of a concentration camp.*

"No. For me," Josef said instead. "I want to be a journalist one day."

"Good!" the news agent said. "We need more writers." He waved a hand at all the magazines and newspapers. "So I have more things to sell!"

He laughed, and Josef smiled. Here they were, talking like two regular people, but Josef hadn't forgotten he was Jewish. He hadn't forgotten that if he were wearing his armband, this man wouldn't be talking and laughing with him. He'd be calling for the police.

Josef was about to leave when he thought to buy Ruthie a piece of candy. Money had been tight since their father lost his job, and she would enjoy the treat. Josef took a hard candy from a jar and fished in his pocket for another pfennig. He found one, put it on the counter, and paid for the candy. But when he'd removed the coin, his armband had slipped out too. It fluttered to the floor, the Star of David landing face up for all the world to see.

A fist closed around Josef's heart, and he dove for the armband.

Stomp. A black shoe covered the armband before Josef could grab it. Slowly, shakily, Josef lifted his eyes from the black shoes to the white socks, brown shorts, brown shirt, and red Nazi armband of a Hitler Youth. A boy about Josef's age, sworn to live and die for the Fatherland. He stood on Josef's armband, his eyes wide with surprise.

The blood drained from Josef's face.

The boy reached down, palmed the armband, and took Josef by the arm. "Let's go," the boy said, and he marched Josef back through the dining car.

Josef could barely walk. His legs were like lead, and his eyes lost their focus.

After Herr Meier had called him in front of the class to show how Jews were inferior to real Germans, Josef had returned to his seat next to Klaus, his best friend in the class. Klaus had been wearing the same uniform this boy did now. Klaus had joined the Hitler Youth not because he wanted to, but because German boys—and their families—were shamed and mistreated if they didn't.

Klaus had winced to show Josef how sorry he was that Herr Meier had done that to him.

That afternoon, a group of Hitler Youth were waiting for Josef outside the school. They fell on him, hitting and kicking him for being a Jew, and calling him all kinds of names.

And the worst part was, Klaus had joined them.

Wearing that uniform turned boys into monsters. Josef had seen it happen. He had done everything he could to avoid the Hitler Youth ever since, but now he'd handed himself right over to one—and all because he'd taken off his armband to walk around a train and buy a newspaper! He and his mother and sister would be put off the train, maybe even sent to a concentration camp.

Josef had been a fool, and now he and his family were going to pay the price.

ISABEL

ISABEL OPENED HER EYES AND LOWERED THE trumpet from her lips. She was sure she had just heard the sound of breaking glass, but cars and bicycles kept streaming by under the bright sun on the Malecón like nothing had happened. Isabel shook her head, convinced she was hearing things, and put her lips back to her trumpet.

Then suddenly a woman screamed, a pistol fired—*pak!*—and the world went crazy.

People rushed out of the side streets. Hundreds of them. They were men, mostly, many of them shirtless in the hundred-degree August heat, their white and brown and black backs glistening in the sun. They yelled and chanted. They threw rocks and bottles. They spilled into the streets, and the few policemen on the Malecón were quickly overwhelmed. Isabel saw the glass window of a general store shatter, and men and women climbed inside to steal shoes and toilet paper and bath soap. An alarm rang. Smoke rose from behind an apartment building.

Havana was rioting, and her father and grandfather were somewhere right in the middle of it.

Some people fled from the chaos, but more people raced toward it, and Isabel ran with them. Car horns beeped. Bicycles swung around and pedaled back. People were as thick on the ground as sugarcane. Isabel weaved in and out among them, her trumpet tucked under one arm, looking for Papi and Lito.

"Freedom! Freedom!" chanted some of the rioters.

"Castro out!"

"Enough is enough!"

Isabel couldn't believe what she was hearing. People caught criticizing Fidel Castro were thrown into jail and never heard from again. But now the streets were full of people yelling, "Down with Fidel! Down with Fidel!"

"Papi!" Isabel cried. "Lito!" Her grandfather's name was Mariano, but Isabel called him Lito, short for *Abuelito*—Grandpa.

Rifles boomed, and Isabel ducked. More police were arriving by motorcycle and military truck, and the protest was turning bloody. The rioters and police traded rocks and bullets, and a man with a bloody head staggered past Isabel. She reeled in horror. A hand grabbed her, making her jump, and she spun around. Lito! She threw herself into her grandfather's arms.

"Thank God you're safe!" he told her.

"Where's Papi?" she asked him.

"I don't know. We weren't together when it started," her grandfather said.

Isabel thrust her trumpet into his arms. "I have to find him!"

"Chabela!" her grandfather cried. He used her childhood nickname, like he always did. "No! Wait!"

Isabel ignored him. She had to find her father. If he was caught again by the police, he'd be sent back to prison—and this time they might not let him out.

Isabel dodged through the crowds, trying to stay away from where the police had formed a line. "Papi!" she called. "Papi!" But she was too short and there were too many people.

High above her, Isabel saw people climbing out onto the big electric sign hanging from the side of a tourist hotel, and it gave her an idea. She worked her way to one of the cars stuck in the riot, an old American Chevy with chrome tail fins, still around from before the Revolution in the 1950s. She climbed up the bumper and onto the hood. The man behind the steering wheel honked his horn and took the cigar out of his mouth to yell at her.

"Chabela!" her grandfather shouted when he saw her. "Chabela, get down from there!"

Isabel ignored them both and turned this way and that, calling out for her father. There! She saw her *papi* just as he reared back and threw a bottle that smashed into the line of police along the seawall. It was the last straw for the police. At a command from their leader, they pushed forward into the crowd, arresting rioters and hitting them with wooden batons.

In all the turmoil, a policeman caught up with her father and grabbed him by the arm. "No!" Isabel cried. She leaped down off the hood of the car and pushed her way through the pandemonium. When she got to her *papi*, he was balled up on the ground and the policeman was beating him with his nightstick.

The policeman raised his truncheon to hit her father again, and Isabel jumped in between them. "No! Don't! Please!" she cried.

The policeman's eyes flashed from anger to surprise, and then back to anger. He reared back again to hit Isabel, and she flinched. But the blow never came. Another policeman had caught his arm! Isabel blinked. She recognized the new policeman. He was Luis Castillo, Iván's older brother.

"What do you think you're doing?" the older policeman barked.

Luis didn't have time to answer. A whistle blew. The police were being summoned elsewhere.

The angry cop yanked his arm free from Luis and pointed his nightstick at Papi. "I saw what you did," he said. "I'll find you again. When all this is over, I'll find you and arrest you, and they'll send you away for good."

Luis pulled the angry policeman away, pausing just long enough to give Isabel a worried look over his shoulder.

Luis didn't have to say anything. As her grandfather arrived and helped Isabel get her father to his feet, she understood.

Papi had to leave Cuba.

Tonight.

MAHMOUD

ALEPPO, SYRIA—2015

THE AFTERNOON *ADHAN* FROM A NEARBY mosque echoed through the bombed-out streets of Aleppo, the melodious, ethereal voice of the *mu'adhdhin* praising Allah and calling everyone to prayer. Mahmoud had been doing his math homework at the kitchen table, but he automatically put his pencil down and went to the sink to wash up. The water wasn't working again, so he had to pour water over his hands using the plastic jugs his mother had hauled from the neighborhood well. Across the room, Waleed sat like a zombie in front of the television, watching a Teenage Mutant Ninja Turtles cartoon dubbed into Syrian Arabic.

Mahmoud's mother came out of the bedroom, where she'd been folding clothes, and turned off the TV. "Time to pray, Waleed. Get washed up."

Mahmoud's mother, Fatima Bishara, held her pink iPhone in one hand, and in her free arm she carried Mahmoud's baby sister, Hana. Fatima had long, dark hair she wore up on her head, and intense brown eyes. Today she was wearing her usual around-the-house attire: jeans and a pink nurse's shirt she used to wear to work. She'd quit the hospital when Hana was born, but not before the war had begun. Not before coming home every day with horror stories about the people she'd helped put back together. Not soldiers—regular people. Men with gunshot wounds. Women with burns. Children with missing limbs. She hadn't gone nearly catatonic like Waleed, but at some point it had gotten bad enough that she just stopped talking about it.

When he was finished washing up, Mahmoud went to the corner of the living room that faced Mecca. He rolled out two mats—one for him and the other for Waleed. Their mother would pray by herself in her bedroom.

Mahmoud began without Waleed. He raised his hands to his ears and said, *"Allahu Akbar."* God is the greatest. Then he folded his hands over his stomach and said a brief prayer before reciting the first chapter of the Qur'an, the most holy book in Islam. He bowed and praised Allah again three times, stood and praised Allah again, then got down on his hands and knees and put his head to the floor, praising Allah three times more. When he was finished, Mahmoud sat back up on his knees and ended his prayers by turning his head right, and then left, recognizing the angels who recorded his good and bad deeds.

The whole prayer took Mahmoud about seven minutes. While he'd been praying, Waleed joined him. Mahmoud waited for his brother to finish, then rolled up their mats and went back to his homework. Waleed went back to watching cartoons.

Mahmoud was just starting a new equation when he heard a sound over the Teenage Mutant Ninja Turtles theme song. A roar like a hot wind rising outside. In the second it took for the sound to grow from a breeze to a tornado, Mahmoud dropped his pencil, put his hands to his ears, and threw himself under the kitchen table.

By now he knew what an incoming missile sounded like.

ShhhhhHHHHHH—THOOOOOOM!

The wall of his apartment exploded, blasting broken bits of concrete and glass through the room. The floor lurched up under Mahmoud and threw him and the table and chairs back against the wall of the kitchen. The world was a whirlwind of bricks and broken dishes and table legs and heat, and Mahmoud slammed into a cabinet. His breath left him all at once, and he fell to the floor with a heavy thud in a heap of metal and mortar.

Mahmoud's ears rang with a high-pitched whine, like the TV when the satellite was searching for a signal. Above him, what was left of the ceiling light threw sparks. Nothing else mattered in that moment but air. Mahmoud couldn't draw a breath. It was like somebody was sitting on his chest. He thrashed in the rubble, panicking. He couldn't breathe. *Couldn't breathe!* He flailed wildly at the debris, digging and scratching at the wreckage like he could somehow claw his way back to a place where there was air.

And then his lungs were working again, raking in great gulps. The air was full of dust, and it scratched and tore at his throat as it went down, but Mahmoud had never tasted anything so sweet. His ears still rang, but through the buzz he could hear more *thuds* and *booms*. It wasn't just his building that had been hit, he realized. It was his whole neighborhood.

Mahmoud's head was hot and wet. He put a hand to it and came away with blood. His shoulder ached and his chest still seared with every hard, desperate breath, but the only thing that mattered now was getting to his mother. His sister. His brother.

Mahmoud pulled himself up out of the rubble and saw the building across the street in raw daylight, like he was standing in midair beside it. He blinked, still dazed, and then he understood.

The entire outside wall of Mahmoud's apartment was gone.

JOSEF

1 day from home

THE HITLER YOUTH LED JOSEF DOWN THE narrow corridor of the German passenger car. Tears sprang to Josef's eyes. The Brownshirt who'd taken his father away on *Kristallnacht* had said, "*We'll come for you soon enough,*" but Josef hadn't waited. He'd gone to *them* with this stupid stunt.

They came to a compartment with a man in the uniform of the Gestapo, the Nazis' Secret State Police, and Josef stumbled. The Gestapo man looked up at them through the window in his door.

No. Not here. Not now. Not like this, Josef prayed—

—and the Hitler Youth boy pushed Josef on past.

They came to the door of the Jewish train car, and the Hitler Youth spun Josef around. He glanced over his shoulder to make sure no one was listening.

"*What were you thinking?*" the boy whispered.

Josef couldn't speak.

The boy thrust the armband at Josef's chest.

"Put that on. And don't *ever* do that again," the Hitler Youth told Josef. "Do you understand?"

"I— Yes," Josef stammered. "Thank you. Thankyou-thankyouthankyou."

The Hitler Youth breathed hard, his face red like he was the one in trouble. He spotted the piece of candy Josef had bought for Ruth and took it. He stood taller, tugged at the bottom of his brown shirt to straighten it, then turned and marched away.

Josef slipped back into his compartment, still shaking, and collapsed onto his bench. He stayed there the rest of the trip, his armband securely in place and as visible as possible. He didn't even leave to go to the bathroom.

Hours later, the train pulled in to Hamburg Central Railway Station. Josef's mother led him and his sister through the crowds to the Hamburg docks, where their ship waited for them.

Josef had never seen anything so big. If you stood the ship on end, it would have been taller than any building in Berlin. Two giant tan smokestacks stuck up from the middle of the ship, one of them belching gray-black diesel engine smoke. A steep ramp ran to the top of the tall black hull, and hundreds of people were already on board, milling around under colorful fluttering pennants and waving to friends and family down on the docks. Flying highest above them all, as if to remind everyone who was in charge, was the red-and-white Nazi flag with the black swastika in the middle.

The ship was called the MS *St. Louis*. St. Louis was the name of a city in America, Josef had learned. That seemed like a good omen to him. A sign that they would eventually get to America. Maybe one day visit the real St. Louis.

A shabby-looking man stumbled out from behind the crates and luggage piled up on the dock, and Ruthie screamed. Josef jumped, and his mother took a frightened step back.

The man reached out for them. "You made it! At last!"

That voice, thought Josef. *Could it really be—?*

The man threw his arms around Mama. She let him hug her, even though she still held her hands across her chest as if to ward him off.

He stepped back and held her at arm's length.

"My dearest Rachel!" he said. "I thought I'd never see you again!"

It *was*. It was him. The shabby man who had lurched from the shadows like an escapee from a mental asylum was Josef's father, Aaron Landau.

Josef shuddered. His papa looked nothing like the man who'd been dragged away from their home six months ago. His thick brown hair and beard had been shaved off, and his head and face were covered with scraggly stubble. He was thinner too. Too thin. A skeleton in a threadbare suit three sizes too big for him.

Aaron Landau's eyes bulged from his gaunt face as he turned to look at his children. Josef's breath caught in his throat and Ruthie cried out and buried her face in Josef's stomach as their papa pulled the two of them into a hug. He smelled so ripe—like the alley behind a butcher shop—that Josef had to turn his head away.

"Josef! Ruth! My darlings!" He kissed the tops of their heads again and again, then jumped back. He looked around manically, like there were spies everywhere. "We have to go. We can't stay here. We have to get on board before they stop us."

"But I have tickets," Mama said. "Visas."

Papa shook his head too quickly. "It doesn't matter," he said. His eyes looked like they were going to pop out of their sockets. "They'll stop us. Take me back."

Ruthie clung to her brother. Papa was scaring her. He scared Josef too.

"Hurry!" Papa said. He pulled the family with him into the stacks of crates, and Josef tried to keep up with him as he darted from place to place, dodging imaginary enemies. Josef gave his mother a frightened glance that said, *What's wrong with Papa?* Mama just shook her head, her eyes full of worry.

When they got close to the ramp, Papa hunkered down behind the last of the crates.

"On the count of three, we make a break for it," he told his family. "Don't stop. Don't stop for *anything*. We *have* to get on that ship. Are you ready? One. Two. *Three*."

Josef wasn't ready. None of them were. They watched as Aaron Landau ran for the ramp, where other passengers had already queued up to hand their tickets to a smiling man in a sailor's uniform. Josef's father threw himself past the sailor and stumbled into the ramp's railing before righting himself and sprinting up the gangway.

"Wait!" the sailor cried.

"Quickly now, children," Mama said. Together they hurried to the ramp as best they could, carrying all the suitcases. "I have his ticket," she told the sailor. "I'm sorry. We can wait our turn."

The startled man at the front of the line motioned for them to go ahead, and Josef's mother thanked him.

"My husband is just . . . eager to leave," she told the sailor.

He smiled sadly and punched their tickets. "I understand. Oh—let me get someone to help you with those bags. Porter?"

Josef stood in wonder as another sailor—a German man without a Star of David armband, a man who wasn't a Jew—put a suitcase under each arm and one in each hand and led them up the gangway. He treated them like real passengers. Like real *people*. And he wasn't the only one. Every sailor they met doffed his cap at them, and the steward who showed them to their cabin assured them that they could call upon him for anything they needed while on board. Anything at all. Their room was spotless, the bed linens were freshly laundered, and the hand towels were pressed and neatly stacked.

"It's a trick," Papa said when the door was closed. He glanced around the little cabin like the walls were closing in. "They'll come for us soon enough," he said.

It was just what the Brownshirt had told Josef.

Mama put her hands on Josef's and Ruthie's heads. "Why don't you two go on up to the promenade," she said softly. "I'll stay here with your father."

Josef and Ruth were only too glad to get away from Papa. A few hours later, they watched from the promenade as tugboats pushed the MS *St. Louis* away from the dock, and passengers threw confetti and celebrated and blew tearful kisses good-bye. Josef and his family were on their way to a new country. A new life.

But all Josef could think about was what terrible things must have happened to his father to make him look so awful and act so scared.

ISABEL

ISABEL AND HER GRANDFATHER SET HER PAPI in a chair in their little kitchen, and Isabel's mother, Teresa Padron de Fernandez, ran to the cabinet under the sink. Isabel hurried after her. Mami was very pregnant—she was due in a week's time—so Isabel knelt down to find the iodine.

Isabel's father, Geraldo Fernandez, had always been a handsome man, but he didn't look it now. There was blood in his hair, and the area around one of his eyes was already turning black. When they pulled his white linen shirt off him, his back was covered with welts.

Isabel watched as Mami cleaned his cuts with a washcloth. Papi hissed as she disinfected them with the iodine.

"What happened?" Isabel's mother asked.

An *Industriales* baseball game played on the television in the corner, and Isabel's grandfather turned down the volume.

"There was a riot on the Malecón," Lito said. "They ran out of food too fast."

"I can't stay here," Papi said. His head was bent low, but his voice was loud and clear. "Not any longer. They'll come for me."

Everyone was quiet at that. The only sound was the soft crack of a bat and the roar of the crowd on the television.

Papi had already tried to flee Cuba twice. The first time, he and three other men had built a raft and tried to paddle their way to Florida, but a tropical storm turned them back. The second time, his boat had a motor, but he'd been caught by the Cuban navy and had ended up in jail.

Now it was even harder to escape. For decades, the United States had rescued any Cuban refugees they found at sea and taken them to Florida. But the food shortages had driven more and more Cubans to *el norte*. Too many. The Americans had a new policy everyone called "Wet Foot, Dry Foot." If Cuban refugees were caught at sea with "wet feet," they were sent to the US naval base at Guantanamo Bay, at the southern end of Cuba. From there, they could choose to return to Cuba—and Castro— or languish in a refugee camp while the United States decided what to do with them. But if they managed to survive the trip across the Straits of Florida and evade the US Coast Guard and actually set foot on United States soil—be caught with "dry feet"—they were granted special refugee status and allowed to remain and become US citizens.

Papi was going to run away again, and this time, whether he got caught with wet feet or dry feet, he wasn't coming back.

"There's no reason to go throwing yourself onto a raft in the ocean," Lito said. "You can just lie low for a while. I know a little shack in the cane fields. Things will get better. You'll see."

Papi slammed a fist on the table. "And how exactly are they going to get better, Mariano? Do you think the Soviet Union is going to suddenly decide to get back together and start sending us food again? No one is coming to help us. And Castro's only making things worse."

As if saying his name made him appear, the baseball game on television was interrupted by a special message from the Cuban president.

Fidel Castro was an old man with liver spots on his forehead, gray hair, a big bushy gray beard, and bags under his eyes. He wore the same thing he did every time he was on television—a green military jacket and flat round cap—and sat behind a row of microphones.

Everyone got quiet as Lito turned up the volume. Castro condemned the violence that had broken out on the Malecón, blaming it on US agents.

Papi scoffed. "It wasn't US agents. It was hungry Cubans."

Castro rambled on without a script, quoting novels and telling personal anecdotes about the Revolution.

"Oh, turn it off," Papi said. But before Mami had reached the set, Castro said something that made them all sit up and listen.

"We cannot continue guarding the borders of the United States while they send their CIA to instigate riots in Havana. That is when incidents like this occur, and the world calls the Cuban government cruel and inhumane. And so, until there is a speedy and efficient solution, we are suspending all obstacles so that those who wish to leave Cuba may do so legally, once and for all. We will not stand in their way."

"What did he just say?" Mami asked.

Papi's eyes were wide as he stood from the kitchen table. "Castro just said anybody who wants to can leave!"

Isabel felt as though her heart had been ripped out of her chest. If Castro was letting anyone leave, her father would be gone before the sun rose the next day. She could see it in his wild look.

"You can't go now!" Lito told Papi. "You have a family to take care of. A wife! A daughter! A son on the way!"

Isabel's father and grandfather yelled at each other about dictators and freedom and families and responsibility. Lito was her mother's father, and he and Papi had never gotten along. Isabel covered her ears and stepped away. She had to think of some answer to all this, some solution that would keep her family together.

Then she had it.

"We'll all go!" Isabel cried.

That shut everybody up. Even Castro stopped talking, and the TV went back to showing the baseball game.

"No," Papi and Lito said at the same time.

"Why not?" Isabel said.

"Your mother is pregnant, for one thing!" Lito said.

"There's no food to feed the baby here anyway," Isabel said. "There's no food for any of us, and no money to buy it with if there was. But there is food in the States. And freedom. And work."

And a place where her father wouldn't be beaten or arrested. Or run away.

"We'll all go, while Castro is letting people out," she went on. "Lito too."

"What? But, I— No," Lito protested.

They were all quiet a moment more, until her father said, "But I don't even have a boat."

Isabel nodded. She could fix that too.

Without saying anything, Isabel ran next door to the Castillos's house. Luis, the older boy who'd saved her from the policeman's nightstick, wasn't home from work yet, and neither was his mother, Juaneta, who worked at the cooperative law office. But Isabel found Iván and his father, Rudi, right where she thought they'd be—working on their boat in the shed.

It was an ugly blue thing cobbled together out of old metal advertisements and road signs and oil drums. It barely qualified as a boat, but it was big enough for the four Castillos—and maybe four more guests.

"Well, if it isn't Hurricane Isabel," Señor Castillo said. He had white hair that he wore swept back on his head, and even though there was no food, he had a middle-aged paunch to his belly.

"You have to take us with you!" Isabel said.

"No, we don't," Señor Castillo said. "Iván, nail."

"People are rioting in Havana!" Isabel said.

"Tell me something I don't know," Señor Castillo said. "Iván, *nail*."

Iván handed him another nail.

"My father was almost arrested," Isabel said. "If you don't take us with you, they'll throw him in prison."

Señor Castillo paused his hammering for a moment, then shook his head. "There's no room. And we don't need a fugitive on board."

Iván looked at him funny, but only Isabel saw it.

"*Please,*" Isabel begged.

"We don't have any gasoline anyway," Iván said. He put a hand to the motorcycle motor they'd mounted inside the boat. "We're not going anywhere soon."

"I can fix that!" Isabel said.

She ran home again. Her father and grandfather were still arguing in the kitchen, so she slipped in the back way. She grabbed her trumpet, gave it one long, sad look, and ran out the back door. She was already in the street when she stopped, ran to her backyard, and snatched up the little mewling kitten too. With the trumpet in one arm and the kitten in the other, she ran the few blocks to the beach, where she banged on the door of a fisherman her grandfather knew. His gas-powered fishing boat rocked gently at a little pier nearby.

The fisherman came to his door, licking his fingers and frowning. Isabel had caught him at dinner. Fried fish, it smelled like. The kitten's nose sniffed eagerly at the air, and it meowed. Isabel's stomach growled.

"You're Mariano Padron's granddaughter, aren't you?" the fisherman said. "What do you want?"

"I need gasoline!" Isabel told him.

"Izzat so? Well, I need money."

"I don't have any money," Isabel said. "But I have this." She held out the trumpet. Isabel regretted that its brass was a little tarnished, but it was the most valuable thing she owned. The fisherman *had* to take it in trade.

"What am I going to do with that?" he asked.

"Sell it," Isabel told him. "It's French, and old, and plays like a dream."

The fisherman sighed. "And why do you need gasoline so badly?"

"To leave Cuba before my father is arrested."

The fisherman wiped his lips on the back of his hand. Isabel stood for what seemed like hours, her insides churning like a waterspout. At last, he reached out and took the trumpet.

"Wait here," he told her.

Isabel held her breath, and soon the fisherman came back with two enormous plastic jugs of gasoline. Each one came up to Isabel's chest.

"Is it enough?" Isabel asked.

"To get you to Miami? Yes. And back again."

Isabel's heart soared, and she hopped up and down.

"*Thankyouthankyouthankyouthankyou!*" Isabel told him. "Oh, and you have to take the kitten too." She held the wiggling creature out to him, but the old fisherman just stared at it.

"Izzat so?" the fisherman said.

"Please," Isabel said. "Or else someone will catch her and eat her. But you have fish to eat. She can eat the scraps."

The fisherman eyed the cat suspiciously. "Izzit a good mouser?"

"Yes!" Isabel said, though she was sure that even a mouse would give the scrawny thing trouble. "Her name is Leona."

The old fisherman sighed and took the squirming kitten from her.

Isabel smiled, then noticed how big and heavy the gas cans were.

"Oh, and I also need you to help me carry these back."

MAHMOUD

ALEPPO, SYRIA—2015

THROUGH THE HUGE HOLE THAT USED TO BE the wall of his apartment, Mahmoud saw gray-white clouds from missile strikes blooming all around. He shook his head, trying to clear the ringing, and spied his little brother. Waleed was sitting right where he had been before the attack, on the floor in front of the TV.

Only the TV wasn't there anymore. It had fallen five stories to the ground below, along with the outside wall. And Waleed was centimeters from joining them both.

"Waleed! Don't move!" Mahmoud cried. He hurried across the room, his ankles turning painfully on broken bits of wall. Waleed sat still as a statue, and he looked like one too. He was covered with a fine gray powder from head to foot, like he'd taken a bath in dry concrete mix. Mahmoud finally reached him, snatching him up and away from the cliff's edge that used to be their wall.

"Waleed—Waleed, are you okay?" Mahmoud asked, turning him around.

Waleed's eyes were alive, but empty.

"Waleed, talk to me. Are you all right?"

Waleed finally looked up at him. "You're bleeding" was all he said.

"Mahmoud? Waleed?" their mother cried. She staggered to the door of her bedroom, Hana crying in her arms. "Oh, thank God you're alive!" their mom said. She dropped to her knees and pulled them both into a hug. Mahmoud's heart was racing, his ears still buzzed, and his shoulder burned, but they were alive. They were all alive! He felt tears come to his eyes and wiped them away.

The floor beneath their feet groaned and shifted.

"We have to get out of here!" Mahmoud's mother said, putting Hana in Mahmoud's arms. "Go, go. Take your brother and your sister. I'll be right behind you. I just have to grab a few things."

"Mom, no!"

"Go," she told Mahmoud, pushing them all toward the door.

Mahmoud clutched Hana with one arm and took his brother's hand. He dragged Waleed with him toward the front door, but Waleed pulled back.

"What about my action figures?" Waleed asked. He looked over his shoulder like he wanted to go back for them.

"We'll buy new ones!" Mahmoud told him. "We have to get out of here!"

Across the hall, the Sarraf family filled the corridor—mother, father, and twin daughters, both younger than Waleed.

"What's happened?" Mr. Sarraf asked Mahmoud, and then he saw the missing wall and his eyes went wide.

"The building's been hit!" Mahmoud said. "We have to get out!"

Mr. and Mrs. Sarraf hurried back into their apartment, and Mahmoud carried Hana down the stairs, pulling Waleed behind them. Halfway to the ground, the building shifted again and the concrete stairs broke away from the wall, leaving a five-centimeter crack. Mahmoud grabbed the railing to steady himself and waited a long, breathless moment to see if the stairs were going to collapse. When they didn't, he ran the rest of the way down and burst out onto the street, Hana still in his arms and his brother right behind them.

Rubble was strewn everywhere. Missiles and bombs thudded nearby, close enough to shake loose parts of walls. A building shuddered and collapsed, smoke and debris avalanching out into the street. Mahmoud jumped when it fell, but Waleed stood still, like this kind of thing happened every day.

With a jolt of surprise, Mahmoud realized this kind of thing *did* happen every day. Just not to them. Until now.

Everywhere around them, people fled into the streets, covered in gray dust and blood. No sirens rang. No ambulances came to help the wounded. No police cars or emergency crews hurried to the scene.

There weren't any left.

Mahmoud stared up at their building. The whole front had collapsed, and Mahmoud felt like he was looking into a giant dollhouse. Each floor had a living room and a kitchen just like theirs, all decorated differently.

The building groaned again, and a kitchen on the top floor began to tip toward the street. It collapsed onto the sixth floor, and then into Mahmoud's apartment, and on down like dominos. Mahmoud barely had time to yell *"Run!"* and drag Waleed and his sister away before the whole building came crashing down into the street, thundering like a jet fighter.

Safe on the sidewalk across the street, clutching Hana and Waleed, Mahmoud suddenly realized his mother had still been in the building. "Mom! *Mom!*" Mahmoud yelled.

"Mahmoud? Waleed?" he heard his mother cry, and she came out from behind the pile of rubble with the Sarraf family, all of them covered in gray dust. She ran toward Mahmoud and embraced him, Waleed, and Hana.

"We went out the back stairs," she told them. "And just in time."

Mahmoud looked up at where his apartment had been. It wasn't there anymore. His home was totally destroyed. What would they do now? Where would they go?

Mahmoud's mother was carrying their school backpacks, and she traded them for Hana. Mahmoud couldn't understand why his mother had bothered to save their backpacks until he saw that they were stuffed with clothes and diapers. She had gone back for whatever she could take from the apartment.

Everything they owned was in these two backpacks.

"I can't reach your father," Mahmoud's mother said, thumbing her phone. "There's no service again."

Mahmoud's father was an engineer with a mobile phone company. If the phones were out, he was probably working on trying to fix them. But what if his father had been hit by one of the bombs? Mahmoud's stomach twisted into knots just thinking about it.

But then there his dad was, running down the street toward them, and Mahmoud felt like he could fly.

"Fatima! Mahmoud! Waleed! Hana!" his father cried. He wrapped them all in a hug and kissed little Hana on the forehead. "Thank God you're all alive!" he cried.

"Dad, our house is gone!" Mahmoud told him. "What do we do?"

"What we should have done a long time ago. We're leaving Aleppo. Now. I parked the car nearby. We can be in Turkey by tomorrow. We can sell the car there and make our way north, to Germany."

Everyone stopped while Mahmoud's father walked ahead.

"*Germany?*" Mahmoud's mother said.

Mahmoud felt as stunned as his mother sounded. Germany? He remembered the map of the world that hung in his classroom. Germany was somewhere up north, in the heart of Europe. He couldn't imagine traveling that far.

"Just for a little while," Mahmoud's father said. "I saw on the TV they're accepting refugees. We can stay there until all this is over. Until we can come back home."

"It's cold in Germany," Mahmoud said.

"*Do you want to build a snowman?*" his father sang. They had seen *Frozen* in a movie theater—back when they could get to the now-government-controlled side of the city that *had* theaters.

"Youssef—" Mahmoud's mom warned.

Mahmoud's dad looked sheepish. "*It doesn't have to be a snowman.*"

"This is serious," Mom said. "I know we've been talking about leaving. But now? Like this? We were going to pack. *Plan.* Buy tickets. Book hotel rooms. All we have now are two backpacks and our phones. Germany is a long way away. How will we get there?"

"By car first." Mahmoud's father shrugged. "Then by

boat? By train? By bus? On foot? I don't know. What choice do we have? Our home is destroyed! Were you able to get the cash we've put away?"

Mahmoud's mother nodded, but she was clearly still worried.

"So we have money! We will buy tickets as we go. More importantly, we have our *lives*. But if we stay in Aleppo a day longer, we may not even have that." Mahmoud's father looked from his wife to Hana to Mahmoud to Waleed. "We've spent too much time talking about it and not doing anything. It's not safe here. It hasn't been for months. Years. We should have gone long ago. Ready or not, if we want to live, we have to leave Syria."

JOSEF

6 days from home

RUTHIE SKIPPED AHEAD OF JOSEF ALONG THE sunny Promenade deck, happier than he'd ever seen her before. And why not? The MS *St. Louis* was a paradise. Banned from movie theaters in Germany because she was a Jew, Ruthie had seen her first cartoon on board during movie night and loved it—even if it *was* followed by a newsreel with Hitler yelling about Jews. Three times a day they ate delicious meals in a dining room laid out with white linen tablecloths, crystal glasses, and shining silverware, and stewards waited on them hand and foot. They had played shuffleboard and badminton, and the crew was putting up a swimming pool, which they promised to fill with seawater once the *St. Louis* hit the warm Gulf Stream.

Everyone on the crew had treated Josef and his family with kindness and respect, despite his father's repeated warnings that all Germans were out to get them. (In five days, Papa hadn't come out of their cabin once, not even for meals, and Josef's mother had barely left his side.)

And the crew wasn't just being nice because they didn't know Josef and his family were Jews. No one wore their Jewish armbands on the ship, and there were no *J*s above any of the passenger compartments, because *all* the passengers were Jews. All nine hundred and eight of them! They were *all* going to Cuba to escape the Nazis, and now that they were finally away from the threats and violence that followed them everywhere in Germany, there was singing and dancing and laughter.

Two girls around Ruthie's age wearing matching flowery dresses were leaning over the railing and giggling. Josef and Ruthie went over to see what they were doing. One of the girls had found a long piece of string and was dangling it over the side, tickling the noses of passengers who were sleeping in chairs down on A-deck. Their current victim kept batting at his nose like there was a fly on it. He bopped his nose hard enough to jerk awake, and Ruthie laughed hysterically. The girls yanked up the string, and they all dropped to the deck behind the rail where the man couldn't see them laughing.

"I'm Josef," he told the other girls when they'd all gathered themselves together. "And this is Ruthie."

"Josef just turned thirteen!" Ruthie told the girls. "He's going to have his bar mitzvah next Shabbos."

A bar mitzvah was the ceremony at which a boy officially became a man under Jewish law. It was usually held on the first Shabbos—the Sabbath, the Jewish day of rest—after a boy's thirteenth birthday. Josef couldn't wait for his bar mitzvah.

"*If* there's enough people," Josef reminded his sister.

"I'm Renata Aber," said the older of the two girls, "and this is Evelyne." They were sisters, and, amazingly, they were traveling alone.

"Our father is waiting for us in Cuba," Renata told them.

"Where's your mama?" Ruthie asked.

"She . . . wanted to stay in Germany," Evelyne said.

Josef could tell it wasn't something they were comfortable talking about. "Hey, I know something funny we can do," he told them. It was a trick he and Klaus had played on Herr Meier once upon a time. Thinking about Klaus made Josef think about other things, but he blinked away the bad memories. The MS *St. Louis* had left all that behind.

"First," Josef said, "we need some soap."

Once they had found a bar, Josef showed them how to soap up a door handle so that it was so slick it was impossible to turn. They used it on the door handles of cabins up and down the passageway on A-deck, then hid around the corner and waited. Soon enough, a steward balancing a large silver tray came down the hall from the other end and knocked on a door. Josef, Ruthie, Renata, and Evelyne had to swallow their snickers as the steward reached down with his free hand and tried and failed to open the door. The steward couldn't see because of the big platter he held, and as he fumbled with the knob he lost his hold on the tray and the whole thing came crashing down with a great clatter.

All four of them burst out laughing, and Josef and Renata pulled the two younger children away before they could be caught. They collapsed behind one of the lifeboats, panting and giggling. As Josef dried his eyes, he realized he hadn't played like this, hadn't laughed like this, for many years.

Josef wished they could stay on board the *St. Louis* forever.

ISABEL

THE BOAT WAS HEAVY IN ISABEL'S ARMS, AND she was afraid of dropping it, even though there were five other people carrying it with her. She and Iván held the middle of the boat on either side, while Iván's parents and Isabel's father and grandfather carried the front and back.

Señora Castillo, Iván's mother, was dark-skinned and curvy, and wore a white kerchief over her dreadlocks. Isabel's mother, almost nine months pregnant, was the only one not helping to carry the boat. It was big and heavy to begin with, and they had packed it with the gas cans, plastic soda bottles filled with fresh water, condensed milk, cheese and bread, and medicine. Everything else had to be left behind.

Nothing was more important than making it to Florida.

It was night, and a waning moon peeked out from behind scattered clouds. A warm breeze lifted Isabel's short curly hair and raised goose bumps on her arms. Fidel Castro had said that anyone who wanted to leave was welcome to go, but that was hours ago. What if he had changed his mind? What if there was a line of police waiting to arrest them at the beach? Isabel hefted the boat to get a better grip and tried to pick up her pace.

They left the village's gravel road and hauled the boat over the dunes to the sea. All Isabel could see was the metal side of the boat in front of her face, but she heard a commotion behind her. There were people on the beach! Lots of them! She panicked, her worst fears come true, and suddenly a blinding light lit her up. Isabel cried out and let go of the boat.

Ahead of her, Señora Castillo staggered and lost her grip too, and the front of the boat slammed into the sand.

Isabel turned, holding a hand up in front of her eyes and expecting to see a police searchlight shining on her. What she saw instead was a television camera.

"You're on CNN," a woman said in Spanish, her face nothing but a silhouette against the light. "Can you tell us what made you decide to leave?"

"Quickly!" Señor Castillo called from the other side of the boat. "Pick it back up! We're almost to the water!"

"I—" Isabel said, frozen in the bright light of the camera.

"Do you have any relatives back in Miami that you want to send a message to?" the reporter asked.

"No, we—"

"Isabel! The boat!" Papi called.

The others had already lifted the boat up out of the sand and were lurching toward the sound of the crashing waves. The bright lights of the camera swung away from Isabel and lit up what looked like a party on the beach. More than half their village was on the sand, clapping, waving, and cheering on the boats.

And there were *so many* boats. Isabel's family had worked in secret all night with the Castillos, worried someone might hear them, but apparently, everybody else had been doing the same thing. There were inflatable rafts. Canoes with homemade outriggers. Rafts made of inner tubes tied together. Boats built out of Styrofoam and oil drums.

A rickety-looking raft made out of wooden shipping pallets and inner tubes raised a bedsheet sail, and as it caught the wind, the villagers on the beach cheered. When another raft made out of an old refrigerator sank, everyone laughed.

The camera lights swung around again, and that's when Isabel saw the police.

There was a small group of them, up on the rocks overlooking the inlet. Not nearly as many as there had been in Havana, but enough. Enough to arrest her family for trying to leave Cuba. But these police weren't doing anything. They were just standing and watching. Castro's order to let people leave must have still been good!

"Chabela!" her mother called. "Chabela, come on!"

Mami was already in the boat, and Papi was helping Iván in. Señor Castillo was trying to get the motor started.

Isabel waded into the water, the waves lapping up to the bottom of her shorts. She was almost to Papi's outstretched arms when she saw her father's eyes go wide.

Isabel looked back over her shoulder. Two of the policemen had broken from the group and were running toward the water.

Toward *them*.

"No no! They're coming for me!" Papi cried. Isabel fell into the water and swam the rest of the way to the boat, but her father was already climbing over the side.

"Start the engine!" he cried.

"No, wait for me!" Isabel yelled, spitting seawater. She got a hand to the side of the boat and looked back. The two policemen had hit the surf and were running high-legged through the waves. Worse, the other policemen were running too—and they were all headed for the Castillos's boat!

Hands grabbed Isabel and helped her climb the side of the boat—Iván! But when he got her aboard, Iván and his mother then reached their hands out for the two policemen who were chasing them. What were they doing?

"No!" Papi cried, scrambling as far away from them as he could. Iván and Señora Castillo grabbed the arms of the two policemen and pulled them on board, and they all collapsed into the bottom of the boat. The policemen pulled off their berets, and Isabel recognized one of them instantly—one was Luis, the Castillos's elder son! The other policeman shook out his long black hair, and Isabel was startled to realize it wasn't a police*man* at all. It was a police*woman*. When she took Luis's hand, Isabel guessed she was his girlfriend.

This must have been the Castillos's plan all along—for Luis and his girlfriend to run away with them! But they had never told Isabel and her family.

Pak! A pistol rang out again over the waves, and the crowd on the beach cried out in panic. The pistol fired again—*pak!*—and—*ping!*—the hull of the Castillos's boat rang as the bullet hit it.

The police were shooting at them! But why? Didn't Castro say it was all right to leave?

Isabel's eyes fell on Luis and his girlfriend, and she understood. They had been drafted into the police, and they weren't allowed to leave. They were deserters, and deserters were shot.

The motor coughed to life, and the boat lurched into a wave, spraying Isabel with seawater. The villagers on the beach cheered for them, and Señor Castillo revved the engine, leaving the charging policemen in their wake.

Isabel braced herself between two of the benches, trying to catch her breath. It took her a moment to process it, but this was really happening. They were leaving Cuba, her village, her home—everything she'd ever known—behind.

Isabel's father pitched across the roiling boat and grabbed Señor Castillo by the shirt. "What are you playing at, letting them on board?" he demanded. "What if they follow us? What if they send a navy boat after us? You've put us all in danger!"

Señor Castillo batted Geraldo Fernandez's arms away. "We didn't ask you to come along!"

"It's our gasoline!" Isabel's father yelled.

They kept arguing, but the engine and the slap of the boat against the waves drowned their words out for Isabel. She wasn't paying any attention anyway. All she could think about was the ninety miles they still had to go, and the water pouring in from the gunshot hole in the side of the boat.

MAHMOUD

1 day from home

MAHMOUD'S FATHER STOPPED THEIR MER-
cedes station wagon for gasoline at a little roadside station north of Aleppo. Waleed and Mahmoud sat in the
car with their mother while she nursed Hana under a
blanket. Fatima had put on a black long-sleeved dress and
a pink flowery *hijab* that covered her head and shoulders.
She and Youssef had agreed she should cover up more than
she usually did in Aleppo, in case they ran into stricter
Muslims outside the city. In some places, women were
being stoned and killed for not covering up their entire
bodies, especially in areas controlled by Daesh—what
the rest of the world called ISIS. Daesh thought they
were fighting the final war of the apocalypse, and anyone who didn't agree with their twisted perversion of
Islam were infidels who should have their heads cut off.
Mahmoud and his family planned to stay as far away from
Daesh as possible, but the radical fighters were coming
farther and farther into Syria every day.

Mahmoud looked out the dusty car window as a jet

fighter streaked by high above them, headed for Aleppo. A mural painted on the side of the gas station showed President Assad, his dark hair cut short and a thin mustache underneath his pointy nose. He wore a suit and tie in front of a Syrian flag, doves of peace and yellow shining light surrounding him.

A jagged line of real bullet holes bisected Assad's face. Mahmoud's father got back in the car.

"I've got a route for us," Mom said. She finally had a signal, and got Google Maps to open on her iPhone. Mahmoud leaned over to see. *This route crosses a country border*, Google Maps told them, marking the alert with a little yellow triangle. That's what they wanted—to get out of Syria using the fastest path possible. Dad started the engine, put the car into gear, and they were off.

An hour later, they were met on the road by four soldiers waving for them to stop. Mahmoud froze. The soldiers might be with the Syrian army, or with the Syrian rebels. They could even be Daesh. It was hard to tell anymore. Some of these soldiers wore camouflage pants and shirts, but others wore Adidas jerseys and leather jackets and track pants. They all had short black beards like Mahmoud's father, and wore head scarves of different colors and patterns.

But each of them had an automatic rifle, which was really all that mattered.

"Your *hijab*," Dad said. "Quickly."

Mahmoud's mother pulled the end of the scarf up over her face so that only her eyes were showing.

Mahmoud sank to the floor of the old Mercedes station wagon and tried to disappear. In the seat beside him, Waleed sat up straight next to his open window, unmoving and unfazed.

"Everybody stay calm," Dad said, slowing the car down, "and let me do all the talking."

One of the soldiers stood in front of the car, his rifle aimed loosely at the windshield, while the others walked around the sides, peering in through the windows. The soldiers were silent, and Mahmoud closed his eyes tight, waiting for the shots to come. Sweat ran down his back.

"I'm just trying to get my family to safety," Dad told the men.

One of the men stopped at the driver's-side window and pointed his rifle at Mahmoud's father. "Which side do you support?"

The question was as dangerous as his gun. The right answer and they lived; the wrong answer and they all died. But what was the right answer? Assad and the Syrian army? The rebels? Daesh? His dad hesitated, and Mahmoud held his breath.

One of the soldiers cocked his rifle. *Chi-CHAK!*

It was Waleed who spoke up. "We're against whoever is dropping the bombs on us," he said.

The soldier laughed, and the other soldiers laughed with him.

"We're against whoever is dropping the bombs too," the soldier at the window said. "Which is usually that dog Assad."

Mahmoud breathed again with relief. Waleed didn't know it, but he'd saved the day.

"Where are you going?" the soldier at the window asked.

"North," Dad said. "Through Azaz."

The soldier opened the back door of the car and slid inside, pushing Waleed into the back of the station wagon. "No, no, you can't go through Azaz anymore," the soldier said. "The Free Syria Army and al-Qaeda are fighting there now."

The door next to Mahmoud opened, and one of the soldiers nudged him up from the floor and into the back with Waleed. Two more soldiers crammed themselves into the backseat, and the last one joined Mahmoud and Waleed in the back with their backpacks. He was dusty and smelled like he hadn't had a bath in months, and the heat of the road radiated off him and his rifle like a stove.

Apparently, they were all coming along for the ride.

One of the soldiers in the backseat snatched up Mom's iPhone and looked at the route.

"Use Apple Maps," another soldier said.

"No, you idiot, Google Maps is better," said his friend. "See here," he told Mahmoud's father, "you'll have to go over to Qatmah, and then north through Qestel Cindo. The rebels and the army and Daesh are all fighting here," he said, pointing to places on the map. "Many guns and artillery. And the Kurds hold all this territory here. Russian airstrikes have hit here and here in support of that Alawite pig Assad, and American drones are attacking Daesh here and here."

Mahmoud's eyes went wide. Everything the soldier was describing stood between them and Turkey.

"Go back south," one of the soldiers told Mahmoud's father. "You can let us off at highway 214."

Dad turned the car around and drove.

The soldier with the iPhone scrolled up the map to see their destination. "You're going to Turkey?"

"I—I went to engineering school there," Mahmoud's father said.

"You shouldn't be leaving Syria," said one of the soldiers. "You should stand up for your country! Fight the tyrant Assad!"

Between Assad and Daesh and Russia and America, Mahmoud thought, there wasn't much of a Syria left to fight for.

"I just want to keep my family safe," Dad said.

"My family was killed in an airstrike," one of the soldiers said. "Maybe when yours is too, you'll take up arms. But by then it will be too late."

Mahmoud remembered the horror he'd felt when his apartment building collapsed and he'd thought his mom was still inside. The fear he'd felt when they couldn't reach his father. If his parents had died in the airstrike, would he want revenge on their killers? Instead of running away, should Mahmoud and his father join the rebels and fight to win their country back?

Mahmoud's dad kept driving. They were almost to the highway when gunfire erupted nearby—*tat-tatatatat! tatatat!*—and bullets pinged into the car. Mahmoud screamed and dropped to the floor as broken glass sprayed him. One of the back tires exploded, and the car swerved wildly and screeched as his dad fought to keep control of it. Mahmoud and Waleed went tumbling, and the soldier in the back rolled on top of them.

The soldier had a hole in his head.

Mahmoud screamed again and pushed the man away as the car skidded to a stop. Bullets whizzed by, then caught the car again—*ping-ping-ping*—and Mahmoud's dad threw open the driver's-side door and pulled Mom and Hana out with him. "Get out of the car!" he cried.

The soldiers in the backseat kicked open the door on the left side of the car and spilled outside. More bullets whizzed by overhead, and soon the rebel soldiers who'd been riding with them were returning fire, their automatic rifles booming in Mahmoud's ears like he was in a barrel and they were beating on the outside of it with hammers.

All Mahmoud wanted to do was curl up into a ball and disappear. But he knew if he and Waleed stayed in the car, they would end up like the dead soldier beside them.

He had to get up. Get out. *Move.* His heart was pounding so hard he thought it would burst right out of his chest, but Mahmoud found the courage to grab Waleed by the arm, drag him over the seat, and dive headfirst out the door. They tumbled into the ditch beside his parents. Hana was wailing, but Mahmoud almost couldn't hear her over the sound of the gunfire.

Mahmoud's dad waited for a pause in the gunfire, then scrambled back up the ridge for the car.

"Youssef, no!" Mom cried. *"What are you doing?"*

Mahmoud's father dove back into the front seat and yanked the iPhone and the charger cord from the Mercedes just as bullets ripped into the car again. He tumbled and slid back down into the ditch.

"Had to go back for the phone," he told them. "How else am I going to play Angry Birds?"

He was joking again. Mahmoud knew they needed

their phones to help them get to Turkey. Without the maps, they'd be lost.

Mahmoud's father waited for another lull in the shooting, and then they all hurried away from the car, leaving everything else they owned behind.

JOSEF

8 days from home

FINALLY, SHABBOS ARRIVED. IT WAS THE DAY Josef would leave his childhood behind and become a man, and he could hardly contain his excitement. The ship's bulletin board announced that the first-class social hall would be converted to a synagogue, a Jewish house of prayer, which meant Josef might have his bar mitzvah after all. He was careful not to show his eagerness in front of his father, however. What would once have been a happy occasion in the Landau home was now fraught with anxiety, thanks to his father's paranoia.

"A synagogue, on board the ship?" Papa said. He shook his head as he paced their little room in his oversized nightclothes.

"The captain himself has arranged it," Mama said.

"Ridiculous! Did no one else see the Nazi flag overhead as we came on board?"

"Will you not go to your own son's bar mitzvah, then?" Josef's mother and Ruthie were already dressed in their nice Shabbos dresses. Josef wore his best shirt and tie.

"Bar mitzvah? There won't be enough men there to form a *minyan!*" Papa said. By tradition, ten or more Jewish men, a minyan, was needed for a public service. "No. No one who has lived in Germany for the past six years would be so foolish as to go to a Jewish service aboard a Nazi ship." Papa ran a hand over his shaved head. "No. It's a trap. Meant to lure us out. That's when they'll snatch us. A trap."

Mama sighed. "All right, then. We'll go without you."

They left him pacing the room, muttering to himself. Josef felt like someone had yanked his heart from his chest. In all the times he'd dreamed of this day, his father had always been there to recite a blessing with him. *But maybe this is what becoming a man is*, Josef thought. *Maybe becoming a man means not relying on your father anymore.*

Josef, his mother, and Ruthie stopped short just inside the first-class social hall. There weren't the required ten men for the service—there were a *hundred* men, probably more, all wearing yarmulkes on their heads and white-and-black *tallisim*—prayer shawls—around their shoulders. The card tables had been pushed to the sides of the room, and stewards were adding more chairs to accommodate the crowd. A table at the front held a Torah scroll.

Josef stood and stared. It felt like ages since he'd been inside a synagogue. It had been before *Kristallnacht*, before the Nuremberg Laws that made Jews second-class citizens, before the boycotts and book burnings. Before Jews were scared to gather together in public places. Josef's parents had always taken him to synagogue with them on Shabbos, even when other parents left their children with their nannies. It all came flooding back to him now— swaying and humming along with the prayers, craning his neck to see the Torah when it was taken out of the ark and hoping to get a chance to touch it and then kiss his fingers as the scroll came around in a procession. Josef felt his skin tingle. The Nazis had taken all this from them, from *him*, and now he and the passengers on the ship were taking it back.

Gustav Schroeder, the ship's diminutive captain, was there to greet them at the door. In the gallery above the room, a number of the off-duty crew had gathered to watch.

"Captain," asked a rabbi, one of the men who was leading the service, "I wonder if we might take down the portrait of the *Führer*, given the circumstances. It seems . . . inappropriate for such a sacred moment to be celebrated in the presence of Hitler."

Josef had seen paintings of the Nazi leader all over the ship, and the first-class social hall was no exception. A large portrait of Hitler hung in the middle of the room, watching over them all. Josef's veins ran with ice. He hated that man. Hated him because of everything he'd done to the Jews, but mostly because of what Hitler had done to his father.

"Of course," Captain Schroeder said. He quickly called over two of the stewards, and soon they had the portrait down and were taking it from the room.

In the gallery above, Josef saw one of the crew slam a fist down on the railing and storm off.

Josef's mother gave him a kiss on the cheek, and she and Ruthie went to sit in the section reserved for the women. Josef took a seat in the section with the men. The rabbi stood in front of the crowd and read from Hosca. Then it was time for Josef to recite the blessing he'd been practicing for weeks. There were butterflies in his stomach as he got up in front of such a large audience, and his voice broke as he stumbled through the Hebrew words, but he did it. He found his mother in the crowd. Her eyes were wet with tears.

"Today," Josef said, "I am a man."

There were many hands to shake and many congratulations after the ceremony, but it was all a blur to Josef. He felt like he was walking in a dream. For as long as he could remember, he'd wanted this. To no longer be a child. To be an adult.

Josef's mother and sister left to go back to visit his father in their cabin. Josef walked the Promenade deck by himself, a new man.

Renata and Evelyne jumped out from behind a lifeboat and grabbed Josef by the hand. Without their parents on the ship, they had skipped synagogue to play.

"Josef! Come stand guard for us!" Renata cried.

Before he could protest, the girls dragged him to a women's restroom. He was afraid they were going to pull him inside, but instead they deposited him by the door.

"Yell if you see someone coming," Renata said breath-lessly. "We're going to latch all the stalls from the inside and crawl out under the doors so no one can use the toilets!"

"No, don't—" Josef tried to tell them, but they were already gone. He stood there awkwardly, not sure if he should stay or go. Soon the sisters ran back outside, hanging on to each other with laughter.

A young woman staggered past them, clutching her stomach and looking green. Renata and Evelyne got quiet, and Josef could hear the woman desperately rattling the stall doors, looking for a toilet. The woman lurched out of the bathroom, looking even more green and desperate, and wobbled away.

Renata and Evelyne burst into laughter.

Josef raised himself up. "This isn't funny. Go in there and unlock those doors this minute."

"Just because you had your bar mitzvah doesn't make

you an adult," Renata told him, and Evelyne stuck her tongue out at him. "Come on, Evie—let's do the bathrooms on A-deck!"

The girls tore away, and Josef huffed. They were right. A bar mitzvah alone didn't make him an adult. Being responsible did. He walked on along the promenade, looking for a steward he could tell about the bathroom stalls. He saw two stewards who had stopped to look over the side at the sea and came up behind them.

"Must be doing sixteen knots, easy," said one of the stewards. "Captain's got the engines maxed out."

"Has to," the other said. "Them other two ships is smaller and faster. They get to Cuba first and unload their passengers, and who knows? Cuba might decide she's full-up with Jews when *we* get there and turn us away."

Josef looked out to sea. There wasn't another ship on the horizon as far as he could see. What other ships were they talking about? More ships full of refugees? And why did it matter which one got there first? Hadn't everyone on board already applied and paid for visas? Cuba couldn't turn them away.

Could they?

One of the stewards shook his head. "There's something they're not telling us, the shipping company. Something they're not telling Schroeder. The captain's in a tight spot, he is. Wouldn't want to be him for all the sugar in Cuba."

Josef backed away. He'd already forgotten about the stalls in the women's bathroom.

If he and his family didn't make it to Cuba, if they weren't allowed in, where would they go?

ISABEL

THE STRAITS OF FLORIDA, SOMEWHERE NORTH OF CUBA—1994

1 day from home

SEÑOR CASTILLO WAS IN CHARGE OF THE BOAT. No one had voted or named him captain, but he had built the boat, after all, and he was the one at the rudder, steering it, so that put him in charge. He didn't look happy about it, though. He kept frowning at the motor and the rudder like there was something wrong, but besides a quick patch job of stuffing a sock into the bullet hole, everything was good. The lights of Havana had faded to a speck on the horizon behind them, and they had left all the other boats behind.

Isabel clung to the wooden bench she sat on, squeezed in between Iván and her grandfather. Their boat was barely big enough for seven people, and with Luis and his girlfriend they were practically sitting on top of each other.

"I think it's time we met the other person on board with us," Isabel's grandfather said. Isabel thought he meant Luis's girlfriend, but instead he pushed some of the sacks of food and jugs of water out of the way and pointed to the bottom of the boat.

Staring back up at them was the huge face of Fidel Castro!

Luis's girlfriend gasped and then suddenly exploded with laughter. Soon all of them were laughing with her. Isabel laughed so hard her stomach hurt.

Even grumpy Señor Castillo chuckled. "I needed something big and thick for the bottom of the boat," he said. "And seeing as there were so many signs around with *El Presidente*'s head on them . . ."

It was true. Castro's face was everywhere in Cuba—on billboards, on taxis, in picture frames on schoolroom walls, painted on the sides of buildings.

Underneath this painting were the words, FIGHT AGAINST THE IMPOSSIBLE AND WIN.

"Well, Fidel *is* thickheaded," Luis said.

Isabel put her hands to her mouth but couldn't help laughing again with everyone else. You weren't allowed to say things like that in Cuba. But they weren't in Cuba anymore, were they?

"Do you know what the greatest achievements of the Cuban Revolution are?" Isabel's father asked.

"Education, public health, and sports," they all said together. It was a constant refrain in Castro's lengthy speeches.

"And do you know what the greatest failures are?" he asked.

"Breakfast, lunch, and dinner!" the adults answered

back, as though they'd heard that one many times before too. Isabel smiled.

That prompted someone to break out food and drinks, even though it was late.

Isabel sipped from a bottle of soda. "How long will it take to get to Florida?" she asked.

Señor Castillo shrugged. "By tomorrow night, maybe. Tomorrow morning we'll have the sun to guide us."

"All that matters now is we get as far away from Cuba as we can," said Luis's girlfriend.

"And what is your name, pretty one?" Lito asked her.

"Amara," she said. She was very pretty, even in her blue police uniform. She had flawless olive skin, long black hair, and full red lips.

"No, no, no," Lito said. He fanned his face. "Your name must be Summer, because you're making me sweat!"

The girl smiled, but Isabel's mother slapped Lito on the leg. "Papi, stop it. You're old enough to be her grandfather."

Lito just took that as a challenge. He put his hands over his heart. "I wish I was your favorite song," he told Amara, "so I could be on your lips forever. If your eyes were the sea, I would drown in them."

Lito was giving her *piropos*, the flirtatious compliments Cuban men said to women on the street. Not everyone did it anymore, but to Lito it was like an art form. Amara laughed and Luis smiled.

"Maybe we shouldn't talk about drowning," Papi said, clutching to the side of the boat as they chopped into a wave.

"What do you think the States will be like?" Isabel's mother asked everyone.

Isabel had to stop and think about that. What *would* the United States be like? She hadn't had much time to even imagine it.

"Shelves full of food at the store," Señora Castillo said.

"Being able to travel anywhere we want, anytime we want!" said Amara.

"I want to be able to choose who I vote for," Luis said.

"I want to play baseball for the New York Yankees!" Iván said.

"I want you to go to college first," his mother told him.

"I want to watch American television," Iván said. "*The Simpsons!*"

"*I'm* going to open my own law office," Señora Castillo said.

Isabel listened as everyone listed more and more things they were looking forward to in the States. Clothes, food, sports, movies, travel, school, opportunity. It all sounded so wonderful, but when it came down to it, all Isabel really wanted was a place where she and her family could be together, and happy.

"What do *you* think *el norte* will be like, Papi?" Isabel asked.

Her father looked surprised at the question.

"No more 'Ministry of Telling People What to Think or Else,'" he said. "No more getting thrown in jail for disagreeing with the government."

"But what do you want to do when you get there?" Señor Castillo asked.

He hesitated while everyone stared at him, his eyes searching Castro's face on the bottom of the boat as though there were answers hidden there.

"Be free," Papi said finally.

"Let's have a song," Lito said. "Chabela, play us a song on your trumpet."

Isabel's chest tightened. She'd told her parents what she'd done, but not Lito. She knew he would never have let her do it.

"I traded my trumpet," she confessed. "For the gasoline."

Her grandfather was shocked. "But that trumpet was everything to you!"

No, not everything, Isabel thought. *It wasn't my mother and father, and you, Lito.*

"I'll get another one in the States," she said.

Lito shook his head. "Here, let's have a song anyway." He began singing a salsa song and tapping out the rhythm on the side of the metal boat. Soon the whole boat was singing, and Lito stood and held out a hand to Amara, inviting her to dance.

"Papi! Sit down! You'll fall out of the boat!" Isabel's mother told him.

"I can't fall out of the boat, because I have already fallen for this princess of the sea!" he said.

Amara laughed and took his hand, and the two of them danced as best they could in the swaying boat. Mami started counting *clave* by clapping, and Isabel frowned, trying to follow the beat.

"Still can't hear it, Chabela?" Lito asked.

Isabel closed her eyes and focused. She could almost hear it . . . almost . . .

And then the motor spluttered and died, and the music stopped.

MAHMOUD

KILIS, TURKEY—2015

2 days from home

MAHMOUD COULD HEAR MUSIC BEYOND the fence.

It was hard to see for all the people. He stood in a long line with his family, waiting at the border to gain admission into Turkey, near the city of Kilis. Around them were countless more Syrian families, all hoping to be let in. They carried everything they owned with them, sometimes in suitcases and duffel bags, but more often stuffed into pillowcases and trash bags. The men wore jeans and T-shirts and tracksuits; the women wore dresses and *abayas* and *hijabs*. Their children looked like miniature versions of them, and acted like miniature adults too—there was very little crying and whining, and none of the kids were playing.

They had all walked too far and seen too much.

After leaving the car behind, Mahmoud and his family had followed the map on their phone, skirting cities held by Daesh and the Syrian army and the rebels and the Kurds as best they could. Google Maps told them it would be an eight-hour walk, and they split the journey up by sleeping in a field. It was hot out by day but it got cold at night, and Mahmoud and his family had left all their extra clothes in the car in their haste to escape.

The next morning they had seen the people.

Dozens of them. Hundreds. Refugees, just like Mahmoud and his family, who had left their homes in Syria and were walking north to Turkey. To safety. Mahmoud and his family had fallen into step with them and disappeared among their ranks. Invisible, just as Mahmoud liked it. Together the shambling throng of refugees was ignored by the American drones and the rebel rocket launchers and the Syrian army tanks and the Russian jets. Mahmoud heard explosions and saw smoke clouds, but no one cared about a few hundred Syrian people leaving the battlefield.

And now they were in line with him, all those hundreds of people and thousands more, and they weren't invisible anymore. Turkish guards in light green camo gear with automatic weapons and white surgical masks over their faces walked up and down the line, staring at each of them in turn. Mahmoud felt like he was in trouble. He wanted to look away, but he was worried that might make the guards think he was hiding something. But if he looked right at them, they would notice him, maybe pull him and his family out of line.

Mahmoud stared straight ahead at his father's back instead. His father's shirt was stained at the armpits, and with a quick sniff of his own shirt Mahmoud realized he stank too. They had walked for hours in the hot sun without a bath, without a change of clothes. They looked tired and poor and wretched. If he were a Turkish border guard, he wouldn't have let in any of these dirty, squalid people, himself included.

Mahmoud's father kept their papers tucked into his pants under his shirt, along with all of their money—the only other things they owned now besides two phones and two chargers. When Mahmoud and his family finally got to the front of the line, late in the day, Mahmoud's father presented their official documents to the border agent. After what seemed like an eternity of looking over their papers, the border guard finally stapled temporary visas onto their passports and let them through.

They were in Turkey! Mahmoud couldn't believe it. Step after step, kilometer after kilometer, he'd begun to think they would never, ever escape Syria. But as relieved as he was, he knew they still had so very far to go.

Ahead of them stretched a small city of white canvas tents, their pointed tops staggered like whitecaps on a choppy sea. There were no trees, no shade, no parks or football fields or rivers. Just a sea of tents and a forest of electric poles and wires.

"Hey, we're in luck!" Mahmoud's dad joked. "The circus is in town!"

Mahmoud looked around. There was a main "street" in the camp, a wide lane where refugees had set up little shops, selling phone cards and camp stoves and clothes and things people had brought with them but no longer wanted or needed. It was like a giant rummage sale, and it seemed like everybody in the camp was there. The path was crammed full of Syrians, all strolling along like they had nothing else to do and nowhere else to go.

"All right," Mahmoud's father was saying. "A man in the group we walked with gave me the name of a smuggler who can get us from Turkey to Greece."

"A *smuggler*?" Mom said. Mahmoud didn't like the sound of that, either—to him, smuggler meant illegal, and illegal meant dangerous.

Dad waved their fears away. "It's fine. This is what they do. They get people into the EU."

The EU, Mahmoud knew, was the European Union. He also knew they were much more strict about letting people in than Turkey was. Once you were *in* one of the EU countries, though, like Greece or Hungary or Germany, you could apply for asylum and be granted official refugee status.

It was getting there that was the hard part.

"I've been talking to him on WhatsApp," Dad continued, holding up his phone. "It will be expensive, but we can pay. And we'll have to get to Izmir, on the Turkish coast. Assuming we stop to sleep every night, that's a nineteen-day walk. Or it's a twelve-hour car ride, non-stop. I'll see if I can find us a bus."

Mahmoud and his mother and sister and brother walked the shopping street. People called out to one another in Arabic, and music from radios and TVs filled the air. Other children darted in and out among the adults, laughing and chasing each other into the alleys of tents off the main drag. Mahmoud caught himself smiling. After Aleppo—the near-constant gunfire and explosions, punctuated by the oppressive quiet of an entire city trying their hardest not to draw attention to themselves—this place felt *alive*, even if it was dusty and cramped.

Mahmoud saw a cardboard box of used toys at one of the shops and knelt to dig in it while his mother and brother and sister walked on. He sifted through it, hoping—yes! A Teenage Mutant Ninja Turtle! It was the one with the red bandanna. The box didn't have any other Ninja Turtles in it, but Waleed would be excited to get it. Mahmoud hoped so, at least. Waleed didn't seem to get excited about much these days. Mahmoud paid ten Syrian pounds for it—about five cents in American money.

A car honked behind Mahmoud, and he turned like everybody else. It was an old blue Opel taxi, traveling so slowly Mahmoud could walk faster. It was the only car Mahmoud had seen in the camp, and the crowd parted for it as it drew closer. A Syrian pop song blared from the radio, and young men and women danced and laughed alongside the taxi. As it passed, Mahmoud saw a young couple sitting in the back. The woman was dressed in a white satin dress and veil.

It was a marriage procession, Mahmoud realized. Back in Syria, it was a tradition to be escorted to your wedding by a parade of cars, to help carry you into your new life. Mahmoud remembered his uncle's wedding, before the war. His uncle had worn a tuxedo and his bride had worn a dress of sparkling jewels and a tiara, and they had been escorted by a dozen cars to a party where Mahmoud had eaten a piece of the delicious seven-tiered cake and danced with his mother to a real band. Here, the couple's only escort was a group of rowdy teenage boys running behind the taxi, and their destination was a dirty white tent with whatever food they'd been able to buy in the camp's market. But everyone seemed to be having fun.

The old taxi's exhaust pipe made a sound like a gunshot—*POK!*—and everybody ducked instinctively. The spell of happiness and safety was momentarily broken by the unforgettable memories of the chaos they had just escaped.

Mahmoud's heart was still racing when someone put a hand on his shoulder, and he jumped.

It was his dad.

"Mahmoud, where's your mother? Where are Waleed and Hana?" his father asked. "I found us a ride, but we have to leave *now*."

JOSEF

10 days from home

JOSEF FOLLOWED THE SMALL GROUP OF KIDS through the raised doorway onto the bridge of the *St. Louis*. The bridge was a narrow, curving room that stretched from one side of the ship to the other. Bright sunlight streamed in through two dozen windows, offering a panoramic view of the vast blue-green Atlantic and wispy white clouds. Throughout the wood-decked room were metal benches with maps and rulers on them, and the walls were dotted with mysterious gauges and meters made of shining brass.

There were a number of crewmen on the bridge, some of them wearing blue-and-white sailor uniforms like the stewards, and three more in brass-buttoned blue jackets with gold bands at the cuffs and blue officers' caps with gold trim. One of the regular sailors stood at a spoked steering wheel the size of a truck tire with handles sticking out all around it. It looked like the steering wheels Josef had seen in paintings of pirate ships, but this one was metal and connected to a big rectangular pedestal.

The shortest of the three men in fancy uniforms strode over to the group with a big smile on his face. Josef recognized him from the Shabbos service.

"Welcome to the bridge, boys and girls," he said. "I'm Captain Schroeder."

The captain shook each of their hands, even though none of them was older than thirteen. One of the parents on board the ship had arranged for a tour of the bridge and engine room for any children who wanted to attend, and eight of them had signed up. Ruthie and Evelyne hadn't been interested, but Renata was there, along with a few of the other older kids.

Captain Schroeder introduced them to his first officer and the other crew on the bridge, and showed them what some of the gauges and dials meant. Josef listened eagerly. "This is the engine control for the *St. Louis*," Captain Schroeder explained. "When we want to change speed, we grip these handles, slide them all the way forward, and then pull them back to the new setting." He smiled. "I'm not going to change the speed now, because we've got the engines set right where we want them."

Josef noticed both handles were set to AHEAD FULL.

"Are we going full speed because we're racing two other ships to Cuba?" Josef asked.

The captain looked surprised, and then a little angry. "Where did you hear that we were racing other ships to Cuba?" he asked Josef.

"Two stewards were talking about it the other day," Josef said, feeling a little nervous. "They said if we don't make it there first, they might not let us in."

The captain pursed his lips and glanced meaningfully at his first officer, who looked concerned.

The captain turned on his smile again. "We're not in any kind of race," he said, looking from Josef to the other kids. "We're just making best possible speed because we have calm seas and a following wind. You've nothing to worry about. Now perhaps Petty Officer Jockl will show you the engine room."

As high up as the bridge was on the ship, the engine room was just as far down. After stepping through a steel fire door that had CREW ONLY painted on it in big letters, Josef and the tour group went down staircase after staircase, and they still weren't to the engine room yet.

Below decks was very different from what Josef was used to above decks. Where everything on A-, B-, and C- decks was airy and comfortable, there were no portholes here, no spacious cabins. The air was damp, and smelled of cigarettes and cabbage and sweat. Peeking into the rooms, Josef could see that the crew quarters below decks had two beds to a room, and barely enough space to turn around. The hallways were narrow, and the ceilings were low. Petty Officer Jockl had to duck as they went through doorways. Josef had never been afraid of tight places before, but the close living conditions made him uneasy. He felt like he was visiting an alien world. The seven other kids must have felt the same way, because they were all silent. Even Renata.

From down the hall came the sound of men singing, and Petty Officer Jockl slowed. As they got closer, Josef recognized the tune. It was "The Horst Wessel Song," the anthem of the Nazi Party. Josef's skin crawled, and he and the other kids looked at each other nervously. Josef had heard "The Horst Wessel Song" hundreds of times in the weeks following his father's abduction. It had gone overnight from an obscure song the Nazis sang at rallies to the unofficial national anthem of Germany— and it was frightening. The last time Josef had heard the song was the day every one of his neighbors had lined the street to salute as Nazi soldiers marched by.

Petty Officer Jockl tried to slip the children past the little common room where the crewmen were drinking and singing, but suddenly someone in the room called out, "Stop! Passengers aren't allowed down here!"

Jockl froze, and so did Josef.

One of the men got up from the table, a scowl on his face. He was a thickset man, with a bulbous nose, bull-dog cheeks, and dark, heavy eyebrows. Josef knew that face from somewhere. Had he been their steward at dinner? Set up their beds one night? No—Josef remembered. This was the man he had seen in the balcony the morning of the Shabbos service. The man who had been angry that the portrait of Hitler had been taken down and removed.

The man staggered a little, bumping into things as he tried to move through the tight little room. Josef had seen drunk people leaving pubs in Berlin the same way.

"The captain has given these children special permission to visit the engine room, Schiendick," Petty Officer Jockl told him.

"The *captain*," Schiendick said, his voice dripping with disapproval. Even from where Josef stood, he could smell the alcohol on his breath.

"Yes," Jockl said, straightening. "The *captain*."

On the wall of the common room, Josef saw a bulletin board with Nazi slogans and headlines from the rabidly anti-Jewish newspaper *Der Stürmer* pinned to it. He felt a shiver of fear.

"*Jewish rats*," Schiendick said, sneering at Josef and the other kids. Many of them looked at their shoes, and even Josef looked away, trying not to draw the big man's attention. Josef clenched his fists, and his ears burned hot with frustration and embarrassment at his helplessness.

After a few tense moments, Schiendick staggered back to his seat, the threat of the captain's rank still worth something even so far away from the bridge.

Petty Officer Jockl hurried the children along, and Schiendick and his friends broke into another Nazi song, even louder than before. Josef heard them sing, "*When*

Jewish blood flows from the knife, things will go much better," before Jockl ushered them down another flight of stairs. Josef's legs felt weak, and he clung to the railing. He thought they had escaped all this on the *St. Louis*. But the hatred had followed them even here, to the middle of the ocean.

With its huge diesel engines and generators and dials and pumps and switches, the engine room should have been fascinating, but Josef had a hard time getting excited about it. None of the other children were excited, either. Not after what had happened with Schiendick. The tour ended solemnly, and Petty Officer Jockl returned them to the surface, being careful to take them back by a different route.

It *was* a different world below decks, Josef thought. A world outside the magic little bubble he and the other Jews lived in above decks on the MS *St. Louis*.

Here, below decks, was the real world.

ISABEL

1 day from home

ISABEL WATCHED AS PAPI, SEÑOR CASTILLO, Luis, and Amara huddled over the boat engine, trying to figure out why it wouldn't start. It had something to do with it overheating, Señor Castillo had said. Amara was pouring seawater over it, trying to cool it. Meanwhile, Iván and Isabel had been tasked with scooping the water back out of the bottom of the boat. The sock stuffed into the bullet hole was soaked through, and it *drip-drip-dripped* water onto Castro's face at the bottom of the boat like a leaky faucet.

They had been drifting north in the Gulf Stream with the motor silent for more than an hour now, and no one was singing or dancing or laughing anymore.

Ahead of Isabel, her mother and Señora Castillo slept against each other on the narrow bench at the front of the boat, where the prow came to a point. Lito sat on the middle bench, right above Isabel and Iván.

"You *do* have family in Miami," Isabel's grandfather told her as she and Iván worked. "When that news lady asked you if you had family in *el norte*, you said no. But you do," Lito said. "My brother, Guillermo."

Isabel and Iván looked up at each other in surprise.

"I didn't know you had a brother," Isabel said to her grandfather.

"He left in the airlifts in the 1970s. The Freedom Flights, when the US airlifted political dissidents off the island," Lito explained. "But Guillermo was no dissident. He just wanted to live in the US. I could have gone too. I was a police officer once, like Luis and Amara. Did you know that? Back before Castro, when Batista was president."

Isabel knew that—and that Lito had lost his job during the Revolution and been sent to cut cane in the fields instead.

"I could have pulled strings," Lito said. "Called in favors. Gotten me and your grandmother off the island."

"Then you would have been born in *el norte*!" Iván told Isabel. She paused in her scooping, thinking how different her life might be right now. Born in the United States! It was almost inconceivable.

"We stayed because Cuba was our *home*," Lito said. "I didn't leave when Castro took over in 1959, I didn't leave when the US sent planes in the '70s, and I didn't leave in the '80s when all those people sailed out of Mariel Harbor."

Lito shook his head at the tight cluster of people worrying over the engine at the back of the boat and thumped his fist against the side.

"It was a mistake, leaving on this sinking coffin. I should have stayed put. All of us should have. How is Cuba worse now than it ever was? We've always been beholden to somebody else. First it was Spain, then it was the US, then it was Russia. First Batista, then Castro. We should have waited. Things change. They always change."

"But do they ever get better?" Iván asked.

Isabel thought that was a good question. All her life, things had only gotten worse. First the Soviet Union collapsing, then her parents fighting, then her father trying to leave. Then her grandmother dying. She waited for Lito to tell her different, to tell her that things would get better, but he looked out at the black water instead. Isabel and Iván shared a glance. Lito's silence was answer enough.

"Someone would have done something," Lito said at last. "We should have waited."

"But they were going to arrest Papi," said Isabel.

"I know you love your father, Chabela, but he's a fool."

Isabel's cheeks burned hot with anger and embarrassment. She loved Lito, but she loved her *papi* too, and she hated to hear Lito say bad things about him. But even worse, he was saying these things in front of her best friend. She glanced quickly at Iván. He kept his eyes on his work, pretending not to have heard. But they were right at Lito's feet. He could hear everything. And Lito wasn't finished.

"He's risking his life for this—he's risking your life, and your mother's life and his unborn child's life—and for what?" Lito asked. "He doesn't even know. He can't say. Ask him why he wants to go to the States and all he can say is 'freedom.' That's not a plan. How is he going to put a roof over your head and food on your table any better than he did in Cuba?" Lito raised his eyebrows at Isabel. "He's taking you away from who you *are. What* you are. How are you ever going to learn to count *clave* in Miami? The US has no soul. In Havana, you would have learned it without even trying. *Clave* is the hidden heartbeat of the people, beneath whatever song Batista or Castro is playing."

"Oh, hush, Papi," Isabel's mother said sleepily. She had been awake enough to hear them after all, at least the last part. "Miami is just North Cuba."

Mami shifted and went back to sleep, but Isabel worried that Lito was right. She had never been able to count *clave*, but she had always assumed it would come to her eventually. That the rhythm of her homeland would one day whisper its secrets to her soul. But would she ever hear it now? Like trading her trumpet, had she swapped the one thing that was really hers—her music—for the chance to keep her family together?

"We should go back," Lito said. He wobbled to his feet. "We're not too far gone, and with Castro being so lenient right now, we won't be punished for leaving."

"No, Lito," Isabel said. No—as much as she feared the loss of her music, her soul, she wouldn't trade that for her family. She grabbed Lito and held him back. "Don't. We can't go back. They'll arrest Papi!"

Panic rose like the distant rumble of thunder in Isabel's ears. But then Iván and Lito both looked up, like they could hear it too.

It wasn't Isabel's fear that shook her deep down to the pit of her stomach.

It was the enormous tanker headed right for them.

MAHMOUD

IZMIR, TURKEY—2015

4 days from home

MAHMOUD STOOD IN A WET PARKING LOT with his family, a light drizzle making everything slick and damp. Down past a pebbly brown beach, the Mediterranean Sea churned like a washing machine. A huge black-and-red cargo ship slid by on the horizon.

"No. No boat today," the Syrian man who was working for the Turkish smugglers told them. "Tomorrow."

"But I was told it would be today," Mahmoud's father said. "We hurried to get here today."

The smuggler raised a hand and shook his head. "No, no. You have money, yes? Tomorrow. You will get a text tomorrow."

"But where are we supposed to go?" Mahmoud's mother asked the smuggler.

Mahmoud couldn't believe it. They had spent two long days in cars and buses, trying to get here on time for the boat Dad had hired to take them across the sea to Greece. And now there was no boat.

"There's a hotel on the next block," the smuggler said. "They take Syrians."

"We're trying to save money. We're going all the way to Germany," Dad told him.

"There's a park nearby," the smuggler said.

"A park? You mean sleep outside? But I have a baby . . ." Mom said, gesturing to Hana in her arms.

The smuggler shrugged as if it didn't matter to him. His phone rang and he turned away to take it. "Tomorrow," he told Mahmoud's parents over his shoulder. "You will get a text tomorrow. Be ready."

Mahmoud's father huffed but immediately turned to his family and put on a smile. "Well, we always talked about taking a Mediterranean vacation," he said. "We've got an extra night in Izmir. Who wants to go out dancing?"

"I just want to find someplace dry where I can sleep," said Mom.

Dad led them in the direction of the hotel. All the shops were closing as they walked back through town, but Mahmoud marveled at how clean everything looked here in Turkey. There was no rubble, no twisted metal. The cobblestone streets were in perfect condition, and flowers grew in front of perfect little houses and shops. Shining cars and vans drove past on the road, and lights glowed in the windows of buildings.

"Do you remember when it used to be like this in Syria?" Mahmoud asked his little brother.

Waleed was gawking just as much as Mahmoud, but he didn't say anything. Mahmoud took a deep, frustrated breath. He and Waleed had had their fights—they were brothers, after all—but ever since Mahmoud could remember, Waleed had been more like his best friend and constant companion. They played together, prayed together, shared a bedroom together. Waleed had been the hyper one, bouncing off walls and hopping on furniture and kicking soccer balls in the hall. As annoying as his brother had been sometimes, Mahmoud wished he would show a little of the old crazy again. Not even the Ninja Turtle that Mahmoud had bought for him in Kilis had cheered Waleed up.

Later, in the hotel lobby, Mahmoud was still thinking about how he could get his brother back when he heard the desk clerk say they had no rooms left.

"Maybe someone will share with us," Mahmoud's father suggested to the clerk.

"You will forgive me," said the desk clerk, "but the rooms already have three families apiece."

Mahmoud's heart sank. Three families in each room! And the hotel was full. What were the chances they would find a room anywhere else?

Dad searched on his phone and tried calling around, but it was the same story everywhere.

"But how can they be so full?" Mahmoud's mother said. "They can't all be leaving tomorrow!"

With nowhere else to go, they found the park the smuggler had told them about. But there was no room for them there, either. All the other refugees who had been turned away from the hotels were there, some sleeping on benches in the rain, others lucky enough to have tents—tents that looked like they had been there for more than a day or two. Mahmoud slumped in the rain. He was so wet. So tired. He just wanted somewhere warm and dry to sleep.

"We should have stayed at the refugee camp!" Mom said.

"No," said his father. "No—we move forward. Always forward. And we don't stop until we get to Germany. We don't want to end up stuck in this place. Let's just see if we can find a dry spot for the night."

Mahmoud spied a thin Syrian boy about his age approaching each of the families in the park, offering them something. Mahmoud wandered closer to have a look. The boy saw his interest and came over to him.

"Want to buy some tissues?" the boy asked. He offered Mahmoud a small unopened plastic pack of tissues. "Just ten Syrian pounds or ten Turkish *kuruş*."

"No, thank you," Mahmoud said.

"Do you need water? Life vests? A phone charger? I can get it for you, for a price."

"We need a place to stay," Mahmoud said.

The boy looked Mahmoud and his family over.

"I know a place," the boy said. "I will show you for two thousand Syrian pounds or twenty-five Turkish *lira*."

Two thousand Syrian pounds was almost ten American dollars—a lot of money when you had a whole continent to cross. But the rain was getting stronger, and there was no place dry left in the park. When Mahmoud told his father the boy's offer, Dad was willing to pay.

The boy led them away from the coast, to a neighborhood where weeds grew up through the cobblestones, and the houses had metal grates on the windows instead of flower boxes. One of the street lamps flickered, giving the street an ominous energy.

The boy lifted a broken chain-link fence that led to a parking lot. "Here," he said.

Mahmoud's father gave the rest of his family a dubious look and led them under the fence. They followed the boy to a large square building with boarded-up windows and graffiti-covered walls. One of the boards blocking the door from trespassers had been ripped off, and they pushed their way inside.

It was a mall. Or it had been once. A large open courtyard with an empty fountain in the middle was ringed with storefronts that went up for four levels. A few of the shops were lit up with lamps connected to extension cords, and others burned kerosene lamps and candles. But most of the shops weren't shops anymore—they were little apartments where people lived. Squatters in an abandoned shopping mall.

The boy led them to an empty yogurt shop on the

third floor, next to a former music store that was home to a Syrian family of six. They looked like they had been there a while. They had a tattered old couch and a hot plate, and sheets hung from ropes to quarter the space into little rooms.

The yogurt shop had no furniture and a broken linoleum floor. Something skittered away in the darkness when they went inside.

"It's just for the night," Mahmoud's father said.

"You leave tomorrow?" the boy said. "On a boat? Then you need life vests. Most definitely. Or else you drown when your boat flips."

Mahmoud's eyes went wide, and he shivered in his soaking-wet clothes. He didn't like any part of this plan.

His father raised his hands to his family. "The boat isn't going to flip," he told them.

"Or run out of gas. Or wreck on the rocks," the boy said. "Then you drown."

Dad sighed. "All right. All right. Where do we buy life vests?"

JOSEF

11 days from home

JOSEF'S MOTHER GRABBED FOR HIS FATHER'S flailing arms, but Aaron Landau was too strong for her, thin as he was.

"No. *No!* They're coming for us," he said, his eyes frantic. "The ship is slowing down. Can't you feel it? We're slowing so they can turn us around, take us back to Germany!"

Josef's father pulled his arm away and knocked over a lamp. It fell to the floor with a crash, and the light went out.

"Josef, help me," his mother begged.

Josef pulled himself away from the wall and tried to grab one of his father's arms while his mother went for the other. In the corner of her bed, Ruthie buried her face in Bitsy's ears and cried.

"No!" Josef's father cried. "We have to *hide*, do you hear me? We can't stay here. We have to get off this ship!"

Josef grabbed his father's arm and held on tight. "No, Papa. We're not turning around," Josef said. "We're slowing for a funeral. A funeral at sea."

Josef's father stopped dead, but Josef kept a tight hold on him. He hadn't wanted to tell his father about the funeral, but now it seemed the only way to calm him down.

Aaron Landau's bulging, haunted eyes swept to his son. "A funeral? Who's died? A passenger? It was the Nazis who did it! I knew they were on board! They're after us all!" He began to thrash again, more panicked than before.

"No, Papa, no!" Josef said. He fought to hold on to his father. "It was an old man. Professor Weiler. He was sick when he came aboard. It's not the Nazis, Papa."

Josef knew all about it. Ruthie had begged him to go swimming in the pool with her and Renata and Evelyne that afternoon. But Josef was a man now, not a boy. He was too old for kids' stuff. He'd been walking the outside boardwalk on B-deck instead, keeping an eye out for the man from the engine room, Schiendick, and his friends, when he'd heard a cry from one of the cabin portholes. Peeking inside, he saw a woman with long, curly black hair and a white dress sobbing as she lay across the body of an old man. Captain Schroeder and the ship's doctor were there too. The man in the bed was perfectly still, his mouth open and his eyes staring blankly at the ceiling.

He was dead. Josef had never seen a dead body so close up before.

"You there! Boy!"

Josef had jumped. A woman walking her little dog on the boardwalk on B-deck had caught him peeping. He had sprinted away as the little dog barked at him, but not before Josef heard the ship's doctor say that Professor Weiler had died of cancer.

In his family's cabin now a few hours later, Josef still clung to his father's arm, trying to calm him down.

"He was an old man, and he'd been sick for a long time already!" Josef told his father. "They're burying him at sea because we're too far away from Cuba."

Josef and his mother hung on to his father until Josef's words finally got through. Papa stopped struggling against them and sagged, and suddenly they were holding him up off the floor.

"He was sick already?" Papa asked.

"Yes. It was the cancer," Josef said.

Josef's father let them guide him to his bed, where he sat down. Mama went to Ruthie to comfort her.

"When is the funeral?" Papa asked.

"Late tonight," Josef told him.

"I want to go," his father said.

Josef couldn't believe it. Papa hadn't left the cabin in eleven days, and now he wanted to go to the funeral of someone he'd never met? In his condition? Josef looked worriedly to his mother, who held Ruthie in her lap.

"I don't think that's such a good idea," Mama said, echoing Josef's thoughts.

"I saw too many men die without funerals at Dachau," Papa said. "I will go to this one."

It was the first time his father had even spoken the name of the place he'd been, and it was like a winter frost covered everything in the room. It ended the conversation as quickly as it had begun.

"Take Josef with you, then," Mama said. "Ruthie and I will stay here."

That night, Josef led his father to A-deck aft, where the captain and his first officer waited with a few other passengers. The passengers' clothes looked shabby, and it was only when he heard his father tearing his shirt that Josef understood—ripping your garments was a Jewish tradition at funerals, and they had torn theirs in sympathy with Mrs. Weiler. Josef pulled on his own collar until the seam ripped. His father nodded, then led him to the sandbox by the pool and had him take a handful of sand. Josef didn't understand, but he did as he was told.

The elevator to A-deck arrived, and Mrs. Weiler emerged first, a candle in hand. Behind her came the rabbi and four sailors, who carried Professor Weiler's body on a stretcher. He was bound up tight in a white sailcloth, like an Egyptian pharaoh.

"Hold on there." The man from below decks, Schiendick, pushed through the small crowd with two fellow crew members. "I'm Otto Schiendick, the Nazi Party leader on this ship," he said, "and German law says that a body buried at sea must be covered with the national flag." Schiendick unfurled the red-and-white Nazi flag with the black swastika in the middle, and the passengers gasped.

Papa pushed his way forward. "Never! Do you hear me? *Never!* It's a sacrilege!" He was shaking worse than ever. Josef had never seen his father this angry, and he was frightened for him. Schiendick wasn't the kind of man you wanted to mess with.

Josef grabbed his father's arm and tried to pull him away.

Papa spat at the feet of Schiendick. "That is what I think of you and your flag!"

Schiendick and his men surged forward to avenge the insult, but Captain Schroeder quickly intervened.

"Stop this! Stop this at once, Steward!" Captain Schroeder commanded.

Schiendick addressed his captain but never took his eyes off Josef's father. "It's German law. And I see no reason for an exception to be made in this case."

"And I do," Captain Schroeder said. "Now, take that flag and leave here, Mr. Schiendick, or I will relieve you of duty and have you confined to quarters."

The steward held Papa's gaze a long moment more. His eyes shifted to Josef, giving him goose bumps, and then Schiendick turned and stormed away.

Josef's chest heaved like he'd been running a marathon.

He was so wound up he was quivering worse than his father. Sand slipped from his shaking fist.

The captain apologized profusely for the disturbance, and the funeral continued. The rabbi said a short prayer in Hebrew, and the sailors slid the body of Professor Weiler over the side of the ship.

After a moment, there was a quiet splash, and the mourners said together, "Remember, God, that we are of dust." One by one they stepped to the rail, where they released handfuls of sand—the sand Josef's father had told him to take from the sandbox. Josef joined his father at the rail, and they scattered their sand in the sea.

Captain Schroeder and his first officer put their caps back on and saluted. They touched the brims of their hats, Josef noticed, instead of giving the Hitler salute.

Without words, the funeral service broke up. Josef expected his father to return to their cabin right away, but instead he lingered at the rail, staring down into the dark waters of the Atlantic. *What is he thinking?* Josef wondered. *What happened to him at Dachau that he's now a ghost of the man he once was?*

"At least he didn't have to be buried in the hell of the Third Reich," his father said.

The ship rumbled softly, and Josef knew the captain had restarted the engines. They were on their way to Cuba again. But how much time had they lost?

ISABEL

THE STRAITS OF FLORIDA, SOMEWHERE NORTH OF CUBA—1994

1 day from home

THE TANKER EMERGED FROM THE DARKNESS like some giant leviathan come to swallow them. It stood at least seven stories tall out of the water and was so wide it filled the horizon. Its pointed bow sent huge waves sluicing away, and two massive anchors stood out from the sides like the horns on a monster. Isabel quailed in fear. It was straight out of a nightmare.

"A ship!" Lito yelled. *"We've drifted into the shipping lanes!"*

But by now everyone had seen it. The rumble of the ship's massive engines had awakened Mami and Señora Castillo, and everyone was scrambling around in the boat in a panic, making it rock dangerously.

"It's coming right for us!" Amara screamed.

Isabel climbed over Iván, trying to get as far away from the tanker as she could. She slipped and fell with a splash into the bottom of the boat.

"Everybody settle down!" Señor Castillo cried, but no one was listening.

"We have to get the engine started!" Papi cried. He yanked frantically on the starter chain, barely giving the engine time to cough and die before he yanked on it again.

"Don't! You'll flood it and it'll never start!" Luis said, trying to wrestle the chain from him.

"Where are the matches?" Lito cried. "We have to start a fire! They can't see us in the dark!"

"Here!" said Iván. He lifted a matchbox from the Styrofoam carton that held the few emergency supplies they'd brought.

"No!" Papi yelled. He lunged for Iván's outstretched hand, and together they fell against the side of the boat, tipping it. Isabel's mother fell into the pool of water on the bottom and slid into the side of the boat with a *thump*. Isabel crawled to help her.

Lito grabbed Papi by the shirt. *"What are you doing?"* he demanded.

Papi held the matchbox out of Lito's reach. "We don't *want* to be seen, you old fool!" he yelled over the growing thunder of the tanker. "If they see us, they'll have to rescue us! It's maritime law! And if they 'rescue' us, they'll send us back to Cuba!"

"Would you rather they send us to the ocean floor?" Lito yelled.

Isabel couldn't help looking up as she pulled her mother out of the water. "It's getting closer!" Isabel cried.

The tanker was still hundreds of meters away, but it was so huge it felt like it was on top of them. They were never getting out of its way. Isabel's heart thumped so hard she thought it was going to burst right out of her chest.

"If we don't want them to know we're here, maybe we shouldn't start the engine!" Amara yelled.

"They'll never hear us no matter what we do!" Señor Castillo said. The tanker was so loud now it sounded like a jet engine. He and Luis flipped a switch on their own engine and yanked the starter chain again. A puff of gray smoke *poofed* out from the engine, but it didn't catch.

The tanker loomed larger. Closer. Isabel cringed. It was going to hit them!

Luis yanked on the chain. A cough. A sputter. Nothing.

Cough. Sputter. Nothing.

Cough. Sputter. Nothing.

The sea swelled in front of the tanker, pushing them higher and away, and for a fleeting moment Isabel's hopes rose with it. But then the swell passed, and they were pulled back in by the tanker's massive draw. Their little blue boat spun sideways, and they zoomed toward the big ship's prow.

The tanker was going to tear them in half, right down the middle.

Isabel looked up into the terrified eyes of Iván as he realized the same thing, and they screamed. Then suddenly they were both thrown to the bottom of the boat, and something buzzed like a mosquito underneath the howl of the tanker.

Luis had gotten the engine to start!

Their little boat shot forward in the water, darting out of the way of the tanker's prow. But the waves thrown off by the big ship lifted up the back end of Isabel's boat and dumped an ocean of seawater on top of them.

Isabel swallowed a mouthful of salty water and tumbled across the boat. She slammed into something hard, and her shoulder exploded with pain. She came up spluttering. She was hip-deep in water and the engine had stopped again, but none of that mattered right now.

Iván's father had fallen overboard.

Isabel saw his white-haired head rise up out of the water. Señor Castillo gulped for air, then disappeared as a wave from the massive tanker's wake rolled over him.

"Señor Castillo!" Isabel cried.

"Papá!" Iván shouted. "Where is he? Do you see him?"

Isabel and Iván frantically searched the dark water, watching for Señor Castillo to surface again. They had missed the huge ship's prow by mere meters, but the waves the behemoth created as it passed were just as dangerous. The ocean heaved and sank, the little boat tipping over sideways as the waves caught it amidships.

Everyone was just getting back up from the floor of the boat when they were sent tumbling again. Iván rolled to the other side of the boat, but Isabel hung on. There!

She saw Señor Castillo's head pop up from under the water, but only for a gasping second—too quick to get enough air.

In a flash, Isabel remembered her grandmother disappearing under the waves just like that two years ago, and without another thought, Isabel dove in after Señor Castillo.

MAHMOUD

IZMIR, TURKEY—2015

11 days from home

MAHMOUD SCREAMED.

He howled louder than a fighter jet, and his parents didn't even tell him to hush. Lights came on in houses nearby, and curtains ruffled as people looked out at the noise. Mahmoud's mother broke down in tears, and his father let the life jackets he carried drop to the ground.

The smuggler had just told them their boat wasn't leaving tonight.

Again.

"No boat today. Tomorrow. Tomorrow," he'd told Mahmoud's father.

It was exactly the same thing he'd told Mahmoud's father the day before. And the day before that. And every day for the last week. A text would come, telling them to hurry—hurry!—out to the beach, and every time they would pack up what few things they owned, grab the life jackets, and rush through the streets of Izmir to this parking lot, and every time there would be no boat waiting for them.

First it was the weather, the smuggler said. Then another family that was supposed to go with them hadn't arrived yet. Then it was the Turkish Coast Guard patrols. Or the boat wasn't ready. There was always some reason they couldn't leave. It was like some cruel school-yard game of keep away.

Mahmoud and his family were at their wits' end. This off-and-on-again business was tearing them apart. All except for Waleed. Lifeless Waleed, who didn't flinch when bombs exploded.

"I want to go back to Syria! I don't care if we die," Mahmoud said after he'd let out his scream. "I just want to get out of here!" Even as he said it, he heard the whine in his voice, the pathetic, toddler-like frustration. Part of him was embarrassed—he was older than that, more mature. He was almost a man. But another part of him just wanted to stomp his feet and pitch a fit, and that part of him was getting harder and harder to keep quiet.

Little Hana started crying too, and Mahmoud's mother tried to calm them both by pulling Mahmoud into a hug.

"Look at it this way," Dad said, "now we have more time to practice our Turkish."

No one laughed.

"Let's get back to the mall before someone takes our place," Mom said wearily.

Mahmoud carried the life jackets so his father could carry Waleed, who quickly fell asleep on his father's shoulder. His mother carried Hana. Even though Mahmoud hated the desperate feeling of defeat in going back to the mall, at least it meant not sleeping outside in the park.

But this time, someone was waiting for them at the mall entrance.

There were two of them, both Turkish men, in matching blue tracksuits. One of them was muscular, with curly black hair, a thin beard, and a thick gold chain necklace. The other was overweight and wore mirrored sunglasses, even though it was night.

He was the one with the pistol stuck in the waist of his pants.

"You want inside, you gotta pay rent," the burly man told them.

"Since when?" Mahmoud's father said.

"Since now," the man said. "We own this building, and we're tired of you Syrians freeloading."

More bullies, thought Mahmoud. *Just like in Syria.* Mahmoud's legs went numb, and he thought he might fall over. He couldn't bear the thought of walking any farther. Looking for a place to live again.

"How much?" Mahmoud's father asked wearily.

"Five thousand pounds a night," the muscular man said.

Dad sighed and started to put Waleed down so he could pay the man.

"Each," the man said.

"*Each?* Per night?" Dad said. Mahmoud knew his dad was doing the math in his head. There were five of them, and they'd already been here a week. How long could they afford to pay twenty-five thousand pounds a day and still have enough for the boat, and whatever came afterward?

"No," Mahmoud's father said. Mom started to protest, but he shook his head. "No—we already have all our things. We'll find someplace else to stay. It's only until tomorrow."

The big man chuckled. "Right. Tomorrow."

Mahmoud staggered along behind his parents as they roamed the streets of Izmir, looking for someplace to sleep. His parents carried Waleed and Hana, but not him. He was too old to be carried anymore, and for the first time he wished he wasn't.

They finally found the doorway of a travel agency set back from the street, and no one else was sleeping there. They were just settling in when a Turkish police car came down the street. Mahmoud shrank back into the corner, trying to be invisible, but the police car's lights came on and it beeped its electronic siren at them—*blurp-blurp.* "You can't sleep there," a police officer told them through a loudspeaker. And so they had to get up and walk again.

Mahmoud was so tired he started to cry, but he did it softly, so his parents wouldn't hear. He hadn't cried like this since that first night when the bombs had started to fall on Aleppo.

Another car came down the road, and at first Mahmoud worried it was another police car. But it was a BMW sedan. On a whim, Mahmoud darted out into the car's headlights and waved the life jackets on his arms.

"Mahmoud! No!" his mother cried.

The BMW slowed, its lights bright in his face. The driver honked at him, and Mahmoud hurried around to the driver's-side window.

"Please, can you help us?" Mahmoud begged. "My baby sister—"

But the car was already shooting away. Another car followed it, and it drove right past Mahmoud.

"Mahmoud! Get out of the street!" his father called. "You'll get yourself killed!"

Mahmoud didn't care anymore. There had to be someone who would help them. He waved the life jackets at the next car, and miraculously it stopped. It was an old brown Skoda, and the driver rolled the window down by hand. He was an elderly, wrinkled man with a short white beard, and he wore a black-and-white *keffiyeh* headscarf.

"Please, can you help us?" Mahmoud asked. "My family and I have nowhere to go, and my sister is only a baby."

Dad jogged up and tried to pull Mahmoud away.

"We're very sorry," Mahmoud's father told the man. "We didn't mean to bother you. We'll be on our way."

Mahmoud was annoyed. He'd finally gotten somebody to stop, and now his father was trying to send him away!

"My house is too small for all of you," the man said, "but I have a little car dealership, and you can stay in the office." Arabic! Mahmoud was thrilled—the man spoke fluent Arabic.

"No, no, we couldn't possibly—" Mahmoud's father started to say, but Mahmoud cut him off.

"Yes! Thank you!" Mahmoud cried. He waved his mother over. "He speaks Arabic, and he says he will help us!"

Dad tried to apologize again and refuse the offer of help, but Mahmoud was already climbing in the backseat with the load of life jackets. Mom got in beside him with Hana, and Mahmoud's father shifted Waleed in his arms so he could reluctantly sit in the front passenger seat.

"Mahmoud . . ." his father said, unhappy. But Mahmoud didn't care. They were off their feet, and they were on their way to someplace they could sleep.

The little Skoda's gears ground as the man got them underway.

"My name is Samih Nasseer," the man told them, and Mahmoud's father introduced them all.

"You are Syrian, yes? Refugees?" the man asked. "I know what it's like. I am a refugee too, from Palestine."

Mahmoud frowned. This man was a refugee, and he owned his own car and his own business? "How long have you lived in Turkey?" Mahmoud asked Mr. Nasseer.

"Sixty-seven years now!" Mr. Nasseer said, smiling at Mahmoud in the rearview mirror. "I was forced to leave my home in 1948 during the first Arab-Israeli war. They are still fighting there, but someday, when my homeland is restored, I will go home again!"

Dad's phone chimed, surprising them all and making Waleed stir. His father read the glowing screen.

"It's the smuggler. He says the boat is ready now."

Mahmoud had learned not to get excited about these texts, but even so, he still felt a little flutter of hope in his chest.

"You take a boat to Greece? Tonight?" Mr. Nasseer asked.

"Maybe," Mahmoud's father said. "If it's there."

"I will take you to it," Mr. Nasseer said, "and if it is not there, you can come back and stay with me."

"You're very kind," Mom said. Mahmoud didn't know why, but his mother pulled Mahmoud close and gave him a hug.

It took very little time for the car to take them back to the beach, and when they pulled to a stop, they were all quiet as they stared.

This time, finally, a boat was there.

JOSEF

SOMEWHERE ON THE ATLANTIC OCEAN—1939

14 days from home

A DAY OUT FROM CUBA, THE *ST. LOUIS* THREW a party. Streamers and balloons hung from the ceiling and decorated the gallery rails of the first-class social hall. Chairs and tables were pushed aside to make room for dancers. There was a feeling of wild relief, as though they were dancing away all the stress of leaving Germany. The stewards smiled with the passengers as though they understood, but none of them could really understand, Josef thought. Not until *their* shop windows had been smashed and *their* businesses had been shut down. Not until the newspapers and radio talked about *them* as sub-human monsters. Not until shadowy men had burst into *their* homes and smashed up *their* things and dragged away someone *they* loved.

Not until they had been told to leave their homeland and never, ever come back.

Still, Josef enjoyed the party. He danced with his mother while Ruthie, Renata, and Evelyne ran in and out between people's legs all evening long. Josef had been nervous about Cuba at first, scared of the unknown, but now he was excited to reach Havana, to start a new life—especially if it was like this.

Josef's father stayed hidden away in their cabin the whole night, sure this was all just another Nazi trick.

The next morning, breakfast in the ship's dining room was interrupted by the thundering, clanking sound of the anchors being dropped. Josef ran to the window. Dawn had broken, and Josef could see the Malecón, Havana's famous seaside avenue. The stewards had told them all about its theaters and casinos and restaurants, and the Miramar Hotel, where all the waiters wore tuxedos. But the *St. Louis* was still a long way off from there. For some reason, the ship had anchored kilometers out from shore.

"It's for the medical quarantine," a doctor from Frankfurt explained to the small crowd who had gathered with Josef at the porthole to look at Cuba. "I saw them run up the yellow flag this morning before breakfast. We just have to be approved by the port's medical authorities first. Standard procedure."

Josef made sure he was on deck when the first boat from the Havana Port Authority reached the *St. Louis*. The Cuban man who climbed the ladder to C-deck from the launch was deeply tanned and wore a lightweight white suit. Josef watched as Captain Schroeder and the ship's doctor met the man as he came aboard. The captain swore an oath that none of the passengers was insane, a criminal, or had a contagious disease. That was apparently all that should have been required, because when the port doctor insisted he still be allowed to examine each and every passenger, Captain Schroeder looked angry. He balled his fists and breathed deeply, but he didn't object. He gave a curt order to the ship's doctor to assemble the passengers in the social hall and then marched away.

Josef ran back to his cabin and burst in on his mother packing the last of their things. Ruthie was helping her while Papa lay on the bed.

"The—the doctor from Cuba—he's going to make all the passengers—go through a medical examination," Josef told his mother, still panting from his run. "They're gathering everybody in the social hall right now."

Mama's shocked look told him she understood. Papa was not well. What if the Cuban doctor said he was too mentally disturbed to be allowed into Havana? Where would they go if Cuba turned them away? What would they do?

"Gathering us?" Papa said. He looked even more frightened by the prospect than Josef's mother had. "Like—like a roll call?" He stood up and backed against a wall. "No," he said. "The things that happened at roll call. The hangings. The floggings. The drownings. The beatings." He wrapped his arms around himself, and Josef knew his father was talking about that place. Dachau. Josef and his mother stood like statues, afraid to break the spell. "Once, I saw another man shot dead with a rifle," his father whispered. "He was standing right beside me. He was standing right beside me, and I couldn't move, couldn't make a sound, or I would be next."

"It's not going to be like that, dear heart," Mama said. She reached out to him, tentatively, gently, and he didn't flinch under her hand. "You were strong once before, in that place. We just need you to be strong again. And then we'll be in Cuba. We'll be safe forever. All of us."

It was clear to Josef that his father was still lost in his memories of Dachau as they led him to the social hall. Papa looked frightened. Jittery. It scared Josef when his father got this way, but he was even more scared that the doctor would see Papa's condition and turn them away.

Josef and his family joined the other passengers standing in rows, and the doctor walked among them. Papa stood beside Josef, and as the doctor got closer, Josef's father began to make a low keening sound, like a wounded dog. Papa was starting to attract the attention of the passengers around them. Josef felt a bead of sweat roll down his back underneath his shirt, and Ruthie cried softly.

"Be strong, my love," Josef heard his mother whisper to his father. "Be strong, like you were before."

"But I wasn't," Josef's father blubbered. "I *wasn't* strong. I was just lucky. It could have been me. Should have been me."

The Cuban doctor was getting closer. Josef had to do

something. But what? His father was inconsolable. The things he said he saw—Josef couldn't even imagine. His father had only survived by staying quiet. By not drawing attention to himself. But now he was going to get them sent away.

Suddenly, Josef saw what he had to do. He slapped his father across the face. Hard.

Papa staggered in surprise, and Josef felt just as shocked as his father looked. Josef couldn't believe what he'd just done. Six months ago, he would never have even dreamed of striking *any* adult, let alone his father. Papa would have punished him for such disrespect. But in the past six months, Josef and his father had traded places. Papa was the one acting like a child, and Josef was the adult.

Mama and Ruthie stared at Josef, stunned, but he ignored them and pulled his father back in line.

"Do you want the Nazis to catch you? Do you want them to send you back to that place?" Josef hissed at Papa.

"I— No," his father said, still dazed.

"That man there," Josef whispered, pointing to the doctor, "he's a Nazi in disguise. He decides who goes back to Dachau. He decides who lives and who dies. If you're lucky, he won't choose you. But if you speak, if you move, if you make even the slightest sound, he will pull you out of line. Send you back. Do you understand?"

Josef's father nodded urgently. Beside him, Mama put a hand to her mouth and wept, but she didn't say anything.

"Now, clean yourself up. Quickly!" Josef told his father.

Aaron Landau dropped his wife's hand, dragged his oversized coat sleeve across his face, and stood rigidly at attention, eyes forward.

Like a prisoner.

The doctor came down their row, looking at each person in turn. When he got to Papa, Josef held his breath. The doctor looked Josef's father up and down, then moved on. Josef sagged with relief. They'd made it. His father had passed the doctor's inspection!

Josef closed his eyes and fought back tears of his own. He felt terrible for scaring his father like that, for making Papa's fears worse instead of better. And he felt terrible for taking his father's place as the man in the family. All Josef's life, he had looked up to his father. Idolized him. Now it was hard to see him as anything but a broken old man.

But all that would change when they got off this ship and into Cuba. Then everything would go back to normal. They would find a way to fix his father.

The Cuban doctor finished his rounds and nodded to the ship's doctor that he approved the passengers. Josef's mother wrapped his father in a hug, and Josef felt his heart lift. For the first time all afternoon, he felt hope.

"Well, that was a sham," said the man standing in line next to him.

"What do you mean?" Josef asked.

"That was no kind of medical inspection. The entire business was a charade. A giant waste of time."

Josef didn't understand. If it wasn't a proper medical inspection, what had it all been for?

He understood when he and his family lined up at the ladder on C-deck to leave the ship. The Cuban doctor was gone, and he'd left Cuban police officers behind in his place. They were blocking the only way off the ship.

"We've passed our medicals and we have all the right papers," a woman passenger said to the police. "When will we be allowed into Havana?"

"*Mañana*," the policeman said in Spanish. "*Mañana.*"

Josef didn't speak Spanish. He didn't know what *mañana* meant.

"Tomorrow," one of the other passengers translated for them. "Not today. Tomorrow."

ISABEL

1 day from home

ISABEL HIT THE WATER AND SANK INTO THE warm Gulf Stream. It was pitch-black all around her, and the ocean was *alive*. Not alive with fish—alive like the ocean was a living creature itself. It churned and roiled and roared with bubbles and foam. It beat at her, pushing her and pulling her like a cat playing with the mouse it was about to eat.

Isabel fought her way back to the surface and gasped for air.

"Isabel!" her mother shrieked, her arms stretching out for her. But there was no way her mother could reach her. The boat was already so far away! Isabel panicked. How was it so far away already?

"We have to get the boat turned!" Isabel heard Luis cry. "If we don't meet the waves head on, they'll roll us over!"

"Dad!" Iván yelled.

Isabel spun in the water, and a wave slammed into her, filling her mouth and nose with salty water and sweeping her under again. The wave passed and she broke the surface, gagging and choking, but she was already moving toward the place where she had seen Señor Castillo's head before it went under.

Her hand struck something in the dark water, and Isabel recoiled until she realized it was Señor Castillo. The sea was tossing him around, but he wasn't moving on his own, wasn't fighting to get back out of the water. Isabel took in as much air as she could and dove down beneath an oncoming wave. She found Señor Castillo's body in the dark, wrapped her arms around him, and kicked as hard as she could for the surface. The ocean fought her, sweeping her legs out from under her and spinning her all around, but Isabel kicked, kicked, kicked until her lungs were about to burst, and at last she exploded up into the cold air, gasping.

"There! There they are!" Iván cried.

Isabel couldn't even try to look for the boat. It was all she could do to keep Señor Castillo's lolling head above water and catch quick breaths before the waves rolled over them both.

But the waves seemed to be smaller now. Still deadly, but not as high and fast. Isabel began to feel the rhythm of the sea, the singsong lullaby of it, and it was easy to close her eyes, to stop kicking, to stop fighting. She was so tired. So very, very tired . . .

And then Iván was there in the water with them, his arms around her, like they were back in their village playing together in the waves on the beach.

"Here! Here! They're here!" Iván shouted. Their boat was now alongside her, and her head thumped into the side of it as a wave washed over her. Hands lifted Señor Castillo from her, and soon they dragged her over the side too. She splashed back down into the half-meter of water that filled the boat. But she was away from the waves, the never-ending waves, and she collapsed into her mother's arms.

"Rudi! Rudi! Oh, God," Señora Castillo cried, clutching her husband's hand. Señor Castillo was unconscious. Luis and Papi had laid him out on one of the benches, and Isabel's grandfather was pumping his stomach like an accordion. Seawater burbled up out of Señor Castillo's mouth, and he suddenly lurched, coughing and spluttering. Lito and Papi and Luis rolled him over, and he retched up the rest of the ocean he'd swallowed.

"Rudi—Rudi!" Señora Castillo said. She wrapped him in her arms and sobbed, and then everything was quiet and still, but for the gentle lapping of the sea against the side of the boat and the sloshing of water inside it.

The tanker had passed.

Amara stood at the back of the boat, keeping the rudder straight against the waves. But the engine was dead again. Like everything else, it had been swamped.

Señora Castillo reached for Isabel's hand and squeezed it. "Thank you, Isabel."

Isabel nodded, but it came out more like a shudder. She was freezing cold and soaked from head to toe, but at least she was back in her mother's arms. Mami hugged her close and Isabel shivered.

"We need to get the water out of the bottom of the boat," Papi said. It was strange to Isabel to hear her father talk about something so normal, so practical, when Señor Castillo had almost drowned and the boat had almost rolled over and sunk. But he was right.

"And get the engine running again," Iván said.

"The water first," Lito agreed, and together they gathered up bottles and jugs and began the tedious work of filling them and pouring the seawater back into the ocean. Isabel stayed buried in her mother's arms, still exhausted, and no one made her get up.

"Where's the box with the medicine in it?" Luis asked.

There weren't too many places it could be in the small boat, and they quickly decided it must have fallen overboard in the confusion. Gone were their aspirin and bandages, and Señor Castillo was still dazed and weak.

It was bad, but if they got the boat bailed out and if they got the engine running and if they got back on track with the sun tomorrow and if they didn't run into any more tankers, they could make it to the States without needing the medicine or matches.

If, if, if.

They bailed water the rest of the night, taking turns dozing in the uncomfortable, crowded little boat. Isabel didn't even realize she'd fallen asleep until she jerked awake from a nightmare about a giant monster coming for her out of the dark sea. She cried out, looking this way and that, but there was nothing but blue-black water and gray skies tinged with the red of the sun all around them for miles and miles and miles. She closed her eyes and took deep breaths, trying to calm down.

The boat rocked again, and Amara struggled to keep the rudder steady. She had taken over as pilot while Señor Castillo recovered, but they still hadn't gotten the motor running again. The Gulf Stream would carry them north, toward Florida, but they would need the engine to reach the shore.

Isabel's mother leaned over the side of the boat and threw up into the sea. When she slid back down inside, she looked green. The boat was rocking so much now Isabel couldn't sit on the bench without holding on. The waves were growing higher and higher.

"What is it?" Iván said sleepily. "Another tanker?"

"No. Red sky at morning, sailors take warning," Lito said, looking up into the red-tinged clouds. "A storm is coming."

MAHMOUD

IZMIR, TURKEY—2015

11 days from home

"GOD HELP US—*THAT* IS WHAT WE'RE TO RIDE in?" Mahmoud's father said.

The boat wasn't a boat. It was a raft. A black inflatable rubber dinghy with an outboard motor on the back. It looked like there was room for a dozen people in it.

Thirty refugees waited to get on board.

They all looked as tired as Mahmoud felt, and wore different-colored life jackets. They were mostly young men, but there were families too. Women with and without *hijabs*. Other children, some who looked to be about Mahmoud's age. One boy in a Barcelona soccer jersey didn't have a life jacket but clung instead to a blown-up rubber inner tube. A few of the other refugees had backpacks and plastic bags full of clothes, but most of them, like Mahmoud's family, carried whatever they owned in their pockets.

"Let's go! Let's go!" one of the smugglers said. "Two hundred and fifty thousand Syrian pounds or one thousand euros per person! Children pay full price, including babies," he told Mahmoud's father. There were two more

Turks in tracksuits like the ones who had turned them away from the mall, and they stood apart, staring at the refugees like they were something disgusting that had just washed up on the beach. Their scowls made Mahmoud want to disappear again.

Dad handed out their life jackets, and they put them on.

Mom stared out at the black dinghy bobbing in the gray-black Mediterranean seawater. She grabbed her husband's arm. "What are we doing, Youssef? Is this the right decision?"

"We have to get to Europe," he said. "What choice do we have? God will guide us."

Mahmoud watched as his father pushed the cash they'd saved into the hands of one of the smugglers. Then Mahmoud and his family followed his dad to the dinghy, and they climbed on board. Waleed and his mother sat down in the bottom of the dinghy, his mother holding Hana tight in her arms. Mahmoud and his father sat on one of the inflated rubber edges, their backs to the sea. Mahmoud was already cold, and the wind off the waves made him shiver.

A big bearded man wearing a plaid shirt and a bulky blue life jacket sat down right next to Mahmoud, almost squeezing Mahmoud right off the edge. Mahmoud slid a little closer to his father, but the big man next to him just settled into the extra space.

"How long will we be on the boat?" Mahmoud asked his dad.

"Just a few hours, I think. It was hard to tell on the phone."

Mahmoud nodded. The phones and chargers were safely sealed away in plastic bags in his parents' pockets, just in case they got wet. Mahmoud knew because he'd been the one who'd dug through the trash for the resealable zipper bags.

"We don't have to get all the way to the Greek mainland," Dad said. "Just the Greek island of Lesbos, about a hundred kilometers away. Then we're officially in Europe, and we can take a ferry from there to Athens."

When the smugglers had packed the dinghy full of refugees, they pushed it out to sea. None of the smugglers came with them. If the refugees were going to get to Lesbos, they were going to have to do it themselves.

"Does anyone know if dinner is served on this cruise?" Mahmoud's father asked, and there were a few nervous laughs.

The outboard motor roared to life, and the refugees cheered and cried. Dad hugged Mahmoud, then reached down to hug Mom, Waleed, and Hana. They were finally doing it. They were finally leaving Turkey for Europe! Mahmoud looked around in wonder. None of this seemed real. He had begun to feel like they were never going to leave.

Mahmoud had been so tired he could barely keep his eyes open before, but now the thrum of the motor and the chop of the boat as it hit wave after wave flooded him with adrenaline, and he couldn't have slept if he'd wanted to.

The lights of Izmir dwindled to glittering dots behind them, and soon they were out in the dark, rough waters of the Mediterranean. Phone screens glowed in the darkness— passengers checking to see if they could tell where they were.

The roar of the engine and the whip-blinding sea spray made it impossible to have any kind of conversation, so Mahmoud looked around at the other passengers instead. Most of them kept their heads down and eyes closed, either muttering prayers or trying not to get sick, or both. The dinghy began to toss not just front to back but side to side, in a sort of rolling motion, and Mahmoud felt the bile rise in the back of his throat. On the other side of the dinghy, a man shifted quickly to vomit over the side.

"Watch out for the Coast Guard!" the big man next to Mahmoud shouted over the noise. "Turks will take us back to Turkey, but Greeks will take us to Lesbos!"

Mahmoud didn't know how anybody could see any- thing in the dark, cloud-covered night. But it helped his seasickness to look outside instead of inside the boat. It didn't help his growing sense of panic, though. He couldn't see land anymore, just stormy gray waves that were getting taller and narrower, like they were driving a boat through the spiky tent tops at the Kilis refugee camp. More people leaned over the side to throw up, and Mahmoud felt his stomach churn.

And then the rain began.

It was a hard, cold rain that plastered Mahmoud's hair to his head and soaked him down to his socks. The rain began to collect in the bottom of the dinghy, and soon Mahmoud's mother and the others were sitting in centimeters of shifting water. Mahmoud's muscles began to ache from shivering and holding the same tight position for so long, and he wanted nothing more than to get off this boat.

"We should turn back!" someone yelled.

"No! We can't go back! We can't afford to try again!" Mahmoud's father yelled, and a chorus of voices agreed with him.

They pushed on through driving rain and roiling seas for what felt like an eternity. It might have been ten hours or ten minutes, Mahmoud didn't know. All he knew was that he wanted it to end, and end now. This was worse than Aleppo. Worse than bombs falling and soldiers shooting and drones buzzing overhead. In Aleppo, at least, he could run. Hide. Here he was at the mercy of nature, an invisible brown speck in an invisible black rubber dinghy in the middle of a great black sea. If it wanted to, the ocean could open its mouth and swallow him and no one in the whole wide world would ever know he was gone.

And then that's exactly what it did.

"*I see rocks!*" someone at the front of the dinghy yelled, and there was a loud *POOM!* like a bomb exploding, and Mahmoud went tumbling into the sea.

JOSEF

A STRONG HAND GRABBED JOSEF BY THE ARM and swung him around. It was a sailor, one of the ship's firemen, and Josef knew right away he was in trouble. The firemen were big, churlish brutes who were supposed to be on board to put out fires. But lately they'd been walking the decks, harassing the Jewish passengers. They'd been making trouble ever since the Cubans had told them they couldn't leave the ship.

For three days the *St. Louis* had sat at anchor kilometers from shore. For three days, while port officials came and went, the Cuban police who guarded the ladder off the ship told the passengers they couldn't leave today.

"*Mañana*," they said. "*Mañana*."

Tomorrow. Tomorrow.

Two days ago, the SS *Orduña*, a smaller English passenger liner, had arrived and anchored nearby. Josef guessed it was one of the other two ships they'd been racing to Cuba. He and the other passengers had watched as launches went to and from the ship, as the yellow quarantine flag went up and then down. And then the

Orduña had lifted anchor and cruised in to dock at the pier and let off passengers! Why had they been allowed to dock and not the *St. Louis*? The *St. Louis* had gotten there first!

Captain Schroeder wasn't around to ask, and the officers and stewards had no answers for the passengers.

And then today the same thing had happened with the French ship SS *Flandre*. It arrived, anchored nearby, passed quarantine, docked at the Havana pier, and let off its passengers. Now it was sailing back out to sea.

The passengers on the *St. Louis* had grown more and more restless, cornering sailors on deck and berating their stewards at dinner. Josef had felt the tension mounting all over the ship, the pandemonium threatening to boil over every time the crew dealt with the passengers. It was as suffocating and oppressive as the 100-degree heat.

Apparently, Schiendick and his Nazi friends had felt the tension too, because that's when the firemen patrols had begun. It was nothing official, Josef was sure, because the captain hadn't made an announcement. It was just certain members of the crew who had taken it upon themselves to police the ship like they were all back in Germany.

"For the safety of the Jews," Schiendick told them, the same way the Gestapo took Jews into "protective custody."

Another fireman stood beside the one who held Josef's arm, blocking out the sun. And between them was Otto Schiendick himself.

"Just the boy we were looking for," Schiendick said. "You are to come with us."

"What? Why?" Josef asked, looking up at the two big men around him. Josef felt guilty, and he was immediately mad at himself for it. Why should he feel guilty? He hadn't done anything wrong! But he remembered feeling this way back home too, whenever he passed a Nazi on the street.

In Germany, just being Jewish was a crime. And here too, apparently.

"Your parents' cabin must be searched," Schiendick said. "You have a key?"

Josef nodded, even though he didn't want to. These men were adults, and they were Nazis. One he'd been taught to respect. The other he'd learned to fear.

The big fireman still had Josef's arm, and he pulled him toward the elevator. Josef couldn't believe he'd let himself be caught. He'd warned his little sister, Ruthie, to avoid the firemen, who loved to intimidate the children on board, and she'd managed to stay out of their way. But he'd lost himself watching the *Flandre* sail out of Havana Harbor, his back turned to the promenade, and that's when they'd caught him.

Schiendick and his firemen hustled Josef down the stairs, and Josef's stomach sank when they ordered him to open the door to his cabin. Josef's hand shook as he put the key in the lock. He wished there was some way he could get out of this, some way he could keep these men away from his mother and father.

Otto Schiendick reached down and turned the handle for him, throwing the door open. Papa lay on a bed in his underclothes, trying to stay cool in the stifling heat. Mama sat in a chair nearby, reading a book. Ruthie, Josef was glad to see, was still up at the pool.

When she saw the men, Rachel Landau stood. On the bed, Josef's father propped himself up, a look of panic on his face.

"What's going on here?" Mama asked. "Josef?"

"They made me bring them here," Josef said, his eyes wide, trying to warn her of the danger.

"Yes," Schiendick said, spotting Josef's father. "There he is."

Schiendick and the two firemen stepped inside. Schiendick closed the door and locked it behind them.

"For your safety, this cabin must be searched," Schiendick said.

"On whose authority?" Mama asked. "Does the captain know about this?"

"On *my* authority," Schiendick told her. "The captain has other things to worry about."

Schiendick nodded, and the two firemen ransacked the room. They swept Mama's makeup and perfume off the vanity and smashed the mirror. They knocked the lamps off the bedside tables and cracked the washbasin. They opened up the family's suitcases, which were carefully packed and ready to go to Cuba, and threw their clothes all over the cabin. They tore the head off Ruthie's stuffed bunny. They snatched the book from Mama's hands and ripped out the pages, tossing them in the air like ashes from a bonfire.

Josef's mother cried out, but not so loudly that anyone else would hear. Papa wrapped himself in a ball and threw his hands over his head, whimpering. Josef huddled against the door, angry at his helplessness but scared that if he fought back, he'd only be punished more.

When there was nothing left to smash or scatter, the firemen stood behind Schiendick at the door.

Schiendick spat on the floor. "That's what I think of you and your race," he said, and suddenly Josef understood—this was payback for his father's words to Schiendick at the funeral.

Schiendick snorted dismissively at the cowering man on the bed. "It's time you had your head shaved again," he told Josef's father.

Otto Schiendick let himself and the two firemen out, leaving the door wide open. Josef's mother slid to the floor crying, and Papa blubbered on the bed. Josef shook as he buried his face in his hands, trying to hide his own tears. He wanted nothing more than to run to his mother's arms, but she felt a million miles away from him. So did his father. They were three lonely islands, separated by an ocean of misery.

Of all the things Schiendick and his fireman had broken, the Landau family was the one thing Josef wasn't sure they could put back together.

"You said if I was quiet, if I stood very still, they wouldn't come for me," Papa said. It took Josef a moment to realize his father was talking to him. Josef's breath caught. His father was talking about the medical inspection. When Josef had scared his father to get him to straighten up.

Papa looked up at him, his eyes red from crying. "You said they wouldn't come for me. You said they wouldn't send me back. You promised, and they came for me anyway."

Josef felt like his father had slapped him, even though Papa hadn't touched him. Josef reeled. He backed into his mother's little makeup table, and one of the bottles Schiendick hadn't smashed rolled off and shattered on the floor beside him. Josef didn't even jump. He had lied to his father. Betrayed him. Made him think he was back at that awful place. Terrified him all over again. But that wasn't the worst thing he had done.

Josef had made his father a promise he couldn't keep.

ISABEL

SOMEWHERE ON THE STRAITS OF FLORIDA—1994

2 days from home

RAIN LASHED ISABEL AS SHE SHOVELED water out of the boat. Scoop, pitch. Scoop, pitch. The bottom of the boat filled as fast as they could bail it out. Isabel, her mother, her father, her grandfather, Luis, Iván, Señora Castillo, they all worked feverishly, none of them talking—not that they could hear each other over the storm. The only ones not bailing were Señor Castillo, who looked like a ghost, and Amara, who clung to the rudder with white-knuckled hands and tried to keep the boat turned into the churning waves so it wouldn't capsize. The engine hadn't worked since their escape from the tanker.

The storm clouds turned the day into night, and the driving rain soaked Isabel to the bone. She shivered in the cold wind, her feet numb in the water sloshing at the bottom of the boat. Sea spray stung her eyes, and in between scoops of water she dragged her arm across her face, trying to wipe away the saltwater tears.

As she watched the surging waves, Isabel remembered the last time she had seen her *abuelita*, her grandma. She remembered Lita's hand reaching out for help as the tide swept her away. Isabel had been nine years old. Her parents had sent her to stay with Lito and Lita in their little shack on the coast. They hadn't said why, but Isabel was old enough to know her parents had been fighting again, and they wanted to be alone while they worked things out. All that spring Isabel had waded without joy in the ocean, waiting for the storm to come that would tear her family apart.

And then the real storm had come.

It wasn't a hurricane. It was bigger than a hurricane— a gigantic cyclone that stretched from Canada down through the United States and across Cuba and into Central America. Later they would call it the Storm of the Century, but to Isabel it was *The* Storm. The shrieking wind ripped roofs off houses and pulled palm trees straight out of the ground. The rain fell sideways. Hail shattered windows like a never-ending shotgun blast. And the ocean, the ocean rose up like a giant hand and reached inland, over Lito and Lita's little house by the sea, smothering the house in its giant paw and dragging the shattered pieces back into its lair.

Lito and Lita hadn't known the storm was coming or they wouldn't have been there. They would have been inland. Found higher ground. Castro had promised he would protect them, but he didn't. Not then. Not Isabel's grandmother.

Lito had been able to hold on to Isabel, but Lita had been swept away. She had slipped under the waves, her arms still reaching for Lito. For Isabel.

And that was the last they had ever seen of her.

Lito's arm found Isabel again now and wrapped her in a hug.

"I know what you're thinking," he said close to her ear where she could hear him. "I'm thinking about it too."

"I miss her," Isabel told her grandfather.

"I miss her too," Lito said. "Every day."

Real tears came into Isabel's eyes now, and Lito hugged her tighter.

"That was her song's end," Lito whispered. "But ours plays on. Come. Keep bailing, or soon it'll be up to our eyeballs."

Isabel nodded and went back to scooping water. What if her life *was* a song? No, not a song. A life was a symphony, with different movements and complicated musical forms. A song was something shorter. A smaller piece of a life.

This journey was a song, Isabel realized, a *son cubano*, and each part of it was a verse. The first verse had been the riot: a blast of trumpets, the rat-a-tat-tat of a snare drum. Then the pre-chorus of trading her trumpet for gasoline—the piano that gave the *son* its rhythm—and then the chorus itself: leaving home. They were still leaving home, still hadn't gotten to where they were going.

They would return to the chorus again and again before they were done.

But what was the refrain? And how many more verses would there be before they got to the climax of the song, that brash moment at the end of a *son cubano* that echoed the refrain, and then the coda, those brief few notes that tied it all together?

She couldn't think about that now. All she could do now was scoop water. Scoop water and pray they didn't drown in the mad conga solo that drummed against the side of their tiny metal boat.

MAHMOUD

SOMEWHERE ON THE
MEDITERRANEAN SEA—2015

11 days from home

THE COLD WATER WAS LIKE A SLAP IN Mahmoud's face. Before he could think, he gasped, sucking in a mouthful of the dark Mediterranean Sea. He tumbled backward, head down in the murky water, his arms and feet thrashing, trying to right himself. Something else—someone else—fell on top of him, pushing him deeper down into the water. He choked. Coughed. Swallowed more water. Bodies tumbled into the water above him, beside him, below him. His knee struck something hard and sharp—a rock—and he felt a cold flash of pain that quickly disappeared into blind, senseless terror.

He was drowning. The rubber dinghy had burst against the rocks, and he was drowning.

Mahmoud kicked. Paddled. Flailed. His face came out of the water and he gulped down air, and then a wave washed over him again and he went down. He kicked his way back to the surface and fought to keep his head above water.

"Mom! Dad!" Mahmoud cried. His yells were mixed with the screams and cries of the other passengers who had made it back to the surface. All around Mahmoud, survivors thrashed and gasped, swamped by the choppy waves. There was nothing left of the dinghy. The engine had dragged the rest of it down.

Mahmoud saw something bobbing along the water, glowing. A cell phone! It was still sealed tight in its plastic bag, the air in the bag keeping it afloat. Mahmoud swam for it, ducking a wave and pawing the bag into his arms.

The glowing phone screen said 2:32 a.m.

"Help—*help*!" Mahmoud's mother sobbed, her voice recognizable in the chaos. Mahmoud spun, oriented himself, and frog-kicked his way through the waves toward the shape he thought was his mother. He picked her pink headscarf out of the swirling pandemonium, and saw that she was fighting to lift something up out of the water.

Hana.

Mahmoud swam to his mother. Hana was crying— she was alive!—but it was all Mahmoud's mother could do to keep the baby and her own face above the relentless waves. One or the other of them was going to drown.

Mahmoud put his arms around his mother and tried to kick her and Hana both to the surface, but half the time he felt like he was dragging them down with him.

"Fatima! Mahmoud!" he heard his father cry. Mahmoud turned to see his father with Waleed in his arms. "The life preservers are useless!" he roared, his head appearing and disappearing behind the waves. "They're fakes!"

Fake?! Mahmoud was furious, but his anger quickly faded. Every ounce of his energy was focused on kicking, swimming. If he stopped, he and his mother and sister would drown.

There were other people around them, yelling, searching, fighting to stay afloat, but as far as Mahmoud was concerned his world was four meters round. Where did they go from here? How did they get out of the sea and onto dry land? They were lost in the stormy Mediterranean Sea in the middle of the night. Their dinghy was sunk, and though it had run into rocks, there wasn't any land in sight.

They were going to die here. All of them.

Mahmoud breathed in seawater through his nose and hacked it up. He fought to breathe, the waves lapping over him, and rain and spray still lashing his face. But his baby sister's cries refocused him. He could *not* lose her. He couldn't lose any of them.

They came together in the water, Mahmoud and his mother and father, all of them helping Hana and Waleed and each other stay afloat. Other families and groups did the same, but eventually the little groups drifted apart from each other, none of them knowing which way they were supposed to go. All they could do was stay on top of the next wave, the next wave, the next wave.

"Kick off your shoes," Mahmoud's father told them. "Anything to lighten you."

Time passed. The rain stopped. The waxing moon even peeked out from behind a cloud. But just as quickly it was dark again, and the cold wind and the salty spray and the swelling sea still tormented them. Mahmoud's legs were numb with cold and exhaustion. They felt like two lead weights he struggled to lift and churn to stay afloat. His mother had been quietly sobbing for what seemed like forever. Her arms no longer held Hana above the water, but just on top of it, like she was pushing along a tiny barge. Mahmoud's father did the same with Waleed, trying to save his strength. Hana had gone as quiet as Waleed, and Mahmoud wondered if they were still alive. He couldn't ask. Wouldn't. If he didn't ask he couldn't know for sure, and as long as he didn't know for sure, there was a chance they were still alive.

Mahmoud slipped beneath the waves once more, longer this time. It was getting so hard to come up again, to keep himself afloat. He rose again, pushing air out his nose, but he was tired. So very, very tired. He wished for a respite from swimming, just a moment to sit without working his arms and legs. To close his eyes and go to sleep . . .

Water was sloshing in and out of Mahmoud's ears, but he thought he heard a drone just above the howl of the wind. In Syria that sound would have sent him ducking for cover, but now it made his eyes widen, his legs kick just a little harder, a little higher. There—coming at them out of the darkness—another dinghy full of people!

Mahmoud and his mother and father waved their arms and cried out for help. At last, the people on board saw them, but as the dinghy came closer it didn't slow down.

They weren't going to stop!

The front of the dinghy chopped past Mahmoud, and he lunged for one of the handholds on the side. He caught it and grabbed his mother before the dinghy pulled him away. He swung Mom to the side of the dinghy and she grabbed hold, the wake from it almost swamping Hana.

Behind them, Mahmoud's father also reached for the dinghy but missed. It churned along, bouncing in the chop, and Mahmoud's father and brother disappeared into the darkness.

"Dad—*Dad*!" Mahmoud cried, still holding on to the dinghy.

"Let go!" a woman in the dinghy yelled down at him. "You're dragging on us!"

"Let us in! Please!" Mahmoud begged. It was all his mother could do to hang on to the dinghy and to Hana.

"We can't! There's no room!" a man inside the dinghy yelled.

"Please," Mahmoud begged. "We're drowning."

"I'll call the Coast Guard for you!" a man said. "I have their number on my phone!"

Another man reached down and tried to pry Mahmoud's hand from the dinghy. "You're tipping us!"

"Please!" Mahmoud cried. He sobbed with the effort of fighting off the man's fingers and hanging onto the dinghy. "Please, take us with you!"

"No! No room!"

"At least take my sister!" Mahmoud begged. "She's a baby. She won't take up any room!"

That caused much yelling and discussion on the boat. A man tried to pry Mahmoud loose again, but he hung on. *"Please . . ."* Mahmoud begged.

A woman appeared at the side of the boat, her arms reaching down to Mahmoud's mother. Reaching for the baby.

Mahmoud's mother lifted the little ball of wet blankets up to the woman. *"Her name is Hana,"* she said, struggling to be heard above the roar of the engine and the splash of the waves.

Someone finally pried Mahmoud's fingers off the side, and he slipped into the water and tumbled in the dinghy's wake. When he came up, he saw his mother had let go of the dinghy too. She was crying great howling tears and tearing at her clothes. Mahmoud swam over to her and wrestled her hands into stillness, and she put her head on Mahmoud's shoulder and sobbed.

Mahmoud's sister was gone, and so were his father and brother.

JOSEF

18 days from home

JOSEF TRIED TO HANG ON TO THE CHAIR, BUT his father was still strong enough to yank it out of his hands. Papa stacked it on the tower of furniture he'd already piled up against the door.

"We can't let them back in!" Papa cried. "They'll come for us again and take us away!"

It had taken Josef and his mother a night and a day to put their cabin back together after Otto Schiendick and his goons had torn the place up. But in the span of fifteen minutes his father had undone it all again, snatching up anything that wasn't nailed down and stacking it against the door.

Ruthie crouched in the corner, crying and hugging Bitsy. Josef's mother had sewed the stuffed bunny back together first thing, before Ruthie had seen it headless.

"Aaron. Aaron!" Josef's mother said now. "You have to calm down! You're scaring your daughter!"

He was scaring Josef too. Josef stared at his father. This skeleton, this crazed ghost, this wasn't his father. The

Nazis had taken his father away and replaced him with a madman.

"You don't understand," Josef's father said. "You can't know what they did to people. What they'll do to us!"

Papa threw an open suitcase on the pile, spilling clothes all over the room. When he'd put everything he could on the barricade, he crawled under the desk at the back of the room like a child playing hide-and-seek.

Mama looked frightened as she tried to figure out what to do. "Ruthie," she said at last, "put your swimsuit on and go to the pool."

"I don't want to go swimming," Ruthie said, still crying in the corner.

"Do as I say," Mama said.

Ruthie pulled herself away from the wall and picked through the clothes on the floor for her swimsuit.

"Josef," Mama said, low enough for just him to hear her, "I'm going to go to the ship's doctor for a sleeping draught for your father. Something to calm him. I'll take Ruthie to the pool, but I need you to stay here and watch your father."

Papa was still curled into a ball under the desk, rocking and muttering to himself. The idea of being here alone with him filled Josef with dread.

"But if the doctor knows he's unwell, they might not let us into Cuba," Josef whispered, desperate to find some reason to keep his mother with him.

"I'll tell the doctor I'm anxious and haven't been sleeping," Mama said. "I'll tell him the draught is for me."

Josef's mother helped Ruthie finish putting her swimsuit on, and together they were able to pull the haphazard pile of furniture far enough away from the door to open it. Josef's father, who'd been so set on building the barricade just minutes before, was so lost in his own mind he didn't even notice.

Josef didn't know what to do with himself, so he started to put the room back together. Papa stayed quiet and still under the desk. Josef hoped he had gone to sleep. Mama came back within minutes, and Josef felt an immense sense of relief—until he saw the dull, panicked look Mama wore, and he got scared all over again. She stumbled as she entered the cabin like she couldn't remember how to walk, and Josef hurried to help her to one of the beds.

"Mama, what is it? What's wrong?" Josef asked.

"I—I told the doctor the sleeping draught was for me," she said, her words slow, "and he made me—he made me take it right there."

"*You drank it?*" Josef said.

His mother's eyelids fluttered. "I had to," she said. "After I told him—after I told him . . . Couldn't let him know Aaron was really the one who . . ."

Mama's eyelids closed, and she swayed.

Josef panicked. She couldn't go to sleep. Not now.

How was he supposed to take care of his father? He couldn't do this alone!

"Mama! Don't go to sleep!"

Her eyes jerked open again, but they had lost their focus.

"Your sister," she said. "Don't forget . . . your sister . . . she's at the pool . . ."

Her eyes flickered closed again, and she rolled back onto the bed.

"No. No no no no no," Josef said. He tried patting his mother on the cheeks to wake her up, but she was out cold.

Josef got up and paced the room, trying to think. With his mother asleep, he had to watch his father every second. Josef glanced at him under the desk. Papa was quiet now, but the slightest thing could set him off. Josef couldn't go for help anyway. If anyone knew his father was unwell, he'd be barred from entering Cuba. But Josef also had to go get Ruthie at some point, and make sure she got dinner and was put to bed.

Suddenly, Josef was the man of the family—the only *adult* in the family—whether he wanted to be or not.

"Have you ever seen a man drown?" Papa asked in a whisper, and Josef jumped. Josef wasn't sure if Papa was talking to him, or just talking, but he was afraid to answer, afraid to break the quiet spell his father was under.

His father kept talking.

"After the evening roll call, they would choose some- one to drown. One every night. They would tie his ankles together and his hands behind his back and tie a gag around his mouth, and then they would hang him upside down, with his head in a barrel. Like a fish. Like a big fish on the pier, hanging upside down by its tail. Then they would fill the barrel with water. Slowly. So they could enjoy the panic. So they could laugh. And then the water would rise high enough to cover his nose, and he would breathe in water because there was nothing else he could do. He would breathe in water like a fish. Only he wasn't a fish. He was a man. He would thrash around and breathe water until he drowned. Drowned upside down."

Josef's breathing stilled. He caught himself hugging Ruthie's stuffed bunny tight.

"Every night they did it, and we all had to stand and watch," his father whispered. "We had to stand and watch, and we couldn't say a word, couldn't move a muscle, or we would be next."

Tears rolled down Josef's cheeks. He thought about how he'd treated his father at the Cuban doctor's exami- nation. How he'd made his father believe he was back in that place, where he'd seen so many awful things.

"I can't go back there," his father whispered. "Can't go back."

His father closed his eyes and put his head between his knees, and soon he was asleep. Josef sat with his sleeping parents until the cabin started to get dark and he couldn't put off finding Ruthie any longer. He would just have to be as quick as he could.

Josef left the cabin and found his sister splashing around in the pool with the other kids. Josef asked a steward to bring their dinners to their cabin tonight, and as he led Ruthie back he congratulated himself on surviving his first day as an adult.

Until he opened the door and his father was gone.

Josef dropped Ruthie's hand and got down on his hands and knees to search under the beds, but his father wasn't there. He wasn't in the cabin at all.

"No. No!" Josef cried. He shook his mother, begged her to wake up, but the sleeping draught was too powerful. Josef spun in the room, trying to figure out what to do.

He snatched up Bitsy and put the little stuffed bunny into Ruthie's arms.

"Stay here," he told Ruthie. "Stay here with Mama, and don't leave the cabin. Understand? I've got to go find Papa."

Josef ran out the door and into the passageway. But where to now? Where would his father go? Papa hadn't left the cabin the whole trip, and *now* he had decided to leave?

Josef heard a commotion, and he sprinted up the stairs to A-deck. Up ahead, a man was helping a woman to her feet, and both of them were looking angrily over their shoulders, the direction Papa must have run.

And that's when Josef remembered: His father had left the cabin before. To watch them bury Professor Weiler at sea.

Somewhere up ahead, a woman screamed, and Josef took off at a run. He felt as though he was outside himself, like he existed outside his own skin, and he watched himself slam into the rail and look over the side.

Someone yelled, "Man overboard!" and the ship's siren shrieked.

Josef's father had jumped into the sea.

ISABEL

SOMEWHERE ON THE CARIBBEAN SEA—1994

3 days from home

ISABEL WOKE TO A WARM ORANGE GLOW ON the horizon and a silver sea stretching out before them like a mirror. It was as though the storm had been some kind of feverish nightmare. Señor Castillo woke from his nightmare too, parched like a man who'd been lost in the desert. He drank almost half of one of the few gallons of water they had left in one long chug, then laid back against the side of the boat.

Isabel worried about her mother. For Mami, the nightmare was just beginning. The illness she'd felt as the storm began had gotten worse in the night, and now she had a fever hotter than the rising sun. Lito dipped a scrap of shirt into the cool seawater and draped it across his daughter's forehead to cool her, but without the aspirin from the lost medicine box there was no way to bring the fever down.

"The baby . . ." Mami moaned, holding her stomach.

"The baby will be fine," Lito told her. "A good strong healthy baby boy."

Lito and Señora Castillo took care of Isabel's mother. Papi and Luis got the engine restarted, and bathed it with water to keep it cool. Amara, at the rudder, steered them north now that the sun was in the sky. Everybody had a job, it seemed, except Isabel and Iván.

Isabel bumped shoulders and stepped on toes as she wobbled her way over to Iván in the prow of the boat. She sat down beside him with a huff.

"I feel useless," she told Iván.

"I know," he said. "Me too."

They sat for a while in silence before Iván said, "Do you think we'll have to do algebra in our new American school?"

Isabel laughed. "Yes."

"Will they have political rallies every day at school in the US? Will we have to work in the fields all afternoon?" His eyes went wide. "Do you think we'll have to carry guns to protect us from all the shootings?"

"I don't know," Isabel told him. Their teachers told them all the time how homeless people starved in the streets of the US, and how people who couldn't afford to pay for doctors got sick and died, and how thousands of people were killed by guns every year. As happy as she had been to go to *el norte*, Isabel suddenly worried that it wouldn't be as magical a place as everyone in the boat believed.

"No matter what, I'm glad you came with us," Iván said. "Now we can live next door to each other forever."

Isabel blushed and looked at her feet. She liked that thought too.

Castro's face was even more submerged now, which meant they were taking on water. Between the tanker and the storm, the little boat had suffered a pounding— and it had never been very seaworthy to begin with. Señor Castillo had only expected the boat to be on the water for a day, two at the most. How much longer would it take them to get to Florida?

And where exactly *were* they?

"Hey, is that land?" Iván asked.

He pointed over the side of the boat. Isabel and the others scrambled so quickly to see that the boat tipped dangerously in the water.

Yes—yes! Isabel could see it. A long, thin, dark green line along the blue horizon. Land!

"Is it Florida?" Iván asked.

"It's on the wrong side of the boat to be the US," Luis said, looking back at the sun. "Unless we got blown into the Gulf of Mexico overnight."

"Whatever it is, I'm steering for it," Amara told them.

Everyone watched in silence as the green line turned into hills and trees, and the water got clearer and shallower. Isabel held her breath. She had never been so excited in her entire life. Was it really the United States? Had they made it? Amara brought them close to shore, then turned and ran south along it. Isabel searched the shore. There! She pointed to red and yellow beach umbrellas with chairs underneath them. And in the beach chairs were white people.

A woman in a bikini lifted her black sunglasses and pointed at them, and the man with her sat up and stared. As the boat rounded the beach, Isabel saw more people, all staring and pointing and waving.

"Yes! Yes! We made it! We made it!" Isabel said, shaking Iván's arms.

Iván hopped up and down so much the boat groaned. "Florida!" he cried.

A black man in a white suit hurried down the beach toward them, waving his arms over his head to get their attention. He yelled something in English, and pointed for them to go farther south.

Amara followed the shore around a bend, and the open ocean gave way to a quiet little bay with a long, wooden pier. The pier had a little café on it with tables and chairs. Fancy two-man sailboats were parked on the beach next to volleyball courts, and more umbrellas and chairs dotted the sand. Isabel's heart leaped—the US was even more of a paradise than she ever imagined!

Luis flipped a switch, and the putter of the engine died. The white people got up from their tables at the bar to help pull them to the dock, and Isabel and the others reached for their hands. Their fingertips were almost close enough to touch when black men in white short-sleeve uniforms pushed their way between the vacationers on the pier and the boat.

One of them said something in a language Isabel didn't understand.

"I think he's asking us if we're from Haiti," Lito said to the others in the boat. "We are from Cuba," he said slowly in Spanish to the uniformed man.

"You're from Cuba?" the officer asked in Spanish.

"Yes! Yes!" they cried.

"Where are we?" Papi asked.

"The Bahamas," the man said.

The Bahamas? Isabel's mind went back to the map of the Caribbean on the wall of her schoolroom. The Bahamas were islands to the north and east of Havana, directly above the middle of Cuba. A long way east of Miami. Had the storm really taken them *that* far off course?

"I'm sorry," the officer said. "But you are not allowed to land. Bahamian law forbids the entrance of illegal aliens to the Bahamas. If you set foot on Bahamian soil, you will be taken into custody and returned to your country of origin."

Behind the officers, one of the tourists who knew Spanish was translating for the others. Some of them looked upset and started arguing with the authorities.

"But we have a sick pregnant woman," Lito said to the officer. He moved so the men on the dock could see

Isabel's mother, and the tourists behind the officers cried out in concern.

The officers conferred, and Isabel held her breath.

"The commandant says that for health reasons the pregnant woman may come ashore and receive medical attention," the Spanish-speaking officer said. Isabel and Iván clutched at each other with hope. "But she cannot have her baby here," the officer said. "As soon as she is well, she will be deported to Cuba."

Isabel and Iván sagged, and everyone else on the little boat was silent. Isabel felt sick. She wanted her mother to get better, but she didn't want them to be sent back to Cuba. Couldn't the Bahamas just let them stay? How was one more Cuban family going to hurt? She looked back at the pier and nice café. They had plenty of room!

The situation was explained to the tourists on the pier, and they gasped and waited.

"All right," Lito said. "My daughter is sick. She needs medical attention."

"No!" Papi said. "You heard him! If we step off this boat, they'll send us back to Cuba. I'm not going back."

"Then *I* will go with her," Lito said. "*I* care for Teresa's life more than I care for *el norte*."

Tears ran down Isabel's cheeks. No. *No!* This wasn't the way things were supposed to happen! Her family was supposed to be *together*. That's why she'd insisted they *all* go on the boat. And if her mother went back to

Cuba and her father went on to the United States, which one was she supposed to go with?

Lito started to lift Isabel's mother, but Mami pushed him away.

"No!" Isabel's mother said.

"But, Teresa—" Lito said.

"No! I don't want my baby born in Cuba."

"But you're ill! You can't take another ocean voyage," Lito argued.

"I will not go back," Mami said. She reached up and took her husband's and her daughter's hands. "I will stay with my family."

Relieved, Isabel threw herself into her mother's arms. She was surprised when she felt her father kneel down in the boat and hug them both.

"It sounds like we're leaving, then," Luis told everyone in the boat.

Before they could get the engine restarted, one of the tourists tossed down a bottle of water to Señora Castillo. Soon the rest of the tourists were hurrying back and forth to the café, buying bottles of water and bags of chips and tossing them into everyone's hands on the boat.

"Aspirin? Does anyone have aspirin? For my mother?" Isabel begged.

Up on the dock, an old white woman understood. She quickly dug around in her big purse and tossed a plastic bottle full of pills to Isabel.

"Thank you! Thank you!" Isabel cried. Her heart ached with gratitude toward these people. Just a moment's kindness from each of them might mean the difference between death and survival for her mother and everyone else on the little raft.

By the time they finally restarted the engine and Amara swung them around to leave, they had more food and water than they had brought with them to begin with. But they were farther away from Florida and freedom than they had ever been before.

MAHMOUD

SOMEWHERE ON THE
MEDITERRANEAN SEA—2015

11 days from home

"MY BABY," MAHMOUD'S MOTHER WAILED. "My Hana is gone."

The Mediterranean was still attacking them, wave after wave trying to drown them, and Mahmoud could tell that his mother didn't want to fight anymore. It was all Mahmoud could do to keep her head above the water.

"I'm still here," Mahmoud told her. "*I* need you."

"I gave my baby to a *stranger*," Mahmoud's mother howled. "I don't even know who she was!"

"She's safe now," Mahmoud told her. "Hana is out of the water. She's going to live."

But Mahmoud's mother would not be consoled. She lay back in the water, her face to the sky, and sobbed.

The dinghy coming by had reenergized Mahmoud, but he could feel the buzz quickly draining away, replaced by a cold exhaustion that left his arms and legs numb. The sea rolled over him and he went under again, coming up spluttering. He could not keep himself and his mother afloat. Not for long.

They were going to die here.

But at least Hana was safe. Yes, he had been the one to convince a stranger to take his little sister away, and yes, his mother might never forgive herself for letting Hana go. But at least neither of them would have to live long with their regret.

The rain began again, the awful, pelting, deadening rain, and it felt to Mahmoud like Allah was crying for them. With them.

They were drowning in tears.

Under the sweeping wash of rain, Mahmoud heard something like a drumbeat. Water on something that was not water. He searched the rising and falling waves until he saw it—the back side of a life jacket still strapped to a man. A man who floated facedown in the water.

In his mind's eye, Mahmoud immediately filled in the drowned man's face with that of his father, and his heart thumped against his own useless life jacket. He flailed in the water, half swimming, half towing his mother toward the body.

But no! The life vest was blue, and his father's had been orange, like Mahmoud's. And this one was a real, working life jacket. Mahmoud let his mother go for just a moment and wrestled the body over. It was the big man who had sat next to him on the dinghy. His eyes and mouth were open, but there was no life in either one. The man was dead.

It wasn't the first dead body Mahmoud had seen. Not after four years of civil war, with his hometown right in the center of the fighting. A man had been killed right next to him in his family's car, he realized with a start. How long ago had that been? Days? Weeks? It seemed like a lifetime ago. But no matter how many times he saw death, it never stopped being horrifying. Mahmoud shuddered and recoiled.

But if the man was dead, that meant he didn't need his life jacket.

Mahmoud fought down his fear and fumbled with the straps on the dead man's life jacket. Mahmoud's fingers moved, but he couldn't feel them. His hands were like blocks of ice. He only knew he was touching the straps because he could see it happening. Finally, he got one strap unbuckled, and another, and as the body began to shift in the vest, Mahmoud realized he was condemning this man to the bottom of the sea. He would never be bathed and wrapped in a *kafan*, never be mourned by those who loved him, never have his friends and family say prayers over him, never be buried facing Mecca. Mahmoud was putting a man in his grave, and he had a duty to him.

Mahmoud had heard funeral prayers too many times in his short life, most recently for his cousin Sayid, who had died when a barrel bomb exploded. Mahmoud quietly recited one now.

"O God, forgive this man, and have mercy on him and give him strength and pardon him. Be generous to him and cause his entrance to be wide and wash him with water and snow and hail. Cleanse him of his transgressions as white cloth is cleansed of stains. Give him an abode better than his home, and a family better than his family, and a wife better than his wife. Take him into Paradise, and protect him from the punishment of the grave and from the punishment of hellfire."

When he was finished, Mahmoud clicked open the last of the straps and the man's body rolled out of the vest and down into the murky depths of the Mediterranean Sea.

"Here, Mom, put this on," Mahmoud said. It took some time to get her into the life jacket, Mahmoud doing most of the work. But at last it was on her, and Mahmoud no longer had to fight to keep her afloat. She lay on her back, eyes closed, muttering about Hana, and Mahmoud clung to her life jacket. He still had to kick his legs to not pull them both under, but not nearly so much.

He didn't know where they would go or how they would get out of the water. Perhaps in the light of day they would see land, and be able to swim for it.

In the meantime, they had to survive the night.

JOSEF

18 days from home

"HELP! MY DAD JUMPED OVERBOARD! HELP!" Josef cried.

Far below him, already a couple hundred yards away from the ship, Josef's father thrashed crazily in the water. He screamed incoherently, but he wasn't calling out for rescue.

On the decks below, passengers ran to the rails and pointed. The ship's siren continued to blow and sailors ran about, but nobody was *doing* anything. Josef spun around helplessly. What was he supposed to do? Jump in after his father? It was such a long way down, and he didn't know how to swim—

Down below on C-deck, one of the Cuban policemen tossed his cap and gun belt aside, kicked off his shoes, and jumped headlong into the green water. He hit the ocean with a slap and a splash, and for many seconds Josef held his breath as though he was the diver himself. Josef's lungs were just about to burst when the man broke the surface a few yards away from where he'd hit, gasping for breath. The man flipped the wet hair out of his face, spun until he had his bearings, and set off swimming for Josef's father.

Josef's heart raced as fast as his feet as he flew down the stairs. He pushed through the crowds and ran to the rail, but the policeman hadn't yet reached his father. A woman screamed, and Josef followed the pointing fingers—two shark fins had appeared in the water.

Josef froze in terror.

There were more screams as his papa sank beneath the waves, and Josef had to cling to the rail not to collapse.

One of the *St. Louis*'s lifeboats hit the water, and the ship's siren had brought motor launches from the shore, but none of them were going to be in time. The only person close enough to save Josef's father was the Cuban policeman. Even though the sharks still circled, the policeman took a deep breath and dived beneath the waves.

Josef counted the long seconds before the man broke the surface again, this time with Papa in his arms.

The passengers on the ship cheered. But Josef's father didn't want to be rescued. He struggled in the man's arms, beating and flailing at him. "Murderers!" he cried. "They'll never take me!"

But Papa was weak and the policeman was strong. One of the motor launches from shore reached them first, and the policeman helped the other men lift Josef's father into the boat.

"Let me die! Let me die!" Josef's father cried. The words struck Josef like slaps to the face, and tears sprang to his eyes.

His father would rather die than be with his son. His daughter. His wife.

The crack of a pistol shot made Josef jump. One of the men in the boat stood aiming a gun down into the water near the policeman. *Pak! Pak!* He shot twice more, and one of the shark fins turned away from the policeman to attack the shark the man had wounded with his pistol.

The men laid Josef's father in the bottom of the boat and helped the weary policeman aboard. There were sighs of relief and whispered prayers on the *St. Louis*. But Josef's heart lurched when he saw his father kick away the man trying to help him. Papa lunged for the side of the small boat, trying to get back to the sea. "Let me die!" he cried out again.

The policeman grabbed him and pulled him back in the boat. Two more of the men restrained him, and the boat quickly turned and sped toward the shore.

The *St. Louis*'s siren stopped blasting, and suddenly it was over.

All around Josef, passengers wept. But Josef now felt more stunned than sad. His father was gone. In many ways, his father had never really come back from the concentration camp. Not the father Josef knew and remembered. Not the father he loved. He had come back in body, but not in spirit.

Josef's father was gone. His mother was unconscious. His little sister was all by herself. And they would never let Josef's family into Cuba now, not after his father had gone mad. Josef and his family would all be sent back to Germany. Back to the Nazis.

Josef's world was falling apart, and he didn't see any way to put it back together again.

ISABEL

4 days from home

THE LITTLE BOAT WAS FALLING APART.

The seams between the sides had cracks in them. The engine rattled in its mounting, constantly weakening the bolts that held it in place. Even the benches were coming loose. Only Castro hadn't cracked. He stared up at Isabel, as stern and confident as ever, commanding her to *FIGHT AGAINST THE IMPOSSIBLE AND WIN.*

But it was hard to fight against the inevitable. The water in the boat was almost to Isabel's knees. She and the others worked sluggishly in the blazing-hot Caribbean sun to scoop, pitch, scoop, pitch, but water was seeping in as fast as they could bail it. The boat was sinking. Every empty water bottle and gasoline can had been tucked up under a bench to help keep them afloat, but if they didn't reach Florida soon, they were all going to drown.

Fight against the impossible and win, Isabel told herself.

"When are we going to get there?" Iván whined.

"*Mañana,*" Lito said wearily. "*Mañana.*"

Suddenly, Isabel's grandfather stopped bailing water. He sat up straighter, like he was looking at something in the distance. "*Mañana,*" he whispered.

"Lito?" Isabel asked.

Her grandfather blinked and his eyes found her again. Was he crying, or was it just sweat and seawater?

"It's nothing, Chabela. Just . . . a memory. Something I haven't thought about in a long time."

Isabel's grandfather gazed around the little boat, and his eyes suddenly looked sadder, Isabel thought. She would have crawled over and hugged him, but there was no room to do it without three people getting up and moving for her to get there.

"Don't stop bailing," Señor Castillo told them from where he lay in the bottom of the boat.

"Maybe you could help," Papi told him.

"I'm recovering!" Señor Castillo argued. "I can barely move in this heat! Besides, I don't see you bailing."

"I'm tending to my wife," Papi said. "Who's *really* sick."

Ever since the Bahamas, something had come over Isabel's father. He'd been more attentive to Mami. More focused on her than anything else. Nobody else noticed, but Isabel did. She'd seen him hold her hand, watched him gently move her hair out of her face, heard him whispering that he loved her, that he needed her.

Things she had never seen or heard him do before.

"Are you saying my father is faking it?" Luis challenged.

"I'm just saying it's very nice for him that everybody else is keeping this metal coffin afloat while he sits back and relaxes," Papi said.

"You wouldn't even have this 'metal coffin' if I hadn't built it!"

"I'm not sure if *built* is the right word," Señora Castillo said, trying to pull two of the side pieces back together. "Cobbled is more like it."

Iván and Señor Castillo erupted at the same time.

"We did the best we could!" Iván yelled.

"Oh, now *you're* telling us how to build things?" Señor Castillo said. "Where were you and Luis when we were up all night putting this thing together, eh? You were at your law office, doing God knows what."

Isabel shrank in her seat and put her hands over her ears. She hated when her parents argued like this, and now everyone on the boat was mad at each other.

"I was *helping people*," Señora Castillo told her husband. "You've never appreciated what I do—"

"And what was I supposed to do," Luis threw in, "tell my police commander I had to stay home and build a boat so I could escape?"

"All of you, *stop it*," Amara yelled from the back of the boat. "Right now. You're acting like children."

Everyone fell quiet and looked appropriately chastised.

"I think it's time for a water break," Amara told them. "Isabel? Will you hand out the bottles?"

It was a little earlier than their rationed water break, but none of them complained. The clear, delicious water was the best thing Isabel had ever tasted, and it settled them all down like mother's milk for a baby.

"We're all hot, and we're all tired, and yes, we're sinking," Amara said. "But if we lose our heads, we're only going to die faster. We can resolve this."

"She's right," Isabel's father said. "I'm sorry."

"I'm sorry too," Señor Castillo said. "I should be helping."

"Only if you're up to it," Papi said, and he sounded like he meant it.

"The boat *is* falling apart, though," Iván said. "We're taking on too much water."

"We have too much weight," Señora Castillo said.

She was right, but what could they lose? There was just the engine, the fuel, the food and water, and the nine of them.

"What if one or two of us slipped out into the water at a time," Papi suggested. "They could hang on to the boat. Floating in the water alongside would help take some of the weight away."

"But it would drag on the boat. Slow us down," Luis said.

"But it might keep the boat afloat longer," Señor Castillo said.

"I think we should try it," Amara said. "We'll take turns in the water. It'll keep us cooler too."

And right now, Isabel thought, cooler heads just might be the most important thing of all.

MAHMOUD

11 days from home

MAHMOUD WAS IN AND OUT OF SLEEP, WAKING every few seconds when the waves washed over him. Minutes—hours?—passed, and Mahmoud dreamed that a boat was coming for them. He could hear its motor over the lapping of the waves.

Mahmoud jerked awake. He ran a wet, cold hand down his face, trying to focus, and he heard it again—the sound of a motor. He wasn't dreaming! But where was it? The rain had stopped, but it was still dark. He couldn't see the boat, but he could hear it.

"*Here!*" he cried. "*Here!*"

But the sound of the motor still stayed frustratingly, agonizingly, far away. If only whoever was on the boat could *see* him, Mahmoud thought. All his life he'd practiced being hidden. Unnoticed. Now, at last, when he most needed to be seen, he was truly invisible.

Mahmoud cried in exhaustion and misery. He wanted to do it all over again. He wanted to go back and stand up for the boy in the alley in Aleppo who was getting beaten up for his bread. To scream and yell and wake the sleeping citizens of Izmir so they would see him and all the other people sleeping in doorways and parks. To tell Bashir al-Assad and his army to go to hell. He wanted to stop being invisible and stand up and *fight*. But now he would never get a chance to do any of that. It was too late. There was no time.

Time. The phone! Mahmoud still had the phone in his pocket! He pulled it out and pushed the button on it through the plastic bag, and the screen with the clock on it lit up like a beacon in the night. Mahmoud held it over his head and waved it in the dark, screaming and yelling for help.

The motor got louder.

Mahmoud wept for joy as a boat emerged from the darkness—a *real* boat this time, not a dinghy. A speedboat with lights and antennas and blue and white stripes on the side—the colors of the Greek flag.

A Greek Coast Guard ship, come to save them.

And on the front of the ship, down on his knees with hands clasped in thanks, was Mahmoud's father.

Waleed was there too, in the back under a foil thermal blanket, and soon Mahmoud and his mother were out of the water and wrapped in the foil blankets too, what little body heat they still had left reflected back at them. Mahmoud's mother was too insensible to speak, so Mahmoud told his father how they had given

Hana away rather than see her drown with them. Mahmoud's father wept, but pulled Mahmoud to him and hugged him.

"Hana's not with us, but she's alive. I know it," his father told him. "Because of you, my son."

The Greek Coast Guard boat swept through the choppy Mediterranean the rest of the night, pulling more people out of the water. The Coast Guard finally set Mahmoud and his family and all the other refugees down on the island of Lesbos. It was almost six o'clock in the morning, and the sky was beginning to lighten with the dawn. Mahmoud wasn't sure, but he thought he and his mother had spent more than two hours in the water.

When they stepped off the boat, Mahmoud's father got down on his hands and knees and kissed the ground and gave thanks to Allah. It was time for morning prayers anyway, and Mahmoud joined him. When they were finished, Mahmoud staggered up the rocky gray shore, squinting at the hills that rose just beyond the beach. Then he realized: They weren't real hills.

They were piles and piles of life jackets.

There were mountains of them, stretching up and down the coast as far as Mahmoud could see. The way Aleppo had its piles of rubble, Lesbos had its piles of life jackets, abandoned by the hundreds of thousands of refugees who had come before them, shedding the vests they no longer needed and moving along on the road to somewhere else.

There were bodies on the beach too. People who hadn't survived the sea in the night, who hadn't been found by the Coast Guard in time. Men, mostly, but a few women too. And a child.

Mahmoud's mother rushed to the infant, howling Hana's name. Mahmoud hurried after her, horrified, but the child wasn't Hana. It was someone else's baby daughter, her lungs filled with seawater. Mahmoud's mother cried into his shoulder until a Greek man in a uniform moved them both away from the body and recorded the infant in a little notebook. Tallying the daily dead. Mahmoud staggered away, feeling as numb as if he were in the freezing water again.

Mahmoud's mother went to all the other refugees who had landed in the night and were still there, asking each of them if they had seen her little Hana. But none of them had. The boat with Mahmoud's little sister on it was gone—it had either reached the island and its passengers had already moved on, or it too had wrecked on the rocks.

Mahmoud's mother fell to her knees on the rocky ground and wept, and Mahmoud's father held her close and let her cry.

Mahmoud felt gutted. It was all his fault. Hana might still be with them if he hadn't gotten someone on that boat to take her. Or she might have died during their two hours in the water.

Either way, they had lost her.

"Mahmoud," his father said quietly over his sobbing mother, "check the other bodies and see if they have any shoes that will fit us."

JOSEF

19 days from home

JOSEF WISHED HE WAS INVISIBLE.

Once the rest of the passengers discovered who had jumped overboard yesterday, everyone stopped to tell him how sorry they were. How everything would be all right.

But how could it be all right? How could it *ever* be all right?

Josef stood at the rail on A-deck where his father had jumped. Down below, the sea was no longer empty. It was dotted with little motorboats and rowboats. Some carried reporters shouting up questions and trying to get pictures of the ship. Other boats offered up bunches of fresh bananas and bags of coconuts and oranges. Passengers on C-deck tossed money down, and the fruit was passed up the ladder by the Cuban policemen guarding the top and the bottom. Lately, though, the boats were full of relatives of people on board. Mostly men, they had come ahead to Cuba to get jobs and find places for their families to live.

One man brought the same little white dog every day and held it up for his wife to wave to.

The boats with relatives came close enough for their families to yell back and forth a little, but they couldn't get any closer. Thanks to Josef's father, a handful of Cuban police boats now surrounded the *St. Louis*. They kept the rescue ships at a distance and watched for anyone else who tried to jump to freedom.

Or death.

At night, the Cuban police boats swept the hull with searchlights, and the *St. Louis*'s crew members, on the captain's orders, patrolled the decks on suicide watch.

"Evelyne, there he is! There's Papa!" Renata cried. She stood a few paces away from Josef down the rail, trying to point out one of the little rowboats to her sister.

"Where? I don't see him!" Evelyne whined.

Josef was more interested in the small police boat that had navigated its way through the flotilla and was pulling up to the *St. Louis*. Any time they had a visitor now it was cause for conversation, and soon word spread throughout the ship that the boat had brought the Cuban policeman who had saved Josef's father.

Josef ran down to fetch his mother and sister, and together they hurried to the social hall, where a group of passengers and crew gathered to give the Cuban policeman a hero's welcome. They parted for the policeman, cheering and slapping him on the back and shaking hands with him as he went. It was the first time he had been back to the ship since jumping overboard to save Josef's father, and Josef and his family strained to get a good look at him over the heads of the other passengers. Josef's mother cried and put a hand to her mouth, and Josef felt a surge of affection for the policeman. This was the man who had saved his father's life.

The policeman seemed genuinely flattered and surprised by all the attention. He was a short, stocky man with olive skin, a wide face, and a thick mustache. He wore blue pants, a gray shirt with epaulets on the shoulders, and a matching gray beret. Around his waist was a leather belt with a nightstick and holster hanging from it.

His name, they were told, was Mariano Padron.

Captain Schroeder arrived to thank Officer Padron on behalf of the passengers and crew. Josef felt a ripple of tension spread throughout the room. Josef had seen the captain less and less as the hot days of waiting at anchor dragged on, and he wasn't the only passenger who had noticed. But they were there to celebrate Officer Padron, not badger the captain about why they were still on the ship. The mood became happy again when the policeman was presented with a gift of 150 reichsmarks that had been collected from grateful passengers. Officer Padron was stunned, and so was Josef—150 reichsmarks was a lot of money, especially for people who might need that money later to pay for visas and entrance fees.

Officer Padron tried to refuse the money, but the passengers wouldn't hear of it.

"I was just doing my job," Officer Padron told the audience through a translator. "But I will never forget this. I will never forget any of you. Thank you."

The passengers applauded again, and while many of them turned their attention to the captain to ask him for a status report, Josef and his mother and sister pushed forward to talk to the policeman.

Officer Padron's eyes lit up at the sight of Josef's mother. He said something in Spanish, and the passenger who had spoken for him in front of the crowd smiled and translated his words.

"Señora! Your father was a thief?"

Josef's mother frowned. "A thief? My father? No—I don't understand."

"Your father, he must be a thief," Officer Padron said through the translator. "Because he stole the stars from the sky and put them in the señora's eyes."

Josef finally understood—it was some kind of compliment about how pretty she was. His mother smiled politely but impatiently. "Officer Padron, what about my husband?" she asked. "Is he all right? They won't let me go ashore and see him."

The policeman took off his hat. "I am so sorry. So very sorry. Señora Landau, yes? Your husband is alive," he said through the interpreter. "He is in the hospital. He has been . . ." Officer Padron said something more, but the translator frowned. It was beyond his limited Spanish. Officer Padron could see his confusion, and he pantomimed what he meant by turning his wrists upside down, closing his eyes, and lolling his head back like he was asleep.

"Sedated," Mama said. There was pain in her voice. Josef knew she blamed herself. The whole reason her husband was gone was because *she* had been sedated and unable to stop him.

Officer Padron nodded. "It's not good," he said through the interpreter. "But he will live."

Josef's mother took both of the policeman's hands in her own and kissed them. "Thank you, Officer Padron." She spoke in German, but the policeman seemed to understand. He blushed and nodded. Then he spied Ruthie half hidden behind her mother's skirt and knelt down to her. He put his policeman's beret on her head and said something in Spanish, and she smiled.

"He says you're the policewoman now," the translator said. "He will be the criminal. You must catch him!"

Officer Padron led Ruthie on a merry chase around the room, Ruthie squealing. Josef's mother laughed through a sob. It was the first time Josef had heard her laugh or seen her smile in months.

Officer Padron let Ruthie catch him, and he plucked the hat off Ruthie's head and put it on Josef's head, speaking in Spanish again.

"He says it's your turn," the translator said.

"Oh, no," Josef said. He waved a hand to make sure the policeman understood. He wasn't in the mood for fun and games, and besides, he was too old for that kind of thing.

Officer Padron tapped Josef's chest with the back of his hand, urging him to play.

"He says he is the passenger," the translator said. Officer Padron raised himself up in mock anger and spoke in Spanish. "You! Señor Policeman!" the translator said. "When will we leave the ship?"

The happy mood suddenly disappeared. Josef and his family and the translator all looked at each other awkwardly. Officer Padron had only meant to mimic what everyone asked him all the time, but the question made Josef sag. It felt like they were *never* getting off this ship. Officer Padron realized his mistake immediately and looked anguished at having brought it up. He nodded in sympathy. Then, in unison, he and Josef spoke the answer all the Cuban guards always gave:

"*Mañana.*"

ISABEL

5 days from home

ISABEL SLIPPED OVER THE SIDE OF THE BOAT into the sea and sighed. The water was warm, but it felt much cooler than being in the boat. The sun was just setting on the western horizon, turning the world into a sepia-toned photograph, but it still had to be close to a hundred degrees outside. If it wouldn't have swamped their boat and drowned them all for good, Isabel would have prayed for rain to break the muggy heat.

Isabel's father had rigged up a makeshift sunshade out of his shirt for her mother, and she seemed better now. The aspirin had kept Mami's fever down, and though she was still exhausted and near to bursting with Isabel's baby brother, she seemed at peace somehow. Hot, but at peace.

If the rest of them wanted relief, they had to wait for their turn in the water.

Again, Isabel thought about their journey as a song. If the riots and trading for the gasoline were the first verse, and the tanker and the storm the second verse, *this* part of their trip—the long, hot, stagnant day and a half they had been traveling from the Bahamas to Florida—this was the bridge. A third verse that was different from the others. This verse was death by slow measures. This was the down-tempo lull before the coming excitement of the climactic last verse and coda.

This was limbo. They could do nothing but wait.

The last sliver of sun finally disappeared below the waves, and Luis cut the engine. The world went silent but for the soft lapping of water against the hull and the creak of their disintegrating boat.

"That's it," Luis said. "With the sun down, we won't be able to navigate as well."

"Can't we use the stars?" Isabel asked. She remembered reading that sailors had used the stars to navigate for centuries.

"Which one?" Luis asked. None of them knew.

Amara lifted one of the gasoline jugs and swished around what little there was left in it. "Saves us gas, anyway," she said. "The thing's been eating it up. We'll be lucky to have enough to get to shore when we see land."

"When will we get there?" Iván asked. He was bobbing in the water just ahead of Isabel, hanging on to the hull like she was.

"Tomorrow, hopefully," Señor Castillo said from inside the boat. It was the same thing he'd said yesterday, and the day before that.

"*Mañana*," Isabel's grandfather whispered. He was treading water on the other side of the boat with Señora Castillo, his head just visible over the side. He'd been whispering that word off and on since yesterday, and still seemed shaken up somehow. Isabel didn't know why.

"We'll see the lights of Miami sometime tomorrow, and we'll head straight for it," Mami said. She shifted and winced uncomfortably.

"What is it? Are you all right?" Papi asked.

Isabel's mother put a hand on her belly. "I think it's begun."

"What's begun?" Papi asked. Then his eyes went wide. "You mean—you mean the baby's coming? Here? *Now?*"

Everyone in the boat perked up, and Isabel and Iván pulled themselves up on the side of the boat to see. Isabel was a jumble of emotions. She was excited to see her brother born after waiting so long, but suddenly she was also afraid. Afraid for her mother to have the baby here, on this fragile raft in the middle of the ocean. And worried too, for the first time, about how her baby brother would change her fragile family.

"Yes, I think I've gone into labor," Isabel's mother said calmly. "But no, I am not having the baby here and now. The contractions are just starting. It took Isabel another ten hours to come after my contractions began, remember?"

Isabel had never heard her mother talk about her birth before, and she was both curious and a little weirded out at the same time.

"What are you going to name him?" Iván asked.

Mami and Papi looked at each other. "We haven't decided yet," she said.

"Well, I have some good ideas, if you want some," Iván said.

"We're *not* naming him after *Industriales* players," Isabel told him, and Iván stuck his tongue out at her.

They were all quiet for a time, and Isabel watched as the golden horizon shifted from orange to purple to deep blue. Would her baby brother be born at sea, or in the United States? Would the end of their song really be a new life in Miami? Or would it end in tragedy for all of them, adrift, out of gas, and dying of thirst in the great saltwater desert of the Atlantic?

"Hey, we never named our boat," Iván said.

Everyone moaned and laughed.

"What?" Iván said, smiling. "Every good boat needs a name."

"I think we all agree this isn't a good boat," Señor Castillo said.

"But it's the boat that's taking us to the States! To freedom!" Iván said. "It deserves a name."

"How about *Fidel*?" Luis joked, kicking up a splash on Castro's face at the bottom of the boat.

"No, no, no," Papi said. *"¡El Ataúd Flotante!"* The *Floating Coffin.* Isabel winced at the name. It wasn't funny. Not with her mother about to have a baby on the boat.

"Too close, too close," Señor Castillo agreed. "How about *Me Piro*," he suggested. It was slang for "I'm out of here" in Cuba.

"¡Chao, Pescao!" Mami said, and everyone laughed. It literally meant "Good-bye, Fish!" but everyone in Cuba said it to each other to say good-bye.

"The *St. Louis*," Isabel's grandfather said softly. Everyone was quiet for a moment, trying to figure out the joke, but no one understood.

"How about *El Camello*?" Luis said. "The Camel" was what they called the ugly humpbacked buses pulled around by tractors in Havana.

"No, no—I've got it!" Amara cried. *"¡El Botero!"* It was perfect, because it was the slang word for the taxis in Havana, but it actually meant "the Boatman." All the adults laughed and clapped.

"No, no," Iván said, frustrated. "It needs a cool-sounding name, like *The—*"

Iván jumped a little in the water, and his eyes went wide.

"The what?" Isabel asked. Then she jumped too as something hard and leathery bumped into her leg.

"Shark!" screamed Isabel's grandfather from the other side of the boat. *"Shark!"*

The water around Iván became a dark red cloud, and Isabel screamed. Something bumped into her again, and Isabel scrambled to climb into the boat, arms and legs shaking, panic thundering in her chest. Her father grabbed her around her middle and they fell back in a tumble inside the boat. Beside them, Amara and Mami helped pull Señora Castillo into the boat as Lito pushed her up out of the water from behind. Isabel and her father scrabbled to their knees and pulled her grandfather in behind her.

On the other side of the boat, Luis and Señor Castillo cried out Iván's name as they hauled his limp body over the side.

Iván's right leg was a bloody mess. There were small bites all over it, as though a gang of sharks had attacked all at once. Raw, red, gaping wounds exposed the muscle underneath his skin.

Isabel fell back against the side of the boat in horror. She'd never seen anything so awful. She felt like she was going to throw up.

Señora Castillo wailed. Iván was so shocked he didn't even cry out, didn't speak. His eyes had a glazed look to them, and his mouth hung open. One of the gashes up near his thigh was pumping blood out like a garden hose, and Isabel watched as Iván's face grew pale. She couldn't speak.

"A tourniquet!" Lito cried. "We have to get something around his leg to stop the bleeding!"

Isabel's father yanked off his belt and Lito tied it as high around Iván's leg as he could, but the blood still flowed, coloring the water all around them in the boat a dark, sickening red.

"No—*NO!*" Señor Castillo cried as the life went out of Iván's eyes. Isabel wanted to scream too, but she was frozen. There was nothing she could do. There was nothing any of them could do.

Iván was dead.

Luis yelled in rage and pulled his police pistol from its holster. *BANG! BANG-BANG!* He fired once, twice, three times at the fin that circled the boat.

"No!" Lito said, grabbing Luis's hand before he could shoot again. "You'll just bring more sharks with the blood in the water!"

Too late. Another fin appeared, and another, and soon the nameless little boat was surrounded.

They were trapped in their own sinking prison.

MAHMOUD

12 days from home

MAHMOUD WAS IN ANOTHER TENT CITY. THE paved parking lot at the pier in Lesbos was full of the kinds of camping tents sold in sporting goods stores— round-topped single-family tents of blue and green and white and yellow and red, all provided by Greek relief workers who knew the refugees had nowhere to stay while they waited for the ferry to Athens to come. Wet clothes were hung out to dry on bicycle racks and traffic signs, and refugees gathered around camp stoves and hot plates.

It should have been a lively place, full of songs and laughter like the Kilis refugee camp, but instead a soft, mournful murmur of conversation hung over the tent city like a fog. Mahmoud wasn't surprised; his family felt exactly the same way. They all should have been excited to finally be in Greece, to be allowed to buy real tickets to travel on an actual ferry to mainland Europe. But too many of them had lost someone in the sea crossing to be happy.

Mahmoud's mother had gone from tent to tent asking after Hana. Mahmoud had helped. It was his fault she was gone, after all. But no one at the dock had her, and no one had been on the dinghy that had taken her.

Refugees came and went but the tents remained, and Mahmoud's mother insisted they miss the next ferry to Athens so she could ask each new round of refugees for word of her daughter. But no one knew anything about her.

Mahmoud felt as sick as he had on the dinghy. He couldn't look at his mother. She *had* to blame him for losing Hana. He certainly blamed himself. He couldn't sleep at night. He kept picturing his sister's dinghy bursting on the rocks. Hana falling into the water. None of them there to help her.

Mahmoud's mother wanted to stay at the dock longer, didn't want to leave without knowing what happened to Hana, but Dad told her they had to move on. There was no telling when the ferry line might suddenly decide to stop selling tickets to refugees, or when Greece might decide to send them all home. They had to keep moving or they would die. Hana had to have gone ahead of them on the morning ferry they'd missed that first day. Or else . . .

No one wanted to think about the "or else."

The huge Athens ferry arrived again that morning. It was the length of a soccer field, and at least five stories tall. The bottom half of it was painted blue, and BLUE STAR FERRIES was written in big words on the side.

A radar bar spun near the bridge, and antennas and satellite dishes sprouted from the roof. It looked like the pictures Mahmoud had seen of cruise ships. Its lifeboats
alone were bigger than the dinghy they had left Turkey
in. Mahmoud tried to get Waleed interested in the big
ship, to get him excited about their first trip on a boat that
big, but his little brother didn't care. He didn't seem to
care about anything.

A big ramp on the back lowered, and refugees streamed
on board the ferry. Mahmoud's mother wept as they
climbed a ramp with the other passengers. She kept
looking back over her shoulder at the tent city, hoping,
Mahmoud was sure, to catch a glimpse of someone carrying a baby who might be Hana. But she never did.

The inside of the ferry was like the lobby of a fancy
hotel. Every floor had little clusters of glass tables and
white upholstered chairs. Snack bars sold chips and sweets
and sodas, and televisions played a Greek soccer game.
Refugees who still had belongings stuffed their backpacks and trash bags under tables and into the overhead
compartments. Mahmoud and his family settled into one
of the booths, and his father searched for a plug to charge
his phone.

"Mahmoud, why don't you take your brother and
explore the ship," Dad told him.

Mahmoud was only too glad to get away from the
sight of his mother's broken face, and he took Waleed by

the hand and pulled him out onto the promenade that ran around the outside of the ship.

Mahmoud and Waleed watched silently as the ferry pulled away from the dock, the ship's huge engines thrumming deep below them. The awful sea that had tried to swallow them was calm and sapphire blue now. The Greek island of Lesbos was actually beautiful when you saw it from the sea. Little white buildings with terra-cotta roofs rose up tree-covered hills, and on top of one of the hills was an ancient gray castle. Mahmoud could see why people visited there on vacation.

Besides the refugees, there were a number of tourists on board. Mahmoud could tell they weren't refugees because they wore clean clothes and used their phones for taking pictures instead of looking up overland routes from Athens to Macedonia.

Another refugee had laid out a mat on the deck, and he was praying. In all the bustle of waiting in line and getting on board, Mahmoud had lost track of what time it was, and he pulled his brother down with him to pray alongside the man. As he kneeled and stood, kneeled and stood, Mahmoud was supposed to be focused only on his prayers. But he couldn't help notice the uneasy looks the tourists were giving them. The frowns of displeasure. Like Mahmoud and his brother and this man were doing something wrong.

The vacationers dropped their voices, and even though

Mahmoud couldn't understand what they were saying, he could hear the disgust in their words. This wasn't what the tourists had paid for. They were supposed to be on holiday, seeing ancient ruins and beautiful Greek beaches, not stepping over filthy, praying refugees.

They only see us when we do something they don't want us to do, Mahmoud realized. The thought hit him like a lightning bolt. When they stayed where they were supposed to be—in the ruins of Aleppo or behind the fences of a refugee camp—people could forget about them. But when refugees did something they didn't want them to do— when they tried to cross the border into their country, or slept on the front stoops of their shops, or jumped in front of their cars, or prayed on the decks of their ferries—that's when people couldn't ignore them any longer.

Mahmoud's first instinct was to disappear below decks. To be invisible. Being invisible in Syria had kept him alive. But now Mahmoud began to wonder if being invisible in Europe might be the death of him and his family. If no one saw them, no one could help them. And maybe the world needed to see what was really happening here.

It was hard not to see the refugees in Athens when Mahmoud got there. Syrians were everywhere in the streets and hotels and markets, most of them, like Mahmoud's family, planning to move on as soon as they could. Mahmoud's father thought he had the right documents to travel freely in Greece, but a woman at an immigration office told him he would need to go to a local police station first to get an official document, and the police told him he would have to wait up to a week.

"We can't wait a week," Mahmoud's father told his family. They had found a hotel for ten euros a night, per person, and the people of Athens were very friendly and helpful. But Mahmoud knew his parents only had so much money, and they still had four more countries to cross before they reached Germany. Mahmoud's mother would have stayed a week, or even longer, to keep asking everyone she met if they had seen a baby named Hana. But it was decided: They would take a train to the border of Macedonia and try to sneak across during the night.

JOSEF

21 days from home

JOSEF WATCHED FROM THE DECK AS ANOTHER little boat snuck through the flotilla of reporters and fruit sellers and Cuban policemen surrounding the MS *St. Louis.* This boat held a familiar-looking passenger, and Josef realized with a start that it was Dr. Aber, Renata and Evelyne's father, who already lived in Cuba. Josef ran through the ship until he found the sisters in the movie theater, watching serials.

"Your dad's coming to the ship!" Josef told them.

Renata and Evelyne hurried after him. When they got back to the ladder at C-deck, they got an even bigger surprise—Dr. Aber had gotten on board the *St. Louis!* Officer Padron was looking over some papers Dr. Aber had brought with him, and a small crowd had gathered to see what was happening.

Renata and Evelyne ran to their father, and he swept them up in his arms. "My beautiful daughters!" he said, kissing them both. "I thought I'd never see you again!"

Officer Padron nodded and said something in Spanish to Dr. Aber, and Dr. Aber smiled at his daughters. "Come! It's time for you to join me in Cuba."

"But what about our things? Our clothes?" Renata asked.

"Forget about them. We'll buy you new clothes in Cuba," Dr. Aber said. His eyes darted to the policemen, and Josef understood. Somehow Dr. Aber had gotten someone official to let him come get his daughters off the ship, but he didn't want to wait around any longer in case the policemen changed their minds. He carried Renata and Evelyne to the ladder, and Renata barely had time to yell "Good-bye!" to Josef and wave before they were gone over the side.

Josef was speechless, but the rest of the crowd wasn't. Angry passengers surrounded Officer Padron and the other policemen, demanding answers.

"How come *they* got off the ship and not us?"

"Can you help us?"

"How did they do it?"

"Let us off the ship!"

"My husband is in Cuba!"

"They have papers! Right papers!" Officer Padron tried to explain in broken German, but that only made the crowd madder.

"We have papers! Visas! We paid for them!"

Josef was scared for Officer Padron, but he shared the passengers' frustration. Why had Dr. Aber been able to take Renata and Evelyne off and none of the rest of them could go? It wasn't fair! Josef clenched his fists and began to shake. Then he realized it wasn't him that was doing the shaking. It was the metal deck of the ship.

The ship's engines were rumbling to life for the first time since they had dropped anchor. Which could mean only one thing: The *St. Louis* was going home to Germany, and they were all going with it.

Without a word from anyone, the passengers rushed the top of the ladder as one.

Officer Padron drew his pistol, and Josef gasped.

"Paren!" the policeman cried. "Halt!" He swept the gun back and forth, and the other policemen drew their pistols and did the same. The angry passengers pulled back but didn't run away. Josef's heart was in his throat. Any second now the mob was going to attack the policemen, Josef knew it. They would rather die than be sent back to Germany. Back to Hitler.

The ship's first officer and the purser arrived and threw themselves in between the guards and the angry crowd. They begged for everyone to remain calm, but no one listened. As the vibrations of the ship's engines below grew louder and more insistent, more people rushed to the ladder to demand to be let off the ship. Josef was caught in the middle now. If the mob pushed forward into the guns of the policemen, Josef would have no choice but to push with them.

It was hot—well over a hundred degrees on deck already—and the temperature of the crowd was rising. Josef was a ball of sweat, and the close-packed mob only made things worse. The situation was just about to boil over when a small white man in a gray suit climbed up the ladder behind the policemen. It was Captain Schroeder! But Josef wondered why was he out of uniform. And why had he been off the ship?

For a moment the mob was so surprised it stopped surging forward. Captain Schroeder was surprised too. As soon as he saw the angry crowd and the guns drawn, he lost his temper. He yelled at the policemen to lower their weapons or he would order them off the ship, and at last they obeyed.

"Why have the engines started?" one of the passengers yelled.

"Tell us what's happening!"

Captain Schroeder put his hands in the air and called for calm so that he could explain. He took off his hat and mopped his brow with his handkerchief. "I have just been to see President Brú, to appeal to him personally for you to be allowed to disembark," the captain said. "But he would not see me."

There were dark mutterings among the passengers, and Josef felt himself getting angrier. What was going on? Why had the Cubans promised the passengers they would let them in, only to turn them away now?

"Worse," Captain Schroeder said, "the Cuban government has ordered us to leave the harbor by tomorrow morning."

Leave by tomorrow? Josef thought. And go where? And what about his father? Would he be leaving with them?

Cries of anger came from the passengers, and Josef joined in. The first officer had disappeared briefly, but now returned with more sailors in case there was violence.

Josef wondered if he should bring his mother to hear this news, but he knew she was in their cabin, most likely in bed, crying. She blamed herself for her husband's suicide attempt, and in the last two days she had become, in a way, as absent a parent as Josef's father.

No, Josef was the one who needed to be here right now. For his mother and for Ruthie.

Captain Schroeder called for quiet again. "We are not going home. We will cruise the American coast and make appeals to President Roosevelt. If any of you have friends or family in the States, I beg you to ask them to exert what influence they can. No matter what, I assure you: I will do everything in my power to arrange a landing outside Germany. Hope must always remain. Now please, go back to your cabins. I must return to the bridge to make the ship ready for our departure."

The crowd mobbed the captain as he tried to leave C-deck, the passengers pushing and shoving their way around Josef. Josef fought his way to the passenger who had translated for Officer Padron the other day and pulled him to where the policemen stood.

"What about my father?" Josef asked Officer Padron through the translator.

"I saw him in the hospital," the policeman told Josef. "He's not well enough to come to the ship."

"Then can we go to him instead?" Josef asked.

The policeman looked pained. "I'm sorry, Little Man. You cannot leave the ship."

"But the *ship* is leaving," Josef said. He could feel the pulsing engines under his feet. "We can't leave my father behind."

"I wish from the bottom of my heart that you will land soon, Little Man," Officer Padron said again. "I'm sorry. I'm just doing my job."

Josef looked deep into Officer Padron's eyes, searching for some sign of help, some hint of sympathy. Officer Padron just looked away.

....

Josef was still standing there in the hot Cuban sun when, right before lunch, the policemen left on a launch. Officer Padron still wouldn't look at him. Once the little boat was clear, the MS *St. Louis* blew its horn, raised its anchor, and left Havana Harbor, destination unknown.

As he stood at the rail with the rest of the passengers saying a tearful good-bye to the only place that had ever promised them refuge, Josef said good-bye to his father as well. He took his shirt collar in both hands and ripped it along the seam, rending his garment as he'd done when Professor Weiler had been buried at sea.

Josef knew Papa was still alive, but it didn't matter. His father was dead to his family. And so, Josef realized, was their dream of joining him in Cuba.

ISABEL

5 days from home

THE NIGHT SKY WAS SO CLEAR ISABEL COULD see the Milky Way.

Her gaze was on the stars, but she wasn't really looking at them. She wasn't really looking at anything. Her eyes were blurry from tears. Next to her, Señora Castillo sobbed in her husband's arms, her shoulders heaving. Like Isabel, she had been crying ever since Iván died. Señor Castillo stared out over his wife's head, his eyes vacant. Luis kicked out at the silent engine, rattling the bolts that held it down. He buried his face in his hands, and Amara hugged him tight.

Iván was dead. Isabel couldn't grasp it. One minute he had been alive, talking to them, laughing with them, and the next he was dead. Lifeless. Like every other Cuban who had ever died trying to get to *el norte* by sea. But Iván wasn't some nameless, faceless person. He was Iván. *Her* Iván. He was her friend.

And he was dead.

Isabel's eyes drifted down to where Iván's body lay, but she still didn't look right at him. Couldn't. Even though Papi had taken down the shirt he'd draped over Mami to shade her and laid it across Iván's face, Isabel couldn't bear to look.

She knew Iván's face. His smile. She wanted to think of him that way.

Lito sang a low, sad song, and Isabel retreated into the arms of her mother and father. The three of them huddled together, as if what happened to Iván might happen to them too if they came too close to his body. But the real threat was the sinking boat and the sharks that still circled it, following the trail of bloody water that started at Isabel's feet.

Fidel Castro had Iván's blood all over him.

Isabel remembered the wake for her grandmother. It had been a quiet, somber occasion. There hadn't even been a body to bury. Those who had come had spent most of their time comforting Lito and Mami and Isabel, hugging them and kissing them and sharing their grief. Isabel knew she should do that now for the Castillos, but she couldn't bring herself to do it. How could she comfort the Castillos when she still needed comforting herself? Iván was their son, their brother, but he was Isabel's best friend. In some ways she knew him better even than his family did. She'd played soccer with him in the alley, swum with him in the sea, sat next to him in school. She had eaten dinner at his house, and he at hers, so many times they might as well have been brother and sister. Isabel and Iván had grown up together. She couldn't imagine a world where she would run next door and he wouldn't be there.

But Iván wouldn't be coming over anymore.

Iván was dead.

The loss of him ached like a part of Isabel was suddenly missing, like her heart had been ripped out of her chest and all that was left was a giant, gaping hole. She shook again as her body was wracked with sobs, and Mami pulled her closer.

After a time, Isabel's grandfather finally spoke.

"We need to do something," he said. "With the body."

Señora Castillo wailed, but Señor Castillo nodded.

Do something with the body? Isabel looked around. But what was there to be done with Iván's body on this little raft? And then Isabel understood. There was only one place for Iván's body to go: into the sea. The thought made her recoil in terror.

"No! No, we can't leave him here!" Isabel cried. "He'll be all alone! Iván never liked to be alone."

Lito nodded to Isabel's father, and the two of them stood to lift Iván out of the small boat.

Isabel fought to get free of her mother, but Mami held her tight.

"Wait," Señora Castillo said. She pulled herself away from her husband, her face streaked with tears. "We have to say something. A prayer. Something. I want God to know Iván is coming."

Isabel had never been to church. When Castro and the communists had taken over, they had discouraged the practice of religion. But Spanish Catholics had conquered the island long before Castro had, and Isabel knew their religion was still there, deep down, the way Lito told her *clave* was buried beneath the audible rhythms of a song.

Lito was the oldest, and had been to the most funerals, so he took charge. He made the sign of the cross over Iván's body, and said, "Eternal rest grant unto him, O Lord, and let perpetual light shine upon him. May he rest in peace. Amen."

Señora Castillo nodded, and Lito and Isabel's father picked up Iván's body.

"No—no!" Isabel cried. She reached out as if to stop them, then pulled her hands back and clasped them to her chest. She knew they had to do this, that they could not keep Iván on the boat with them. Not like this. But as she watched Lito and Papi lift up Iván's body, the empty place inside got bigger and bigger, until she was more empty than full. She wished she was dead too. She wished she was dead so they would put her into the water with Iván. So she could keep him company in the deep.

Señora Castillo reached out and took her son's hand one last time, and Luis stood and put a hand to Iván's chest—one last connection to his brother before he was gone for good. Isabel wanted to do something, to say something, but she was too overcome with grief.

"Wait," Luis said. He pulled his pistol from his holster. His face turned mean as he aimed it over the other side of the boat, at one of the fins that skimmed the surface. Isabel was ready for the shots this time, but they still made her jump. *BANG! BANG! BANG!*

The shark died in a bloody, thrashing spasm, and the other sharks that had been following the boat fell on it in a frenzy. Luis nodded to Lito and Isabel's father, and Señora Castillo looked away as they slipped Iván off the other side of the boat, away from the sharks, where he sank into the black sea.

No one spoke. Isabel cried, the tears coming without end, flowing up from the hollow place in her chest that threatened to consume her. Iván was gone, forever.

Isabel suddenly remembered Iván's *Industriales* cap. Where was it? What had happened to it? It hadn't been on him when he'd been put back in the water, and Isabel wanted to find it. Needed to find it. That was something she could do. A piece of him she could keep close to her. She pulled away from her mother and searched the little boat for it. It had to be somewhere . . . Yes! There! Floating upside down in the bloody water, underneath one of the benches. She plucked it up and held it to her chest, the only part of Iván she had left.

"I wanted to open a restaurant," Señor Castillo said. He was right next to her, and the sound of his voice, almost a whisper, made Isabel jump. "When we were talking that first night, everybody was telling each other what they wanted to do when we got to the US," Señor Castillo went on, "but I never said. I wanted to open a restaurant with my sons."

Something sparkled on the dark horizon, and at first Isabel took it to be one of the stars in the white scar of the Milky Way twinkling in her watery eyes. But no—it was too bright. Too orange. And there were others just like it, all clustered in a horizontal line, separating the black waters from the black sky.

It was Miami, at last. Iván had just missed seeing Miami.

MAHMOUD

MACEDONIA TO SERBIA—2015

14 to 15 days from home

MAHMOUD FELT LIKE HE WAS BACK IN SYRIA. Policemen with guns guarded the border from Greece into Macedonia, and he felt dirty again. Unwanted. Illegal.

Even without travel papers, Mahmoud and his family had been able to exchange their Syrian pounds for euros and buy train tickets from Athens to Thessaloniki, and from there to a little Greek town near the border of Macedonia. Now they were headed for the Macedonian town of Gevgelija, where they hoped to catch a train north to Serbia, and from there to Hungary. But first they had to find a way to sneak across the border.

Mahmoud pointed out a little tangle of tents and laundry lines just off the gravel road, and Mahmoud's father pulled them into the camp to plan their next move. It was another little refugee village, the kind of makeshift town Mahmoud had seen again and again on the road out of Syria. Mahmoud and his father hunkered down behind a trash barrel and watched the border crossing. The Macedonian police weren't turning people away, but they might be checking papers, and Mahmoud's family hadn't waited in Athens for official travel permits.

Mahmoud's dad pulled out his iPhone and consulted the map. "This whole area is farmland," his father said. "Flat land. Too easy to be caught." He scrolled sideways on the map, and Mahmoud leaned in closer. "It looks like there's a forest here, to the west," Dad said. "They can't have every meter of the border guarded. We'll slip through at night. Once we're in Macedonia, we'll be all right. Where's your mother?"

Mahmoud looked up. Mom was where she always was, working her way through the tents. Looking for Hana.

Hana wasn't there, though, and she wasn't at any of the other little clusters of refugee tents they passed as they hiked farther into the countryside. At some place he'd picked from the map on his iPhone, Mahmoud's father led them off a dirt road into a dark forest. It was late, well after midnight, and Mahmoud was weary from walking. But they still had two hours to walk to the Macedonian border.

Waleed raised his arms to be carried, and Dad hefted him up against his shoulder. Mahmoud bristled. Waleed was being a baby. He was too big to be carried. Mahmoud was tired too, but nobody was carrying *him*.

They walked along in silence, their way lit only by the occasional glow of the phone screen as Dad checked their position. The forest was full of tall pine trees that crowded almost everything else out, and the ground was covered with brown pine needles that smelled like a car freshener. Somewhere in the forest an owl screeched, and Mahmoud heard the scurrying of small animals. Every rustle made Mahmoud jump, every scuffle gave him goose bumps. He was a city boy, used to the lights and sounds of traffic. Here, every sound was like a gunshot in the unearthly dark and quiet. It terrified Mahmoud.

At last they emerged from the dark woods and found the train station. It was a small, two-story, mustard-colored building, with a burgundy roof and rounded gables.

It was also packed with people.

Hundreds of people slept outside, using their backpacks and trash bags as pillows. They filled the train platform and the sidewalks in front of the station, and some even slept between the tracks. Plastic bottles and empty bags and discarded wrappers littered the ground.

Mahmoud watched his father's shoulders sag. Mahmoud felt the same way. But then his father stood taller and hiked Waleed up higher on his shoulder.

"Hey, at least we know we're on the right track," he said. He grinned at Mahmoud. "The right *track*. Get it?"

Mahmoud got it. He just didn't think any of this was funny.

"No? Nothing?" his father said. "I guess I need to *train* you better."

Mahmoud still didn't laugh. He was too tired.

Mahmoud's mother had already left them, stepping carefully among the sleeping refugees like a ghost. Searching for Hana.

"The train station looks closed," Mahmoud's father told him. "We'll have to find someplace to sleep. We'll come back in the morning and see if we can buy tickets."

They found a nearby hotel listed on TripAdvisor, and they collected Mahmoud's mother and set out for the inn on foot. Mahmoud couldn't wait to climb into a real bed. He felt like he could sleep for days.

A car came up behind them, and this time Mahmoud didn't jump out in front of it. But it slowed down and stopped beside them anyway.

"You need taxi?" the man said in broken Arabic.

"No," Mahmoud's father said. "We're just going to the hotel."

"Hotel much money," the man said. "You go to Serbia? I take you in taxi. Twenty-five euros each."

Mahmoud did the math. A hundred euros was a lot of money—almost 24,000 Syrian pounds. But a taxi ride straight to Serbia, without spending the night—or longer—in Macedonia? Mahmoud's parents huddled together, and Mahmoud listened in. Train tickets were likely cheaper, and Mom worried about accepting a ride from a strange man in a country they didn't know, but Dad argued there wasn't another train until at least tomorrow, and there were already so many people waiting for the train at the station.

"We're all tired, and a taxi gets us closer to Germany. Sleeping on the ground doesn't," Mahmoud threw in.

"That's the deciding vote, then," Dad said. "We'll take the car."

It was a good decision. Two hours and one hundred euros later, they were at the Serbian border. It was still dark, but there were no border guards where the driver dropped them off. No roads, either. Mahmoud had slept a little in the car, but he felt like a zombie as he shambled with his family along the railroad tracks that would take them across the border from Macedonia to the nearest Serbian town. Since they were traveling, they were permitted to skip their early-morning prayers.

They staggered into a town just after sun up. Mahmoud thought that if he didn't lie down somewhere and sleep he would pass out on his feet and fall flat on his face. But there were even more refugees at this train station than there had been in Macedonia, and here there were no tents and no hotel rooms. People slept on the platform of the station or outside in the fields. There were no toilets, either, and no markets or restaurants. What little the local Serbs had they were charging a fortune for. One man was selling water bottles for five euros apiece.

A group of men sat around a power strip charging their phones as though they were huddled around a campfire. Mahmoud had seen scenes like this every-where along the route from Athens to Germany. He and his family paused just long enough to recharge their own phones again, and then they were on the move once more.

Mahmoud was so tired he wanted to cry. His father found them a bus to Belgrade, and Mahmoud was thankful for the few hours' sleep, uncomfortable though they were. It was almost sundown when they arrived in the Serbian capital, but they still couldn't stop. The police there were raiding hotels for illegal refugees, so Dad found another taxi driver who promised to take them the two hours farther to the Hungarian border.

Taxis were expensive, but so was trying to stay over-night in a city that didn't want you.

The silver four-door Volkswagen was driven by a middle-aged, olive-skinned Serbian man with a neatly trimmed black beard. He promised to get them to Hungary and keep them away from the police for thirty euros apiece—more than it had cost them to cross all of Macedonia.

It was a tight fit in the car, with Mahmoud, his mother, and his father crammed into the back seat and Waleed in his father's lap. This new driver seemed to find every rut and hole in the road and send them flying into each other. But none of that mattered to Mahmoud. He was asleep almost as soon as he'd closed his eyes, and he only woke again when he realized the car wasn't moving. Had it really been two hours already? He felt like he'd just gone to sleep.

Mahmoud's eyelids fluttered and he looked out the windows. He expected to see the lights of a Serbian border town. Another tent city. Instead, they were stopped in the middle of a lonely stretch of highway surrounded by dark, empty fields.

And the taxi driver was leaning over the backseat with a pistol aimed straight at them.

JOSEF

21 days from home

MIAMI! THEY WEREN'T EVEN A DAY OUT OF Havana, and already the *St. Louis* was passing the American city. It was so close you could see it from the ship without binoculars. Josef and Ruthie hung over the rails like everyone else, pointing out hotels and houses and parks. Josef saw highways and white square office buildings—skyscrapers!—and hundreds of little boats at harbor. Why couldn't they just pull in to Miami and dock there? Why wouldn't the United States just let them in? There was so much land that didn't have buildings on it. Miles and miles of palm trees and swamp as far as the eye could see. Josef would take it. He would live there. He would live anywhere so long as it was away from the Nazis.

An airplane circled the ship, its propeller buzzing like a hornet. Newspaper photographers, one of the other passengers guessed out loud. Josef knew by now that the *St. Louis* was big news the world over. Newsreel camera crews had followed the ship out of Havana Harbor on little boats, yelling out the same questions all the passengers had: Where would they land? Who would take the Jewish refugees?

Would they end up back in Germany?

That afternoon, a US Coast Guard cutter cruised alongside the *St. Louis*, its officers watching them through binoculars. One of the other children guessed the cutter was there to protect them, to pick up anyone who jumped overboard.

Josef thought it was to make sure the *St. Louis* didn't steer for Miami.

Some of the children, like Ruthie, still played games and swam in the pool, and they were close enough to America for some of the teenagers to pick up a New York Yankees game on their radios. But most of the adults walked around like they were at a funeral. The happy mood of the voyage to Cuba was gone forever. People spoke little, and socialized less. The movie theater was deserted. No one went to the dance hall.

Except for Josef's mother.

For days she had mourned Josef's father, had *become* Josef's father by locking herself in their cabin. But with the announcement that the *St. Louis* was leaving Cuba—leaving without her husband—something in her flipped like a light switch. She cleaned herself up. Put on makeup. Did her hair. Dumped the contents of her suitcase on her bed, put on her favorite party dress, and went straight to the dance hall.

She'd been there ever since.

Josef's mother was dancing by herself when he went to find her. A paper moon and stars still hung from the ceiling, decorations left over from the party when they all thought they'd be leaving the ship for Cuba. Josef's mother saw him in the doorway and hurried over to him. She pulled Josef with her onto the dance floor.

"Dance with me, Josef," she said. She took his hands in hers and led him in a waltz. "We didn't pay for all those dance lessons for nothing."

The dance lessons had been a lifetime ago, back before Hitler. Back when his parents thought Josef would be going to dances as a teenager, not running from the Nazis.

"No," Josef said. He was too old to dance with his mother, too embarrassed. And there were more important things to think about right now. "What's going on, Mama? Why are you doing this? It's like you're happy Papa's gone."

She twirled in his arms. "Did I ever tell you why you're named Josef?" she asked.

"I— No."

"You're named after my older brother."

"I didn't know you had a brother."

Josef's mother danced like her life depended on it.

"Josef died in the Great War. My brother, Josef. At the Battle of the Somme, in France."

Josef didn't know what to say. His mother had never talked about her brother before. His *uncle*, he realized. He would have had an uncle.

"You can live life as a ghost, waiting for death to come, or you can *dance*," she told him. "Do you understand?"

"No," said Josef.

The song ended, and Josef's mother took his face in both her hands. "You look just like him," she said.

Josef didn't know what to say to that.

"I'm sorry for the interruption," the bandleader said, "but I've just been told there will be a special announcement in the A-deck social hall."

Josef's mother pouted because the music had stopped, but Josef knew it was worse than that. He couldn't have said why, but he was sure, deep down in the pit of his stomach, that this would only be bad news.

The worst.

His mother took his hand and squeezed it. "Come on," she said with a smile.

The social hall was already full when they got there. In the front of the room, under the giant portrait of Adolf Hitler, stood a committee of passengers who had been working with the captain on a solution to their problem. From the looks on their faces, they had not come up with one. When the head of the committee spoke, he confirmed all of Josef's worst fears.

"The United States has refused us. We are heading back to Europe."

The outburst was instantaneous. Cries, gasps, tears. Josef cursed—the first time he had ever cursed in front of his mother. She didn't react at all, and it made Josef feel both a little ashamed and a little bolder at the same time.

"You mean we're going back to Germany!" someone yelled.

"Not necessarily," a committee member said. "But we must stay calm."

Calm? Josef thought. Was the man insane?

"*Calm?* How can we stay calm?" a man asked out loud, echoing Josef's thoughts. The man's name was Pozner. Josef had seen him before on the ship. "A lot of us were in concentration camps," Pozner went on. His face was twisted in anger, and he spat his words. "We were released only on condition that we *leave* Germany immediately! For us to return means one thing—going back to those camps. That could be the future of every man, woman, and child on this ship!"

"We will not die. We won't return. We will not die," the crowd chanted.

Out of the corner of his eye, Josef saw Otto Schiendick lingering in the doorway. Schiendick grinned at the panic in the room, and Josef felt his blood begin to boil.

"Ladies and gentlemen," said the head of the committee, "the news is bad. That we all realize. But Europe is still many days away. That gives us, and all our friends, time to make new attempts to help us."

Josef's mother pulled him away. "Come, Josef. Somebody will think of something. Let's dance."

Josef didn't understand why his mother wasn't upset, why she suddenly didn't seem to care anymore. They were about to be taken back to Germany. *Back to their deaths.* Josef let his mother pull him to the door, then broke away. "No, Mama, I can't."

She smiled sadly at him and ducked past Otto Schiendick, who leaned against the doorframe.

"You should do as your mother says, boy," Schiendick said. "These are your last free days. Enjoy them. When you go back to Hamburg, nobody'll ever hear from you again."

Josef went back to the yelling passengers, his anger rising like the tide. There had to be something they could do. Something *he* could do.

The passenger who'd spoken up, Pozner, pulled him aside.

"You are Aaron Landau's son, Josef, yes? I'm sorry about your father," he said.

Josef was tired of hearing people's condolences. "Yes, thank you," he said, trying to move on.

The man grabbed his arm.

"You were among the children who went to the engine room and the bridge, yes?"

Josef frowned. What was this about?

"And you're a man now. You had your bar mitzvah that first Shabbos on the ship."

Josef stood taller, and the man let go of his arm.

"What of it?" Josef asked.

The man looked around to make sure no one else was listening.

"There's a group of us who are going to try to storm the bridge and take hostages," he whispered. "Force the captain to run the ship aground on the American coast."

Josef couldn't believe what he was hearing. He shook his head.

"It'll never work," Josef said. He'd seen how many crew there really were on this ship, and what a lot of them below decks really thought about Jews. They wouldn't go down without a fight, and they knew this ship better than any passenger.

Pozner shrugged. "What choice do we have? We can't go back. Your father knew that. That's why he did what he did. If we succeed, we're free. If we fail, at least the world will realize how desperate we are."

Josef looked to the floor. If they failed—*when* they failed—the captain would take the ship back to Germany, and then Pozner and the rest of the hijackers were sure to be sent to concentration camps.

"Why are you telling me this?" Josef asked.

"Because we need you with us," Pozner told him. "We need you to show us the way up to the bridge."

ISABEL

OFF THE COAST OF FLORIDA—1994

5 days from home

MIAMI.

It was like a dream. Like a glittering vision of heaven, as if Iván had opened the gates for them. Everyone stared, stunned, as though they had never thought they would ever actually see it. When the lights on the horizon became the faint shapes of buildings and roads and trees and they knew for sure they were looking at Miami, they cried and hugged each other again.

Isabel cried again for Iván, cried because he had been so close and hadn't made it. But her tears for him were mixed with relief that she would make it to the States, and that made her feel guilty and cry even harder. How could she be sad for Iván and happy for herself at the same time?

Crunk. Something bent and broke under Papi's foot, and the boat lurched. Water streamed in from a new crack in the hull, and suddenly all feelings of relief ended.

The boat was sinking.

"No!" Papi cried. He dove to try to shore up the hole, but there was nothing he could do. The weight of the ship and its passengers was pulling it apart at last. They all scrambled to the front of the boat, but the back end sank deeper and deeper under the weight of the heavy engine. The top of the hull was almost to the waterline at the back. When the two met, the ocean would flood in over the side and there would be no going back. They would drown.

Or end up like Iván.

Terror rose in Isabel like the water filling the boat. She couldn't drown. Couldn't disappear beneath the waves like Lita. Like Iván. No. *No!*

"Bail!" her grandfather cried.

Mami was lying in the prow of the boat, as far away from the rising water as possible, her breath coming harder and shorter now. But everyone else dove for their cups and jugs. It wasn't going to be enough, though. Isabel could see that. There was too much water. Too much weight.

The engine. Isabel suddenly remembered the way it had been working itself loose from its bolts. She threw herself at it, trying to knock it loose. When she couldn't wrench it free by hand she wedged herself in between it and the next bench, down in the water, and kicked at it with her feet.

"Chabela! Leave the engine alone and help us bail!" her father called. Isabel ignored him and kicked. If she could just get the engine free—

Another foot joined hers. Amara! She understood! Together they kicked at the engine until Isabel finally felt the wet wood around the bolts give. The engine tumbled to the bottom of the boat, covering up Fidel Castro's commandment to them.

Fight against the impossible and win, Isabel thought.

"One, two, three!" Amara said. Together she and Isabel rolled the motorcycle engine up the side and almost over—until Isabel slipped and it rolled back down with a splash into the water inside the boat.

"Again!" Amara told her. "One, two, *three!*"

Up, up, up they rolled the engine, and onto the top of the side, where it pushed the hull down below the surface of the sea. Water gushed in, and Isabel felt the boat sinking under her feet, pulling her with it down into the black depths, down with Iván and the sharks—

"No—wait!" Señor Castillo cried—

—and with one last good push Isabel and Amara tipped the engine over the side. It slipped into the water with a *slurp* and dropped like a stone, and the back end of the boat shot back up out of the water, the weight of the engine no longer dragging it down.

"What have you done?" Señor Castillo cried. "Now we'll never make it to shore!"

"We weren't going to make it if we sank!" Amara told him.

"We'll row," Lito said. "When we're close enough in, the tide will take us the rest of the way. Or we'll swim."

Swim? Isabel worried. *With the sharks?*

"Just bail, or we won't be doing anything!" Luis cried. "Bail!"

BWEEP-BWEEP!

An electronic siren made them all jump, and a red swirling light came on a few hundred meters to their left.

A person speaking English said something over a bullhorn. Isabel didn't understand. From the confused looks on everyone else's faces in the boat, they didn't, either. Then the same voice repeated the message in Spanish.

"Halt! This is the United States Coast Guard. You are in violation of US waters. Remain where you are and prepare to be boarded."

MAHMOUD

SERBIA TO HUNGARY—2015

15 to 16 days from home

MAHMOUD STARED AT THE GUN POINTED AT him. Was this real, or was he still asleep and having a nightmare?

The Serbian taxi driver waved the pistol at Mahmoud's family. "You pay three hundred euros!" he demanded.

This wasn't a dream. *It was real.* Mahmoud had been groggy just seconds before, but now he was wide-awake, his heart hammering. His eyes felt dry even though his shirt still clung to him with sleep-sweat, and he blinked rapidly as he looked at his parents. They were already awake, his father hugging the still-sleeping Waleed protectively.

"Don't shoot—please!" Mahmoud's father said. He threw one of his arms protectively across Mahmoud and his mother.

"Three hundred euros!" the taxi driver said.

Three hundred euros! That was more than twice what they had agreed to pay the driver!

"Please—" Dad begged.

"You not die, you pay three hundred!" the taxi driver yelled. His arm shook, and the gun danced between the two front seats. Mahmoud's mother closed her eyes and shrank away.

Mahmoud's father threw up his hand. "We'll pay! We'll pay!" They were being held at gunpoint in the middle of nowhere in a foreign country. What else could he do? Mahmoud's heart thundered in his chest as his father handed Waleed to Mom and fumbled with the money hidden inside his shirt under his belt. Mahmoud wanted to do something. To stop this man from threatening his family. But what could he do? Mahmoud was helpless, and that made him even madder.

With shaking hands, Mahmoud's father counted out three hundred euros and shoved them at the taxi driver. Why he didn't demand the whole stash of money, Mahmoud didn't understand.

"You get out. Get out!" the taxi driver said.

Mahmoud and his family didn't have to be told twice. They threw open the car doors and scrambled outside, and before the doors were even fully closed again the Volkswagen tore off down the dark road, its red taillights disappearing around a curve.

Mahmoud trembled with anger and fear, and his mother shook with quiet sobs. Mahmoud's father pulled them all into a hug.

"Well," Mahmoud's father said at last. "I'm definitely giving that driver a bad review on TripAdvisor."

Mahmoud's quivering legs gave out, and he sank to the ground. Tears streamed down his face, as though they'd been held back by a dam before and now the floodgates had suddenly been opened. *He'd had a gun pointed right at his face.* As long as he lived, Mahmoud would never forget that feeling of paralyzing terror, of powerlessness.

His mother sat down in the road with him and hugged him. Mahmoud's tears came harder, fueled by everything that had come before—the bombing of their house, the attack on their car, struggling to live in Izmir, the long hours in the sea, and of course, Hana. Mostly Hana.

"I'm so sorry, Mom," Mahmoud blubbered. "I'm so sorry I made you give Hana away."

His mother stroked Mahmoud's hair and shook her head. "No, my beautiful boy. If the boat hadn't come along when it did, if you hadn't convinced them to take her, she would have drowned. I couldn't keep us above water. You saved her. I know you did. She's out there somewhere. We just have to find her."

Mahmoud nodded into his mother's shoulder. "I'll find her again, Mom. I promise."

Mahmoud and his mother cried and held each other until Mahmoud remembered they weren't getting any closer to Hana or to Germany. He dragged a sleeve across his wet mouth and nose, and his mother kissed him on the forehead.

"That thief took us about halfway to Hungary, at least," Mahmoud's father said, looking at his phone. "We're on a back road about an hour's drive from the border. I think we're close to a bus stop. It means we have to walk again, though."

Mahmoud helped his mother stand, and his father hefted Waleed up higher on his shoulder.

Mahmoud's little brother had slept through the whole thing.

Mahmoud worried again about his brother. Air raids, shoot-outs, taxi holdups—nothing seemed to faze him anymore. Was he just keeping all his tears and screams pent up inside, or was he becoming so used to horrible things happening all around him that he didn't notice anymore? Didn't care? Would he come to life again when they got to Germany?

If they got to Germany?

They made it to the bus stop in time to catch the late bus to Horgoš, a Serbian city on the Hungarian border. Even more Syrian refugees had collected there, but no one was getting through. Not by road or rail, or even out in the countryside the way Mahmoud and his family had crossed into Macedonia and Serbia.

The Hungarians had a fence.

It wasn't finished yet, but even now, at night,

Hungarian soldiers were hard at work driving four-meter-tall metal poles into the ground along the border and stretching chain-link fencing between them. Once the fence was hung, another group came behind them and attached three tiers of razor-wire coil to it, to keep people from climbing over.

The Hungarians were closing their border.

"But we don't even *want* to go to Hungary," Mahmoud said. "We just want to get through to Austria."

"The Hungarians don't care, I guess," Dad said. "They don't want us in their country, whether we're coming or going."

A group of refugees suddenly rushed a part of the unfinished fence, trying to get through before it was done. "We're not terrorists!" someone cried. "We're refugees!"

"We just want to get through to Germany! They'll take us!" someone else cried.

There were more shouts and screams, and before Mahmoud knew what was happening he and his family were caught up in the press of refugees trying to get across the border. Mahmoud was jostled from every side. He clung to the back of his father's shirt, hanging on like Dad was a life preserver and they were going over a waterfall.

As frightening as the stampede was, Mahmoud was excited too—the refugees were finally *doing* something. They weren't just disappearing into their tent cities. They were standing up and saying, "Here we are! Look at us! Help us!"

But the Hungarian soldiers weren't interested in helping. As the refugees swarmed the border, soldiers in blue uniforms with red berets and red armbands hurried to stop them, firing tear gas canisters into the crowd. One of the canisters exploded near Mahmoud with a bang, and people screamed as a gray-white cloud erupted around them.

Mahmoud's eyes burned like someone had sprayed hot pepper juice in them, and mucus poured from his nose. He choked on the gas, and his lungs seized up. He couldn't breathe. It was like he was drowning on land. He fell to his knees, clutching at his chest and gasping uselessly for air.

I'm going to die, Mahmoud thought. *I'm going to die. I'm going to die. I'm going to die.*

JOSEF

22 days from home

JOSEF WATCHED HIS SISTER SPLASHING around happily in the swimming pool on A-deck. Other kids chased each other around the promenade. Watched movies. Played shuffleboard. For as much as he'd wanted to grow up, Josef wished now that he could join them. Be a little kid again, cheerfully oblivious to what was going on around him.

But he wasn't a kid anymore. He had responsibilities. Like keeping his sister and his mother safe. Papa had told him what the concentration camps were like. He couldn't let that happen to Ruthie and his mother.

"Are you ready?"

It was Pozner. He stood in the shadow of a smoke-stack, looking around nervously.

Josef nodded. He had agreed to help take over the ship. He had to do something, and this was the only thing he could do.

"What about Schiendick and his firemen?" Josef asked as they walked.

"We've got a distraction for them down on D-deck. But we have to move fast."

The rest of the group came together near the social hall. There were ten men, including Josef, and they all carried metal candlesticks and pieces of pipe. Some of the men were Papa's age, like Pozner, and some of them were in their twenties. Josef was by far the youngest.

Ten men, Josef thought. *A minyan.*

Ten Jews come together not to worship, but to mutiny.

Pozner put a small length of lead pipe in Josef's hand, and suddenly the weight of what Josef was about to do was very real.

"Lead on," Pozner said.

Josef took a deep breath. There was no turning back now. He led his fellow mutineers into the maze of crew corridors.

Just outside the bridge, in the chart room where all the maps were stored, they came across Ostermeyer, the first officer. He looked up from the map cabinet with surprise, but before he could do anything, Pozner and one of the other men grabbed him and pushed him through the door to the bridge. Josef was startled by how rough they were being with Ostermeyer, but he tried to swallow his fear. Taking over the ship wasn't going to be easy, and this was only the start.

There weren't as many people on the bridge as there had been when Josef visited—just one officer and three sailors.

The sailor at the ship's helm saw them first, and he let go of the steering wheel to dive for an alarm. One of the passengers got to him first, slamming into the helmsman and sending him tumbling to the floor. The mutineers quickly surrounded the other sailors, threatening them with their makeshift clubs.

And they had done it. Just like that, they had taken the bridge.

Josef's heart raced as he looked around, wondering what was next. Stretched out before them was the great green-blue Atlantic Ocean, and beyond that, still days away, Germany and the Nazis. Up on the little platform at the back of the room, the steering wheel teetered back and forth, and Josef wondered crazily if he should jump up there and turn the ship around himself.

"Send for the captain," Pozner told the first officer.

Warily, Ostermeyer went to the ship's intercom and summoned Captain Schroeder to the bridge.

As soon as Captain Schroeder stepped onto the bridge, he understood what was happening. He spun to leave, but Josef and one of the other men blocked his exit.

"Who's in charge here?" Captain Schroeder asked. "What do you mean by all this?"

Pozner stepped forward. "We mean to save our lives by taking over the ship," he said, "and sailing it to any other country but Germany."

Captain Schroeder put his hands behind his back and walked to the middle of the bridge. He looked out at the ocean, not Pozner.

"The other passengers will not support you, and my crew will overpower you," he said matter-of-factly. "All you are doing is laying yourselves open to a charge of piracy."

Pozner and the others looked around at each other nervously. Josef couldn't believe they were so easily losing their resolve.

"We'll hold you here as hostages!" Josef said. "They'll have to do as we say!"

Even Josef was surprised he'd spoken up. But his words seemed to put a little more steel back in the mutineers' resolve.

Captain Schroeder turned to look at Josef. "The crew will obey only me," he said calmly, "and I will give no order, no matter what you do, that will take my ship off its set course. And without that order, you can do nothing. What will you do, pilot the ship yourself?"

Josef blushed and stared at the ground, remembering his crazy urge to take the wheel when he didn't even know how it worked or where to go.

Captain Schroeder helped his fallen helmsman back to his feet and led him to the steering wheel. The man was still shaking from the attack, but he took the helm and straightened the ship on course.

"You have done enough already for me to prefer serious charges against you," Captain Schroeder said, still frustratingly even-keeled. "If I do, I can assure you that you will most certainly be taken back to Germany. And you know what that means."

Josef steamed. He *did* know what that meant, but did Captain Schroeder know? *Really* know? How many Germans really understood what was happening in the concentration camps? Josef knew, because his papa had told him. Had *shown* him when he jumped overboard and tried to kill himself.

Josef wasn't about to let his mother and sister end up in one of those camps.

"You would do that to us?" one of the men asked the captain.

"You are doing it to yourselves," Schroeder said. "Listen: I understand and sympathize with your desperation."

Pozner huffed. "You have no idea what we've been through. Any of us."

Captain Schroeder nodded. "No. You're right. But no matter what's been done to you, what you're doing now is a real criminal act. By law I should have you all thrown in the brig. But I'm willing to overlook all this if you leave the bridge right now and give me your word you will take no such further action."

Josef scanned the faces of his co-conspirators and saw only panic. Fear.

Surrender.

"No," Josef told them. *"No,"* he told Captain Schroeder. "My father told me what happened to him in those camps. I can't let that happen to my mother and my little sister. We can't go back to Germany!"

The first officer took that moment to try to pull free from the men holding him. There was a struggle. The other sailors moved to help him, and the other mutineers flinched, ready to fight.

"Ostermeyer! No!" Captain Schroeder commanded. "Cease and desist. That's an order."

The first officer froze, and Pozner froze too, the lead pipe in his hand still raised in threat.

Nobody moved.

The captain raised his hands. "I promise you men," he said quietly, his voice almost a whisper, "I promise you on my honor as a sea captain that I will do everything possible to land you in England. I will run the ship aground there if I must. But you must stand down and promise me no further trouble."

Pozner lowered his pipe. "Agreed," he said.

No. *No!* Josef wanted to argue, but everyone else agreed.

Josef threw his pipe to the ground and left without the other men. They were going back to Europe, and there was nothing he could do about it.

ISABEL

OFF THE COAST OF FLORIDA—1994

5 days from home

THEY WERE GOING BACK TO CUBA, AND THERE was nothing any of them could do about it.

So this was the last verse, Isabel thought. After everything they'd been through, after everything they'd lost, their climactic ending wasn't going to be climactic after all. Theirs wasn't a *son cubano*, with its triumphant finale; theirs was a fugue, a musical theme that was repeated again and again without resolution. Their coda was to be forever homeless, even when returned to their own home. Forever refugees in their own land.

The US Coast Guard had found them.

"Geraldo," Isabel's mother said, but Papi didn't answer. He sat frozen with all the others as a bright white searchlight clicked on. A ship motor—a real motor, attached to a real propeller—roared to life.

"Geraldo," Mami said again, "it's started."

"No," he said. "It's over. For all of us. They're going to take us to Guantanamo."

The searchlight swung around toward them.

"No," Mami said, hands on her bulging stomach, her voice tinged with alarm. "No, I mean, it's *started*. The baby's coming!"

The head of every single person in the little boat turned in surprise. Isabel sat down with a splash in the water. She didn't know what to think. How to feel. She'd been put through the wringer—the elation of leaving Cuba, the exhaustion of the storm, the horror of Iván's death, the relief at seeing the lights of Miami, the despair of running into the Coast Guard ship and knowing they would never get to *el norte*. And now her mother was having a baby. Isabel's baby brother. Isabel could only sit lifelessly and stare. She had nothing left to give.

"I'm not staying in that refugee camp at Guantanamo behind a barbed-wire fence," Lito said. "That's just trading one prison for another. I'll go back to Cuba. Back to my home. Castro said he won't punish anyone who tried to leave."

"Unless he's changed his mind again," Amara said.

It was Luis who saw the Coast Guard searchlight sweep past them on the water and point somewhere else.

"Maybe none of us will have to go to Guantanamo!" Luis said. "Look! They're not after us! The Coast Guard is after someone else!"

Isabel watched as the searchlight found another craft on the water a few hundred meters away. It was a raft full of refugees, just like them!

"More Cubans?" Amara asked.

"It doesn't matter!" Señor Castillo said. "Now's our chance! Paddle for shore! Quickly!"

Isabel spared her mother a look, then grabbed a water jug carved into a scoop and started rowing as hard as she could. So did Lito, Amara, and the Castillos.

"But be quiet," Lito whispered. "Sound carries a long way on the water."

"Ohhh!" Isabel's mother cried.

"Shhh, Teresa," Papi said, holding her hand. "Don't have the baby yet—wait until we get to Florida!"

Isabel's mother gritted her teeth and nodded, tears welling in her eyes.

The lights of Miami got closer, but they were still so far away. Isabel glanced behind her. In the darkness, she could pick out the lights of the Coast Guard ship, alongside another dark craft. Shadowy figures were moving back and forth between the two.

They were taking the refugees on board to send them back to Cuba.

"*Ohhh!*" Isabel's mother cried, her voice like a cannon shot in the quiet.

"*Row, row,*" Señor Castillo whispered.

They were so close! Isabel could see which hotel rooms had their lights on and which were off, could hear bongos beating out a rhythm over the water. A rhumba.

"The current's taking us north," Luis whispered. "We're going to miss it!"

"It doesn't matter—as long as we're standing on land, we're safe!" Lito said, his voice thin from exertion. "We just can't be caught on the water! *Row!*"

"*OHHHH!*" Isabel's mother screamed, her voice booming out across the water.

BWEEP-BWEEP!

The Coast Guard cutter made the same sound as before, and its searchlight lit up their little boat. They'd found them!

"*No!*" Isabel's mother sobbed. "No! I want to have my baby in *el norte!*"

"*ROW!*" Señor Castillo yelled, giving up entirely on being quiet.

Behind them, the Coast Guard cutter's motor roared to life.

Isabel churned at the water, bending her flimsy jug-paddle in her desperation. Tears streamed down her face, from sorrow or fear or exhaustion, she didn't know.

All she knew was that they were still too far from shore.

The Coast Guard ship was going to catch them before they reached Miami.

MAHMOUD

HUNGARY—2015

16 days from home

SIRENS. SOLDIERS SHOUTING THROUGH BULL-
horns. Screams. Explosions. Mahmoud was barely aware
of everything that was happening around him. He lay on
the ground, curled into a ball. Trying desperately to draw
a breath that would not come. His eyes felt like bees had
stung them, and his nose was a streaming cauldron of
burning chemicals. He made a choking, gurgling sound
that was somewhere between a shriek and a whimper.

After everything, he was going to die here, on the
border between Serbia and Hungary.

Rough hands pulled Mahmoud from the ground and
dragged him away, his sneakers twisting and scraping
on the dirt road. He still couldn't see a thing, couldn't
force his eyes to open, but he felt his chest beginning to
work again, the barest tendrils of air reaching his lungs.
He drank the air in greedily. Then he was thrown to the
ground, and someone pulled his hands behind him and
tied them together with a thin piece of plastic. It cinched
painfully tight, and Mahmoud was lifted again and
rolled onto the flat metal bed of a truck. He lay there,

still gasping for breath, the plastic zip tie cutting angrily into his wrists as more people were tossed into the truck beside him. Then Mahmoud heard the truck's doors slam and the engine start, and they were moving.

Mahmoud's breathing finally came back to something like normal, and he was able to sit up and open his bleary eyes. There were no windows in the van and it was dark, but Mahmoud was able to see the other nine men with him, all of them red-eyed and crying and coughing from the tear gas, and all of them handcuffed with zip ties. Including Mahmoud's father.

"Dad!" Mahmoud cried. He worked his way across the floor of the bouncing van on his knees and fell into his father. They put their heads together.

"Where are Mom and Waleed?" Mahmoud asked.

"I don't know. I lost them in the chaos," Dad said. His eyes were red-ringed and his face was wet from tears and snot. He looked terrible, and Mahmoud realized he must look just as bad.

Mahmoud thought the van would stop soon, but it drove on and on.

"Where do you think we're going?" Mahmoud asked.

"I don't know. I can't reach my phone," Dad said. "But we've been in this van for a long time. Maybe they're taking us to Austria!"

"No," one of the other men said. "They're taking us to prison."

Prison? For what? Mahmoud wondered. *We're just refugees! We haven't done anything wrong!*

The van stopped, and Mahmoud and the other refugees were unloaded into a building one of the soldiers called an "immigration detention center." But Mahmoud could tell it was really a prison. It was a long, single-story building with a barbed-wire fence surrounding it, guarded by Hungarian soldiers with automatic rifles.

A soldier cut the zip tie off Mahmoud's wrists. Mahmoud expected the relief to be instant, but instead his hands went from numb to on fire, like the tingling needles he felt in his leg after it fell asleep, times a thousand. He cried out in pain, hands shaking, as he and his father were hurried into a cell with cinder-block walls on three sides and metal bars on the front. Eight other men were pushed inside with them, and up and down the hall more prison cells were filling with refugees.

A soldier slammed the barred door shut, and it locked with an electronic bolt.

"We're not criminals!" one of the other men in the cell yelled at him.

"We didn't ask for civil war! We didn't want to leave our homes!" another man yelled.

"We're refugees!" Mahmoud yelled, unable to stay silent any longer. "We need help!"

The soldier ignored them and walked away. Mahmoud felt helpless all over again, and he kicked the bars in anger. There were similar cries of innocence and rage from the other cells, but soon they were overtaken by separated families trying to find each other without being able to see from cell to cell.

"Fatima? Waleed?" Mahmoud's father called, and Mahmoud yelled their names with him. But if his mother and brother were here, they didn't answer.

"We'll find them," Dad assured Mahmoud. But Mahmoud didn't understand how his father could be so sure. They hadn't found Hana, so what made him think they would find Mom and Waleed? What if they had lost them forever? Mahmoud was beside himself. This trip, this odyssey, was pulling his family apart, stripping them away like leaves from the trees in the fall. It was all he could do not to panic. His breath came quick and his heart hammered in his chest.

"I don't believe it. They took us almost all the way to Austria," Mahmoud's father said, checking his iPhone at last. "It's just another hour by car. We're outside a little town in the north of Hungary called Győr."

Almost all the way to Austria, Mahmoud thought. But instead of helping them along, the Hungarians had thrown them in prison.

Hours passed, and Mahmoud went from panic to frustration to despair. They sat in the cell without food or water, and only one metal toilet attached to the wall. All Mahmoud could think about was Mom and Waleed.

Were they in some Hungarian prison somewhere too, or had they been pushed back across the border into Serbia? How would he and Dad ever find them again? He slumped against the wall.

"I have to say, this is the worst hotel I've ever stayed in," Dad said. He was trying to joke again. His father was always joking. But Mahmoud didn't think that any of this was funny at all.

At last, soldiers with nightsticks came to their cell and told them in Arabic to line up to be processed.

"We don't want to be processed," Dad said. "We just want to get to Austria. Why not just take us all the way to the border? We never wanted to stay in Hungary anyway!"

A soldier whacked him in the back with his nightstick, and Mahmoud's father collapsed to the ground. "We don't want your filth here, either!" the guard yelled in Arabic. "You're all parasites!" He kicked Mahmoud's father in the back, and another soldier hit Mahmoud's father again and again with his stick.

"*No!*" Mahmoud cried. "No! Don't! Stop!" Mahmoud begged. He couldn't bear to see his father beaten. But what could he do?

"We'll do it! We'll be processed!" Mahmoud told the guards. That was all it took—to surrender. The guards stopped beating his father and ordered everyone to line up.

Mahmoud helped his father to his feet. Dad leaned

heavily against him, needing his son for support. Together they shuffled in line along the far side of the hallway, away from the cells. Men and women and children watched them with hopeful eyes as they passed, looking for their husbands and brothers and sons.

And then Mahmoud saw them—his mother and Waleed. They were in a cell with other women and children!

"Youssef! Mahmoud!" Mahmoud's mother cried.

"Fatima!" Mahmoud's father cried with relief, and he stepped toward her.

Whack! A soldier clubbed Mahmoud's father with his nightstick, and Dad went down again in a heap. Mahmoud and his mother cried out at the same time.

"Stay in line!" the soldier yelled.

Mahmoud's mother reached for them through the bars. "Youssef!" she cried.

"No, Mom—don't!" Mahmoud cried. A soldier clanged his nightstick against the metal bars, and she retreated inside her cell.

Mahmoud got his father up again and helped him into what the soldiers called the "processing center." There, clerks sat behind long tables, taking down information from the refugees. When Mahmoud and his father got to the front of their line, a man in a blue uniform asked them if they wanted to claim asylum in Hungary.

"Stay here? In Hungary? After you have beaten me? Locked my family up like common criminals?"

Mahmoud's father asked, fists clenched and shaking. Mahmoud still had to help him to stand. *"Are you joking? Why can't you just let us go on to Austria? Why do we need to be 'processed'? We don't want to stay here one second longer than we have to!"*

The policeman shrugged. "I'm just doing my job," he said.

Mahmoud's father slammed his hand flat on the table, making Mahmoud jump. "I wouldn't live in this awful country even if it was made of gold!"

The policeman filled in an answer on a form. "Then you will be sent back to Serbia," he said without looking up at them. "And if you return to Hungary, you will be arrested."

Mahmoud's father didn't speak again, not even to make a joke. Mahmoud answered the rest of the clerk's questions about their names and birthdates and places of birth, then helped his father back to their cell with the other inmates. Mahmoud's mother cried out for them again as they passed, but Mahmoud's father didn't acknowledge her, and Mahmoud didn't respond. He knew that would only bring down the wrath of the guards again.

Head down, hoodie up, eyes on the ground. Be unimportant. Blend in.

Disappear.

That was how you avoided the bullies.

JOSEF

36 days from home

THE *ST. LOUIS* WAS THROWING A PARTY. EVEN bigger than the one it had thrown the night before they'd reached Cuba. This one had the euphoria of more than nine hundred people who had been at death's door and were suddenly, miraculously, saved.

Belgium, Holland, France, and England had agreed to divide the refugees among them. None of the passengers were going back to Germany.

Josef's mother wasn't alone on the dance floor anymore. She was joined by dozens of couples, all dancing with giddy abandon. Josef had even taken a turn around the floor with her. Passengers sang songs and played the piano with the orchestra, and one man who knew magic tricks entertained Ruthie and the other little kids in the corner of the social hall. In another corner, Josef laughed as passengers took turns telling jokes. Most of the jokes were about taking holiday cruises to Cuba, but the best was when one of the passengers got up and read from the brochure that advertised the MS. *St. Louis*.

"'The *St. Louis* is a ship on which everyone travels

securely, and lives in comfort,'" he read. You could barely hear him over the hooting. "'There is everything one can wish for,'" the man read, gasping for breath, "'that makes life on board a pleasure! *We hope you'll want to travel on the* St. Louis *again and again!'*" Josef laughed so hard he cried. If he never saw the MS *St. Louis* again in his life, he would die happy.

The next morning, the ship docked at a pier in Antwerp, Belgium. Negotiations between Captain Schroeder and the four countries still took time, and it was a full day later when, under the grim portrait of Adolf Hitler, Josef and his family joined the other passengers in the social hall again to find out where they would be going.

Representatives from the four countries sat at a long table at the front of the hall, arguing over which passengers each would take. Every country wanted only the passengers with the best chances of getting accepted by America, so they could ship the refugees back out as quickly as possible.

Josef hoped they would get England, because it was the farthest away from Nazi Germany, safe across the English Channel. But when everything was settled, he and his family were assigned to France. They would be among the third group to disembark—after the Jewish refugees going to Belgium and the Netherlands were delivered, but before the last group sailed for Great Britain.

The first group left that afternoon.

Josef watched with most of the other passengers as the refugees going to Belgium disembarked. Josef didn't want to go to Belgium, but he was jealous nonetheless. Like everybody else, he was ready to get off this ship.

"Think of it—we traveled ten thousand miles on board the *St. Louis*," one of the men leaving for Belgium told the other passengers as he stepped onto the gangplank, "only to end up three hundred miles from where we started!"

The line got a laugh, but a sad one. Josef was all too aware of the long shadow cast by Nazi Germany, and so was everyone else. Still, as long as the Nazis stayed in Germany, they would all be safe. Wouldn't they?

The next day, 181 passengers disembarked in the city of Rotterdam, even though Holland wouldn't let the *St. Louis* dock at their pier, just like in Havana. The refugees were taken into town by another ship and escorted by police boats.

As they sailed on to France, Josef wandered the decks. The ship had a strange, empty feeling to it. Half the passengers were gone. The morning they arrived in Boulogne, France, the 288 passengers who were traveling on to England gathered on C-deck to say farewell to Josef and the others who were disembarking.

"We're due into England tomorrow," Josef heard one of them say. "June twenty-first. That's exactly forty days and forty nights in a boat. Now, where have I heard that story before?"

Josef smiled, remembering the story of Noah from the Torah. But he felt less like Noah and more like Moses, wandering in the desert for forty years before reaching the Promised Land. Was that France? The Promised Land, at last? Josef could only pray it was. He picked up his suitcase in one hand, took Ruthie's hand with his other, and led her and their mother down the ramp into Boulogne.

"You see?" Mama said. "I told you somebody would think of something. Now, stay close, and don't lose your coats."

At the bottom of the ramp, Josef watched as one of the other passengers got down on his hands and knees and kissed the ground. If he hadn't had his hands full, Josef might have done the same thing.

The secretary general of the French Refugee Assistance Committee officially welcomed them to France, and the porters on the docks moved quickly to carry the passengers' luggage for them, refusing any and all tips offered.

Maybe this was the Promised Land after all.

••

Josef and his mother and sister spent the night in a hotel in Boulogne, and then they were taken by train to Le Mans, where they were put up in a cheap lodging house. Days passed, and life went on. Josef's mother got work doing other people's laundry. Ruthie went to kindergarten at last, and Josef went to school for the first time in months—but because he couldn't speak French they put him in the first grade. Thirteen years old—a man!—and they put him in a classroom with seven-year-olds! It was humiliating. Josef promised himself he would learn to speak French over the summer, or die trying.

He never got the chance. Two months later, Germany invaded Poland, touching off a new world war.

....

Eight months after that, Germany invaded France, and Josef and his mother and sister were on the run again.

ISABEL

OFF THE COAST OF FLORIDA—1994

5 days from home

ISABEL'S MOTHER CRIED OUT. "IT'S COMING—it's coming!"

Isabel didn't know if she meant the baby, or the Coast Guard ship.

Or both.

"*Paddle!*" Amara cried.

Isabel paddled harder. She could see the shore, could see the beach umbrellas folded up for the night but still stuck in the sand. Strings of lights. Palm trees. More music—a salsa now. It was all so close!

But so was the Coast Guard ship. It bore down on them, its red light flashing, its powerful motor thrumming, water sluicing from its bow.

Isabel's heart hammered. It was going to catch them. They weren't going to make it!

Lito froze. "It's happening again," he said.

"What? What do you mean?" Isabel asked, panting.

"When I was a young man, I was a policeman," Lito said, his eyes wild. "There was a ship—a ship full of Jews, from Europe. And we sent them back. *I* sent them back!

Sent them back to die when we could so easily have taken them in! It was all politics, but they were *people*. Real people. I met them. I knew them by name."

"I don't understand," Isabel said. What did her grandfather's story have to do with anything?

"Paddle!" Isabel's father cried. The Coast Guard boat was almost on top of them.

"Don't you see?" Lito said. "The Jewish people on the ship were seeking asylum, just like us. They needed a place to hide from Hitler. From the Nazis. *Mañana*, we told them. We'll let you in *mañana*. But we never did." Lito was crying now, distraught. "We sent them back to Europe and Hitler and the Holocaust. Back to their deaths. How many of them died because we turned them away? Because I was just doing my job?"

Isabel didn't know what ship her grandfather was talking about, but she knew about the Holocaust from school. The millions of European Jews who had been murdered by the Nazis. And now her grandfather was saying that a ship full of Jewish refugees had come to Cuba when he was a young man? That he had helped to send them away?

Mañana. Suddenly, Isabel understood why her grandfather had been whispering that word over and over again for days. Why it haunted him.

When would the Jews be let into Cuba? *Mañana*.

When would their boat reach America? *Mañana*.

Mañana had never come for the Jewish people on that ship, Isabel realized. Would *mañana* never come for Isabel and her family either?

A calm came over Lito, as though he'd come to some sort of understanding, some decision. "I see it now, Chabela. All of it. The past, the present, the future. All my life, I kept waiting for things to get better. For the bright promise of *mañana*. But a funny thing happened while I was waiting for the world to change, Chabela: It didn't. Because I didn't change it. I'm not going to make the same mistake twice. Take care of your mother and baby brother for me."

"Lito, what are you—?"

"Don't stop rowing for shore!" Isabel's grandfather yelled to everyone else. He kissed Isabel on the cheek, surprising her, and then stood and jumped into the ocean.

"Lito!" Isabel cried. *"Lito!"*

"Papá!" Isabel's mother cried. "What's he doing?"

Isabel's grandfather popped back up a few meters away, his head appearing and disappearing in the waves.

"Lito!" Isabel cried.

"Help!" he cried, waving his arms at the Coast Guard ship while at the same time swimming away from it. "Help me!" he yelled.

"He jumped in to distract them!" Papi realized.

"They'll come for us first!" Señor Castillo said.

"No, he's in danger of drowning. They have to rescue him!" Amara cried. "This is our chance. Row—*row*!"

Tears rolled down Isabel's cheek where her grandfather had just kissed her good-bye. "Lito!" she cried again, reaching out for him over the waves.

"Don't worry about me, Chabela! If there's one thing I'm good at, it's treading water," Lito yelled back. "Now, row! *Mañana* is yours, my beautiful songbird. Go to Miami and be free!"

Isabel sobbed. She couldn't paddle. Couldn't row. Couldn't do anything but watch as the Coast Guard ship veered away from their little boat and steered toward her grandfather. Went to save him and send him to Guantanamo. Back to Cuba.

MAHMOUD

HUNGARY—2015

17 days from home

THEY CAME FOR MAHMOUD AND HIS FATHER again the next morning, this time to take them to a crowded refugee camp in a cold, muddy field surrounded by a wire fence. Multicolored camping tents stood among heaps of trash and discarded clothes, and Hungarian soldiers in blue uniforms and white surgical masks guarded the entrances and exits. There was only one real building, a windowless cinder-block warehouse filled with row after row of metal cots.

Mahmoud and his father found Mom and Waleed among the newly arrived refugees, and they shared a tearful reunion. They were each given a blanket and a bottle of water, and found cots for themselves. But when the food was delivered, they missed out. The Hungarian soldiers stood at one end of the room, tossing sandwiches into the crowd like zookeepers throwing food to the animals in a cage, and Mahmoud and his family didn't know enough to rush the tables to catch their lunch.

Mahmoud expected his father to laugh it off, but he wasn't joking anymore. Instead, Dad sat on his cot, his face and arms purple and bruised, staring off into space. Getting beaten and thrown into prison by the Hungarians had finally broken his spirit.

It scared Mahmoud. Of the four members of his family who were left, he was the only one who *wasn't* broken. His mother had snapped the moment she had handed her daughter away, and now she wandered the maze of mattresses and blankets in the detention center, asking people she had already asked if they had seen or heard of a baby named Hana.

Mahmoud's brother, Waleed, was broken too, but unlike his mother he had been broken piece by piece, over time, like someone snapping off little bites of a chocolate bar until there was nothing left. He lay listless on a foam mattress, disinterested in the card games or soccer games the other children were playing. Whatever childish joy he had once possessed had been sucked out until there was nothing left.

And now his father was dead inside too.

Mahmoud fumed. Why were they even here? Why did the Hungarians care if they were just passing through? Why had they taken them all the way to the Austrian border only to throw them in a detention center? It felt personal somehow. Like the whole country was conspiring to keep them from finding a real home. There were policemen with guns at every door. They were more like prisoners than refugees, and when they got out of here it would just be to go back to Serbia. Back to another country that didn't want them.

After everything they had been through, they weren't going to make it to Germany after all.

But Mahmoud wasn't ready to give up. He wanted life to be like it was before the war had come. They couldn't go back to Syria. Not now. Mahmoud knew that. But there was no reason they couldn't make a new life for themselves somewhere else. Start over. Be happy again. And Mahmoud wanted to do whatever it took to make that happen. Or at least try.

But making something happen meant drawing attention. Being visible. And being invisible was so much *easier*. It was useful too, like in Aleppo, or Serbia, or here in Hungary. But sometimes it was just as useful to be visible, like in Turkey and Greece. The reverse was true too, though: Being invisible had hurt them as much as being visible had.

Mahmoud frowned. And that was the real truth of it, wasn't it? Whether you were visible or invisible, it was all about how *other people* reacted to you. Good and bad things happened either way. If you were invisible, the bad people couldn't hurt you, that was true. But the good people couldn't help you, either. If you stayed invisible here, did everything you were supposed to and never made waves, you would disappear from the eyes and minds of all the good people out there who could help you get your life back.

It was better to be visible. To stand up. To stand out.

Mahmoud watched as a door on a nearby wall opened, and a group of men and women in light blue caps and vests with the letters *UN* written on them came inside, escorted by some important-looking Hungarian soldiers. Mahmoud knew that the UN was the United Nations— the same group that had been helping people at the Kilis refugee camp. The UN people carried clipboards and cell phones, and made notes and took pictures of the living conditions. This place was run by the Hungarians, not the UN, so Mahmoud guessed they were there to observe. To document the living conditions of the refugees.

Mahmoud decided right then and there he was going to make sure the observers saw him.

Mahmoud got up from his cot and walked to the door. All he had to do was push his way through, and he would be outside. But a Hungarian soldier stood guard next to it. She wore a blue uniform, a red cap, and a thick black leather belt that held a nightstick and had all kinds of compartments. Over her shoulder she carried a small automatic rifle on a strap, the barrel pointed at the gymnasium floor.

The guard ignored Mahmoud. He stood right in front of her, but she looked over him. Past him. Mahmoud was invisible as long as he did what he was supposed to do, and as long as he was invisible he was safe, and she was comfortable.

It was time for both of those things to change.

Mahmoud took a deep breath and pushed the door open. *Chuk-chunk.* The sound echoed loudly in the big room, and suddenly all the kids stopped playing and all the adults looked up from their mattresses at him. It was green outside, and sunny, and at first Mahmoud had to squint to see.

"Hey!" the guard cried. She saw him now, didn't she? The UN observers did too.

"Stop! No! Not allowed!" the soldier said in bad Arabic. She struggled to find the right words and said something in Hungarian that Mahmoud didn't understand. She started to raise her gun at him, and then she glanced up and saw the frowns on the faces of the UN observers.

Mahmoud stepped outside. The woman looked around at the other guards and called out to them, as if asking what to do. Mahmoud took another step, and another, and soon he was away from the building, walking toward the road.

Waleed ran through the door after him, followed by the rest of the children. The Hungarian guards yelled after them, but they didn't do anything to stop them.

"Mahmoud!" Waleed said, panting as he ran up alongside his brother. His eyes were bright and alive for the first time Mahmoud could remember. "Mahmoud! What are you doing?"

"I'm not staying in that place and waiting for them to send me back to Serbia. Come on," Mahmoud said. "We're walking to Austria."

JOSEF

VORNAY, FRANCE—1940

1 year, 1 month, and 10 days from home

GUNFIRE CRACKLED. AN ARTILLERY SHELL whistled overhead and hit with a shuddering *thoom* somewhere nearby. Ruthie cried, and Josef's mother hugged her close.

Josef peeked out the window. They were hiding in a tiny schoolhouse in a village called Vornay, somewhere south of Bourges, in France. The desks were all in perfect rows, and a long-forgotten assignment was still written on the chalkboard. It was dark outside, and the trees surrounding the schoolhouse made it even darker. That was good—it helped them hide. But it also made spotting German storm troopers harder.

Josef ducked back down inside, and his eyes fell on a map of Europe on the wall, the various countries shaded different colors. How wrong that map was now, just a year after he and his family had come to France as refugees. Germany had absorbed Austria, and conquered Poland and Czechoslovakia soon after. Holland and Belgium and Denmark had fallen to Hitler, and the Nazis occupied the northern half of France, including Paris. All of France had surrendered, but there were still pockets of Free France Forces resisting the Nazis throughout the countryside. The countryside where Josef and his family were now.

The only refugees from the *St. Louis* who were still safe, Josef realized, were the ones who had made it to Great Britain—though word was that Hitler was going to try to cross the English Channel any day now.

Josef and his mother and sister were trying to get to Switzerland in the hope that the Swiss would give them refuge. They'd made it this far traveling by night, sleeping in hay barns and out in fields under the stars, but the Nazis had finally caught up to them.

A light played across the window above him, and Josef chanced a look out again. Storm troopers! Headed toward the school!

"They're coming!" Josef told his mother. "We have to go!"

His mother picked up Ruthie and headed for the door, but Josef stopped her. There was only one door to the schoolhouse, and the Nazis would be using it. "No—this way!" he said.

Josef kept low as he scurried to the back wall of the classroom. There was a window there. They could climb out and run for the woods.

He tried the handle. It was stuck! Josef looked over his shoulder. He could see the beam of a flashlight in the hall outside, could hear the familiar German language of his homeland. They had to get out of there!

Josef threw his elbow against the glass, and it shattered. That brought a cry from the hallway. Josef knocked the rest of the glass out of the window in a panic. He felt his coat sleeve rip, felt something cold and sharp against his skin, but he didn't have time to think about that. He helped his mother out first, then handed Ruthie out to her through the window.

"Go, go!" Josef said before he was even all the way out the window, and his mother picked up Ruthie and ran for the darkness of the woods. None of them carried suitcases anymore—those had been left behind long ago—but they all still wore their coats, even though it was the height of summer. His mother had insisted.

The only thing any of them still carried was Bitsy, the little stuffed bunny Ruthie had never parted with. It was tucked tightly under Ruthie's arm.

Josef leaped down from the window, stumbled, got back up, and ran.

"There! There!" The beam of the flashlight found him. A pistol cracked, and a bullet blew the bark off a tree less than a meter away from him. Josef stumbled again in panic, righted himself, and kept running. Behind him, the storm troopers were yelling to each other, barking like dogs after a fox.

They were on the scent now, and wouldn't let up. Not until Josef and his family had been caught.

"There's a house up ahead!" his mother yelled over her shoulder. She swerved onto a small dirt lane, and Josef overtook her, beating her to the door. It was a little French country house, with two windows on either side of a double door in the middle and a chimney on one side.

Josef caught a faint whiff of smoke from the kitchen fire, and a curtain fluttered in the window.

Someone was inside!

Josef pounded on the door. He glanced over his shoulder. Three flashlight beams were bouncing up the lane toward them.

"*Help. Please, help us,*" Josef whispered frantically, still pounding.

No one answered, and no lights came on inside.

"Halt!" came a young man's voice.

Josef spun around. There were four German soldiers behind them. Three of them pointed flashlights at them, making Josef squint. He could still see well enough to know that two of them had rifles pointed at them. A third carried a pistol.

"Hands up. Put the child down," the storm trooper told Josef's mother. Ruthie tried to cling to her, but Mama did as she was told.

Dully, Josef realized that he'd lost some of the feeling in his right arm, and that his sleeve was coated in blood. He'd cut himself on the window glass. Badly. He squeezed the place where his arm had grazed the glass, and the pain was so blinding it almost made him pass out.

Ruthie had her head down, crying, but she raised her little bunny's right arm and said, "Heil Hitler!"

One of the soldiers laughed, and as he blinked the pain of his arm away, Josef thought maybe the soldiers would let them go. But one of them said, *"Papers."*

They were in trouble now for sure. Their papers had big letter *J*s stamped all over them. *J* for *Jew*.

"We—we don't have papers," Mama said.

One of the soldiers gestured at her, and a storm trooper with a rifle marched up to them and checked her coat pockets. He quickly found the papers she carried for her and Ruthie, and just as easily found Josef's papers on him.

The soldier brought them back to a man with a flash-light, and he unfolded them.

"Jews," the man said. "From Berlin! You've run a long way from home."

You have no idea, thought Josef.

"We're going to Switzerland," Ruthie said.

"Hush, Ruthie!" Josef hissed.

"Switzerland? Is that so? Well, I'm afraid we cannot allow that," the soldier said. "You will be taken to a con-centration camp, like the rest of the Jews."

Why? thought Josef. *Why bother hunting us down and taking us back to prison? If the Nazis want us Jews gone so badly, why don't they just let us keep going?*

One of the soldiers came toward them with a gun.

"No! Wait!" Josef's mother cried. "I have money. Reichsmarks. French francs." She fumbled inside her shirt, where she kept their money hidden. The bills fluttered to the ground.

The soldier moved the bills around with his feet and made a *tsk*ing sound. "It is not enough, I'm afraid."

Josef's heart sank.

At the chance she might really be able to buy their way out, Josef's mother became hysterical. "Wait! Wait! I have jewelry. Diamonds!" She yanked at Ruthie's coat, pulling it off over her head.

"Mama! What are you doing?" Ruthie cried.

Josef's mother ripped at the seams, the way his father had when he'd rent his garments for old Professor Weiler on the ship. From Ruthie's coat she pulled something that glittered in the light of the electric torches.

Earrings. The diamond earrings Josef's father had bought her for their anniversary one year. Josef remembered Papa giving them to her. Remembered the smile on Mama's face, the light in her eyes, both long gone now. Mama had sewn her earrings into the lining of Ruthie's coat! That was why she had never let Ruthie take it off.

The soldier took the earrings from Josef's mother

and examined them in the light. Josef held his breath. Maybe they would let his mother buy their way out of this after all.

"Everything I was able to keep," his mother said, "it's all yours. Just please—let us go."

"These are very nice," the soldier said. "But I think there is only enough here to buy freedom for one of your children."

"But—but that's all I have left," Mama said.

The soldier looked at her expectantly. At first Josef didn't understand what he wanted—they didn't have anything else to give him. But then the Nazi pulled Josef and Ruthie to him and turned them around for Mama to see, and that's when Josef understood. The Nazi didn't care how much money they had, how many jewels. It wasn't about that. He was playing with them. This was another game, like a cat playing with a mouse before he ate it.

I think there is only enough here to buy freedom for one of your children.

One of Rachel Landau's children would go free, and one of her children would go into the camps.

The Nazi soldier smiled at Josef's mother. "You choose."

ISABEL

5 days from home

HERE, IN THIS BOAT THAT HAD BEEN HER HOME for four days and four nights, Isabel's little brother was born.

Not right away. First had come her mother's frantic pushing, pushing, pushing to bring the baby into the world, while the rest of them paddled, paddled, paddled. All but Señora Castillo, who sat on the bench next to Mami, holding her hand and talking her through it. Behind them, the Coast Guard had finished picking up Isabel's grandfather and was headed their way, lights flashing.

Their little blue boat was close to the shore. The waves around them were breaking with white caps. Isabel could see people dancing on the beach. But they weren't close enough. Weren't going to make it. That's when Mami's cries had mixed with Amara's yell to "Swim for it!" and Luis and Amara hopped over the side, half swimming, half tumbling toward shore.

"No, wait!" Isabel cried. Her mother couldn't swim

for the beach. Not like this. They had to paddle in or her mother would never make it to the US.

Isabel and Papi and Señor Castillo rowed as hard as they could, but the Coast Guard ship was faster. It was going to catch them.

"Go!" Isabel's mother told her husband between pants. "If you're caught, they'll send you back."

"No," Papi said.

"*Go!*" Mami said again. "If I'm caught, they'll just— they'll just send me back to Cuba. Go, and take Isabel. You can—you can send money, like you always planned!"

"No!" Isabel cried, and amazingly, her father agreed.

"Never," he insisted. "I need you, Teresa. You and Isabel and little Mariano."

Isabel's mother sobbed at the name, and tears sprang to Isabel's eyes too. Like the boat, they had never settled on a name for the baby. Not until now. Naming the baby after Lito was the perfect way to remember him, no matter where they were.

"But they'll send us back," Mami sobbed.

"Then we'll go back," Papi said. "Together."

He put his forehead to his wife's temple and held her hand, taking Señora Castillo's place as Mami made her last push.

The Coast Guard ship bounced in the waves. It was almost on top of them.

"It's time!" Señor Castillo said. "We have to swim for it. Now!"

"No, please," Isabel begged, paddling helplessly against the tide, tears running down her face. They were so close. But Señor Castillo was already helping his wife over the side into the water.

They were abandoning ship.

Isabel's mother cried out louder than before, but Papi was with her. He would take care of her. All that mattered now was rowing. Rowing as hard as Isabel could. She was her mother's last hope.

"Take—take Isabel *with you*," she heard her mother say between pushes. But Isabel wasn't worried. She knew her father wouldn't listen. That he would never leave. Neither of them would. They were a family. They would be together. Forever.

But then suddenly arms were picking her up, lifting her over the side!

"Say good-bye to Fidel," Señor Castillo said. *He* was the one Mami had been talking to. He had come back, and *he* was the one lifting Isabel out of the boat and into the water!

"No—*no!*" Isabel cried.

"You saved my life once, now let me save yours!" Señor Castillo told her.

Isabel didn't listen. She kicked and screamed, trying to get free. She didn't want to go to the States if it meant leaving her parents—*her family*—behind. But Señor

Castillo was too strong. He tossed her in the water, and she sank under the waves in a tangle of arms and legs and bubbles before quickly hitting bottom.

Isabel found her footing and pushed herself back up out of the water. It was chest deep, and the waves that slid by her toward shore lifted her up and set her down again on the sand. Iván's cap had come off her head in her splashdown, and she snatched it up before it disappeared in the surf.

Then she grabbed the side of the boat to climb back in.

Señor Castillo's arm went around her waist and pulled her away.

"No!" Isabel cried. "I won't leave them!"

"Hush! We're not going anywhere," Señor Castillo said. "Help us pull the boat to shore!"

Isabel looked around, and for the first time she saw that Señora Castillo was still there, and Luis and Amara were there too. They all stood waist-deep in the water around the boat. They had come back!

They all found somewhere to grab on to the boat and pull, churning up the sand at their feet. Isabel sobbed with relief and grabbed hold. It was harder for her to pull when the waves kept lifting her, but the sight of the Coast Guard boat bearing down on them helped motivate her.

So did the cheering.

The other refugees on the Coast Guard ship were

hopping up and down and clapping and yelling encouragement, just like the crowd on the beach had when they'd left Havana. Isabel saw her grandfather running up and down the ship, waving them toward shore like a baseball player urging a home run ball around the foul pole. She laughed in spite of herself. The water was just below Isabel's waist. They were almost there!

The Coast Guard ship cut its engines to run up to them, and that's when Isabel heard her baby brother cry out for the first time.

The sound stunned Isabel and the others into stillness. It took her father a moment to cut the umbilical cord with his pocket knife. Then he stood up in the boat with something tiny and brown, staring down at it like he held the world's most incredible treasure in his arms. Isabel gaped. All this time, she had known her mother was having a baby. Isabel had seen plenty of babies before. They were cute, but nothing special. But this—this wasn't just a baby. *This was her brother.* She had never met him before this moment, but she loved him now with a deepness she had never felt before, not even toward Iván. This was Mariano, her little brother, and she suddenly wanted to do anything and everything she could to protect him.

Papi finally looked up from his newborn son. "Help me get Teresa out of the boat," he told the others.

The Coast Guard ship was almost alongside the boat, and the adults scrambled for the other side.

Papi bent down over the bow and held out her crying baby brother to Isabel. As if in a dream, Isabel's arms reached up and took him. He was covered with something slimy and gross and was screaming like somebody had slapped him, but he was the most amazing thing Isabel had ever seen.

Little Mariano.

Isabel hugged him protectively against the push and pull of the waves. He was so tiny! So light! What if she stumbled? What if she dropped him? How could her father have put something so new, so precious, in her arms? But then she understood—Isabel had to carry little Mariano to shore so her father and the others could carry Mami behind them.

"Go, Isabel," her father told her, and she went.

Isabel held the baby up high to keep him out of the waves that pushed them both to shore, stumbling as the water crashed against the back of her legs, but step by step she staggered up onto the beach.

Onto United States soil.

Isabel turned in the sand, soaking wet and exhausted, to look behind her.

Papi and Amara and the Castillos were on their feet, carrying Isabel's mother through the shallow water, where the Coast Guard boat couldn't go. The ship had cut its lights and was backing out to sea. On the rear of the boat, among the waving, cheering refugees, was Isabel's grandfather.

Isabel held the screaming baby up high for him to see, and Lito fell to his knees, hands clasped to his chest. Then the engines roared, the sea churned, and the Coast Guard ship disappeared out to sea.

The Castillo and Fernandez families helped each other up onto the sandy beach, and their wet feet became dry feet. Señor Castillo fell to his knees and kissed the ground.

They had made it to the States. To freedom.

Still in a dream, Isabel wobbled up the sand toward the flashing lights and thumping music and dancing people. She stepped into the light, and the music stopped and everyone turned to stare. Then suddenly people were running to help her and her family.

A tan young woman in a bikini dropped into the sand beside Isabel.

"Oh, my God, *chiquita*," she said in Spanish. "Did you just come off a boat? Are you Cuban?"

"Yes," Isabel said. She was trembling, but she clung to Mariano like she would never let him go. "I'm from Cuba," Isabel said, "but my little brother was born here. He's an American. And soon I will be too."

MAHMOUD

17 days from home

HUNGARIAN PEOPLE ON BOTH SIDES OF THE road stopped and stared as Mahmoud and the rest of the refugees marched down the middle of the highway. Men, women, children, they had all come pouring out of the detention center after Mahmoud, joined by the UN observers, and the police had done nothing to stop them.

The refugees stretched from one side of the northbound lane to the other, blocking cars from passing them. Packs of young Syrian men walked and laughed together. A Palestinian woman pushed a stroller with a sleeping girl in it. An Afghan family sang a song. The refugees wore jeans, and sneakers, and hoodies tied around their waists, and carried what little they still owned in backpacks and trash bags.

Mahmoud's father and mother found him and Waleed in the crowd.

"Mahmoud! What are you doing?" his father cried.

"We're walking to Austria!" Waleed said.

Dad showed them the map on his phone. "But it's a twelve-hour walk," he said.

"We can do it," Mahmoud said. "We've already come this far. We can go just a little farther."

Mahmoud's mother pulled him into a hug, and then Waleed, and soon their father had joined them. Refugees streamed around them, and when Mahmoud's mother let them all go she was smiling and crying at the same time.

Cars honked behind the marchers, trying to get past. More cars stopped on the other side of the highway to honk and cheer them on or boo them. A police van pulled up on the opposite side of the road, and through a loud-speaker a policeman told everyone in Arabic, "Stop, or you will be arrested!" But no one stopped, and no one was arrested.

Mahmoud and his family walked with the crowd for hours. Visible. Exposed. It was scary, but energizing too. They marched quietly, calmly, flashing peace signs at people who cheered them on from the sidelines. Police cars with spinning red lights paced them on the other side of the road, occasionally *bweep-bweeping* to warn some car away. News helicopters flew overhead, and a woman from the the *New York Times* worked her way through the crowd, asking Mahmoud questions and interviewing refugees.

See us, Mahmoud thought. *Hear us. Help us.*

Twelve hours had seemed like nothing when Mahmoud added up all the time they'd been walking since they'd left Aleppo. But this walk quickly seemed endless. They had no water and no food, and Mahmoud's stomach growled and his lips were dry. He felt like one of the zombies from his favorite video game. All he wanted to do was lie down and sleep, but Mahmoud knew they couldn't stop. If they stopped, the Hungarians would arrest them. They had to keep moving forward. Always forward. Even if it killed them.

Later that night, Mahmoud and his family at last reached the border of Austria. There was no fence, no wall, no border check post. Just a blue traffic sign by the side of the road with the words REPUBLIK OSTERREICH inside the EU's circle of gold stars, and above it a sign with the red-and-white flag of Austria.

The Hungarian police cars stopped following them as soon as they stepped across the border, and the refugees paused to hug each other and celebrate their escape. Mahmoud fell to his knees, fighting back tears of exhaustion and happiness. *They had made it.* It wasn't Germany, not yet, but Germany was just one country away. The refugees were still laughing and congratulating each other when the phone Mahmoud's father carried beeped an alarm. So did another phone, and another, until the whole crowd was a chorus of alarms.

It was time for the *Isha'a* prayer, the last prayer of the day.

Mahmoud's dad used an app called iSalam to find the exact direction they should face to pray to Mecca.

Mahmoud's family found a patch of grass all to themselves and the hundreds of other refugees did the same, and soon they were all bowing and praying together. It wasn't ideal—they were supposed to wash themselves and pray in a clean place—but it was more important to pray at the right time than in the right place.

As he recited the first chapter of the Qur'an, Mahmoud thought about the words. *Thee alone we worship, and thee alone we ask for help. Show us the straight path.* Their path had been anything but straight, but Allah had delivered them to this place. With his blessings, they might actually reach Germany.

When Mahmoud finished his prayers and opened his eyes, he saw a small group of Austrians had gathered at the edges of the praying refugees. There were police officers there too, and more cars with flashing lights. Mahmoud sagged. *They only see us when we do something they don't like,* he thought again. The refugees had stopped to get down on their knees and pray, and these people watching them didn't do that. Didn't understand. Now the refugees looked foreign again, alien. Like they didn't belong.

Mahmoud worried what the crowd might do when the Austrians told them they didn't want them. Their march through Hungary had been peaceful until now. Would this turn into another fight that would see them gassed and handcuffed and thrown into prison again?

"Welcome to Austria!" one of the Austrians said in heavily accented Arabic, and others yelled *"Willkommen!"* and applauded. Actually applauded them. Mahmoud looked around at Waleed, who was as stunned as Mahmoud. Was there some mistake? Did these people think they were something other than Syrian refugees?

Suddenly, they were surrounded by Austrians—men, women, and children all smiling and trying to shake their hands and give them things. A woman gave Mahmoud's mother a handful of clean clothes, and a man worried over his father's cuts and bruises. A boy about Mahmoud's age wearing a New York Yankees jersey handed him a plastic shopping bag with bread and cheese and fruit and a bottle of water in it. Mahmoud was so thankful he almost wept.

"Thank you," Mahmoud said in Arabic.

"Bitte," the boy said, which Mahmoud guessed was German for "You're welcome."

The Austrians, they learned, had seen their march on the television, and had come out to help them. It was like that all the way up the road to Nickelsdorf, the closest Austrian town with a train station. White, native-born Austrians and olive-skinned Arab Austrians who had recently immigrated to the country filled the overpasses, throwing bottles of water and food down to them—bread, fresh fruit, bags of chips. A man next to Mahmoud caught a whole grilled chicken wrapped in aluminum foil.

"We are with you! Go with God!" a woman shouted down to them in Arabic.

Mahmoud's heart lifted. They weren't invisible anymore, hidden away in the detention center. People were finally *seeing* them, and good people were helping them.

At last, Mahmoud and his family reached the Nickelsdorf train station, where they bought tickets to Vienna, the capital of Austria. They traveled overnight by train, and when they arrived in Vienna the next morning they bought tickets to Munich, a large city in Germany. In Munich, the response was the same as in Austria, only bigger. There were thousands of refugees at the train station, and moving among them were hundreds of regular German people offering bottles of water and cups of coffee and tea. One couple had brought a basket full of candy and were handing pieces out to children. Mahmoud and Waleed joined the happy mob of kids around them and each got a couple of candies, which they wolfed down. A more organized effort was unloading a truck full of fresh fruit, and another group was handing out diapers to anyone with babies.

Seeing the diapers reminded Mahmoud of Hana, and he looked up at his mother. He could tell she was thinking of his baby sister too. She put a hand to her mouth, and soon she was working her way through the crowd again, asking anyone and everyone if they had seen her daughter. But no one had seen or heard of a baby plucked from the water. If the people who had rescued her made it to safety, though, they were likely somewhere here in Germany. Mahmoud and his family would just have to keep looking.

An official-looking German man with a name tag that said Serhat—a Turkish name—approached Mahmoud's father with a clipboard in hand. "Are you and your family seeking asylum in Germany?" he asked in perfect Arabic.

Mahmoud held his breath. Was this it? Was the end of their long, horrible nightmare near? Could they finally stop moving, stop sleeping and praying in doorways and bus stations? In Germany, Mahmoud and his family could make new lives for themselves. Mahmoud could finally find a way to reconnect with Waleed. They could find Hana. Get his dad laughing and joking again. Find peace for his mom. After coming so far, after losing so much, it felt like Mahmoud and his family were almost to the Promised Land.

All they had to do was make room in their hearts for Germany the way it had made room for them, and accept this strange new place as their home.

"Yes," Mahmoud's father said, a smile slowly growing on his face. "A thousand times yes."

ISABEL

MIAMI, FLORIDA—1994

Home

THIS WAS THE CODA TO ISABEL'S SONG.

She stood with a trumpet in hand—a gift from Uncle Guillermo, Lito's brother. She wasn't on a sidewalk in Havana, but in a classroom in Miami. It was her second week of school, and the first day of band class. The day they auditioned for their places in the orchestra.

Isabel twiddled her fingers on the trumpet's keys. She couldn't believe she was standing here, in this classroom, less than a month after stumbling onto Miami Beach with her baby brother in her arms.

So much had changed, so quickly. After her mother and brother had been taken to the hospital and given a clean bill of health, Lito's brother, Guillermo, took them in until they found a little apartment of their own. His apartment was smaller than their house in Cuba, and not near the beach, but if Isabel never saw the ocean again that was fine by her.

Little Mariano was at home, getting fat and happy

along with the other babies Mami was paid to watch at the little in-house daycare she ran. Papi had gotten a job driving a taxi and was saving up for a car of their own. Señora Castillo planned to go back to school to become an American lawyer, and Señor Castillo was already talking to someone about getting a loan to open a restaurant. Luis got work in a little bodega, and Amara in a dress shop, and once Amara became a US citizen she planned to become a Miami police officer. They were going to be married in the winter.

And Isabel, she had started the sixth grade. It was hard because she didn't speak English yet. But there were other Cuban kids there, lots more Cuban kids, a few who had come to America by boat, like her, but more who had been born here, *Cubanoamericanos* who still spoke Spanish at home. Isabel had quickly made friends, girls and boys who were warm and welcoming, and she knew she would learn to speak English like her teachers soon enough. She was practicing by watching lots and lots of television. (At least that's what she told her parents.) She would learn, and in the meantime math and Spanish and art class all still made sense.

And so did music.

Señor Villanueva and the other students waited for her to play. Isabel had practiced for weeks for this moment. At first she couldn't decide what song to play, but then, while watching a baseball game with her father, she had figured it out.

Isabel adjusted Iván's *Industriales* baseball cap on her head, took a deep breath, and began to play "The Star-Spangled Banner," the national anthem of the United States. But she didn't play it like she'd heard it at baseball games on the television. She played it like a *son cubano*, offbeat with a *guajeo* melody.

Isabel played it salsa for Iván, lost at sea, and for Lito, back in Cuba. She played it salsa for her mother and her father, who had left their homeland, and for her little brother, Mariano, who would never know the streets of Havana the way she had. And Isabel played it salsa for herself, so she would never forget where she came from. Who she was.

Soon, Isabel had everyone in the room clapping along to the beat with her, but as she played she heard a different rhythm, a beat underneath the one everyone else was clapping to. Her foot tapped in time with the hidden cadence, and she realized with a thrill that she was finally hearing it.

She was finally counting *clave*.

Lito was wrong. She didn't have to be in Havana to hear it. To feel it. She had brought Cuba with her to Miami.

Isabel finished with a flourish, and Señor Villaneuva and the other students cheered. She thought she might cry for happiness, but she bit back her tears. She had done enough crying over Iván and Lito.

The song of her leaving Cuba to find a new home was over.

Today it was time to start a new song.

MAHMOUD

BERLIN, GERMANY—2015

Home

A GERMAN SONG MAHMOUD HAD NEVER heard before played on the radio of the van that took him and his family through the streets of Berlin. The capital of Germany was the biggest city he had ever seen, far bigger than Aleppo. It was filled with nightclubs and cafés and shops and monuments and statues and apartments and office buildings. Almost all the signs were in German, but here and there he saw a sign in Arabic advertising a clothing store or a restaurant or a market. Buildings lined the sidewalks like ten-story walls of brick and glass, and cars and bicycles and buses and trams rattled and honked and clanged by in the streets.

This strange, frightening, exciting place was to be Mahmoud's new home.

The German government had taken in Mahmoud and his family. For the past four weeks the four of them had lived in a school in Munich that had been turned into simple but clean housing for refugees. They had stayed there—free to come and go as they pleased—until a host family agreed to let them share their home while Mahmoud's parents got on their feet.

A host family here, on this street, in the capital of the country.

The van pulled up to the curb outside a little green house with white shutters and an A-frame roof. Flowers filled the window boxes like Mahmoud had seen in Austria, and two German cars were parked in the driveway. Across the street in a park, teenagers did tricks on skateboards.

Mahmoud's father slid open the side door for them to climb out, and Mahmoud and his mother and brother grabbed the backpacks filled with the clothes, toiletries, and bedrolls the German relief workers had given them. The relief worker who'd driven them led Mahmoud's mother and father and brother up the steps to the front door of the little house, but Mahmoud stood for a moment on the sidewalk, looking around at the neighborhood. Mahmoud knew from his history class back in Syria that Berlin had been all but destroyed by the end of World War II, reduced to a pile of rubble like Aleppo was now. Would it take another seventy years for Syria to return from the ashes the way Germany had? Would he ever see Aleppo again?

Cries of joy and welcome came from the porch, and Mahmoud followed his family up the steps. His mother was being hugged by an elderly German woman, and an elderly German man was shaking hands with his father. The German relief worker had to translate everything everyone said to each other. Mahmoud and his family didn't speak German yet, and the family apparently didn't speak any Arabic. The German family had at least managed a sign written in Arabic that said WELCOME HOME on it, even if the expression they had used was a bit formal. Mahmoud still appreciated the effort—it was better than he could do in German.

The man shaking hands with his father turned to Mahmoud and Waleed, and what Mahmoud saw surprised him. He was a *really* old man! He had wrinkly white skin and thin white hair that stuck out a bit on the sides, like he'd tried to comb it but it wouldn't stay put. When the relief worker had told them they'd be staying with a "German family," Mahmoud had imagined a family like his own, not like his grandparents.

"His name is Saul Rosenberg," the relief worker translated, "and he says welcome to your new home." As Mahmoud shook the old man's hand, he spotted a small, thin, ornate wooden box attached to the frame just outside the front door. Mahmoud recognized the symbol on the box—it was the Star of David! The same symbol on the flag of Israel. Mahmoud tried not to show his surprise. Not only was this couple old, they were Jewish! Back in the Middle East, Mahmoud knew, Jews and Muslims had been fighting each other for decades. This *was* a strange new world.

Herr Rosenberg's wife broke away from Mahmoud's mother and bent down to say hello. She was a wide woman, white-haired like her husband, with big round glasses and a gap-toothed, friendly smile. From the pockets of her frock she withdrew a little stuffed rabbit made of white corduroy and offered it to Waleed. His eyes lit up as he took it from her.

"Frau Rosenberg made it herself. She's a toy designer," the translator explained.

The old woman said something, directly to Mahmoud.

"She says she would have made one for you too," the translator said, "but she thought you might be too old for stuffed animals."

Mahmoud nodded. "She can make one for my little sister, though, when we find her," he told the relief worker. "We had to hand her off to another boat to save her when we were drowning in the Mediterranean Sea. It was my fault. I'm the one who told my mother to do it, and now I have to find her and bring her back."

Frau Rosenberg looked questioningly at the relief worker as he translated, and her bright smile faded. Waleed ran off to show his mother his new toy, and the old woman led Mahmoud into the hallway just inside the house, where family pictures hung on the wall.

"I was a refugee once, just like you," the old woman said through the interpreter, "and I lost my brother." She pointed to an old brown photograph in a picture frame, of a mother and father and two children: a boy about Mahmoud's age in glasses, and a little girl. The father and son wore suits and ties, and the mother wore a pretty dress with big buttons. The girl was dressed like a little sailor. "That's me there, the girl. That's my family. We left Germany on a ship in 1939, trying to get to Cuba. To escape the Nazis. I was very little then, and I'm very old now, and I don't remember too much about that time. But I do remember my father being very sick. And a cartoon about a cat. I remember that. And a very nice policeman who let me wear his hat.

"My father was the only one to make it to Cuba. He lived there for many years, long after the war, but I never saw him again. He died before we could find each other. The rest of us couldn't leave the ship with him. And no other country would take us. So they brought us back to Europe just in time for the war. Just in time to go on the run again.

"The Nazis caught us, and they gave my mother a choice—save me, or save my brother. Well, she couldn't choose. How could she? So my brother chose for her. His name was Josef." Mahmoud watched as she reached out and gently touched the boy in the photograph, leaving a smudge on the glass. "He was about your age,

I think. I don't remember much about him, but I do remember he always wanted to be a grown-up. 'I don't have time for games,' he would tell me. 'I'm a man now.' And when those soldiers said one of us could go free and the other would be taken to a concentration camp, Josef said, 'Take me.'

"My brother, just a boy, becoming a man at last."

She paused a moment, then took the picture down off the wall reverently, with both hands.

"They took my mother and my brother away from me that day, and left me alone there in the woods. I only survived because a kind old French lady took me in. She told the next Nazis who came knocking that I was family. When the war was over and I was old enough, I came back here, to Germany, to look for my mother and brother. I searched for them a long time, but they had died in the concentration camps. Both of them." The woman drew a breath. "I only have this picture of them because a cousin kept it, a cousin who was hidden away by a Christian family throughout the war. Here in Germany I met my husband, Saul. He had also survived the Holocaust. We stayed because he had family here. And we made a family of our own," Frau Rosenberg said. She spread her arms wide and turned in the little hallway, showing Mahmoud the dozens of pictures of her children and grandchildren and great-grandchildren. She put her hand to the old yellowed picture of her family again.

"They died so I could live. Do you understand? They died so all these people could live. All the grandchildren and nieces and nephews they never got to meet. But you'll get to meet them," she told Mahmoud. "You're still alive, and so is your little sister, somewhere. I know it. You saved her. And together we'll find her, yes? I promise. We'll find her and bring her home."

Mahmoud started to cry, and he turned away and tried to blink back his tears. The old Jewish woman put her arms around him and pulled him into a tight hug.

"Everything's going to be all right now," she whispered. "We'll help you."

"Ruthie, *komm hier*," Frau Rosenberg's husband called to her. Mahmoud didn't need the translator to tell him that Herr Rosenberg wanted them to join him in the living room.

Mahmoud dragged a sleeve across his wet eyes, and Frau Rosenberg tried to hang the picture back on the wall. Her old hands were too shaky, though, and Mahmoud took it from her and hung it back on its nail for her. His gaze lingered on the picture. He was filled with sadness for the boy his age. The boy who had died so Ruthie could live. But Mahmoud was also filled with gratitude. Josef had died so Ruthie could live, and one day welcome Mahmoud and his family into her house.

The old woman gave Mahmoud's arm a squeeze, and

she led him into the living room. Mom and Dad were there, and Waleed and Herr Rosenberg, and the space was bright and alive and filled with books and pictures of family and the smell of good food.

It felt like a home.

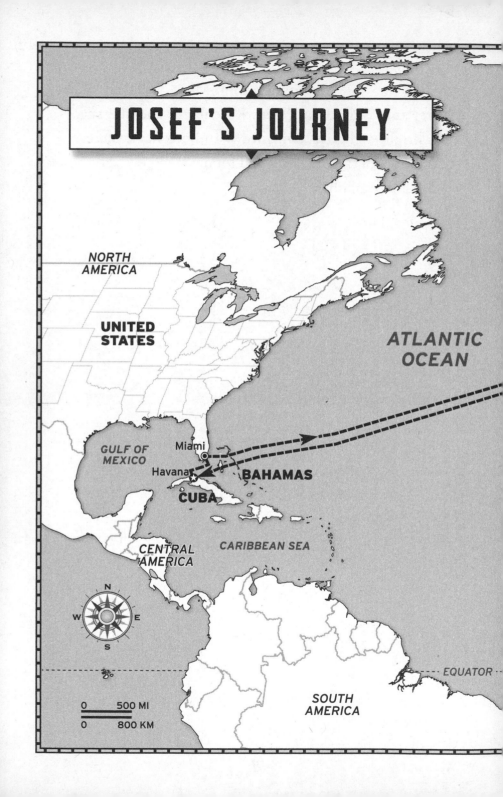

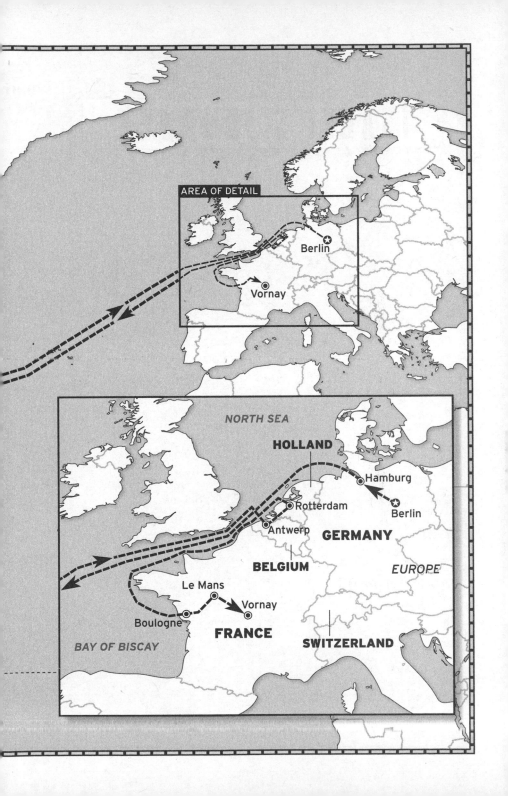

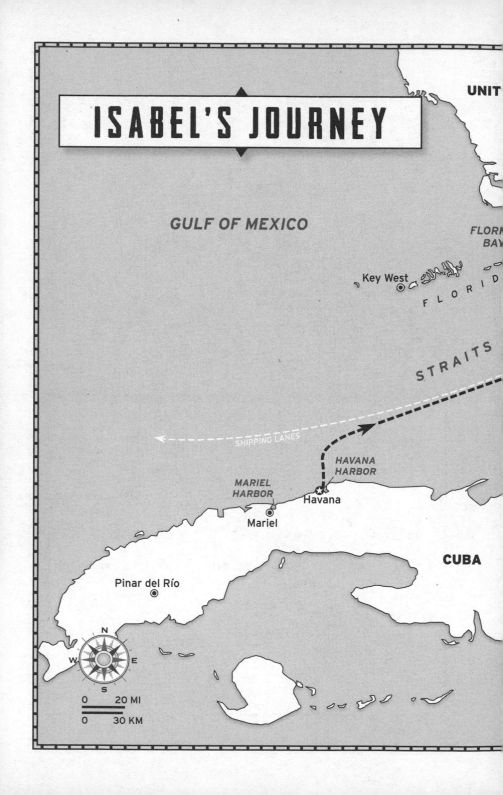

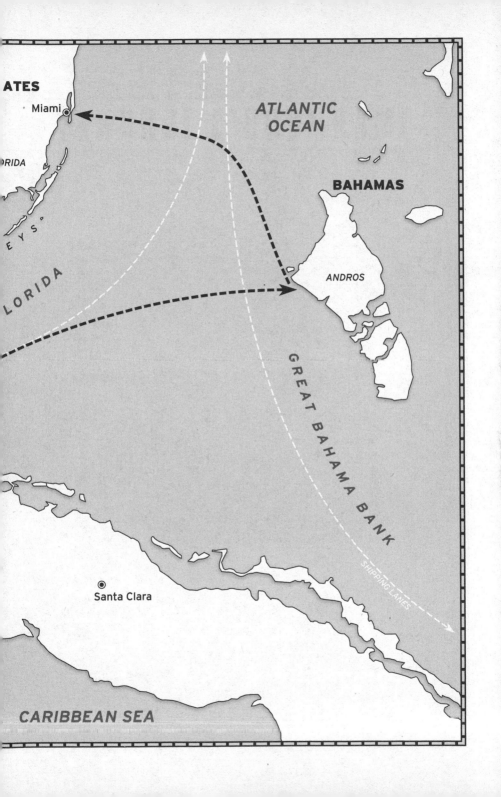

MAHMOUD'S JOURNEY

NORTH SEA

BALTIC SEA

ATLANTIC OCEAN

GERMANY
Berlin ✪

Munich

Vienna

AUSTRIA

HUNGARY

Horgoš

EUROPE

ADRIATIC SEA

MEDIT

AFRICA

0   200 MI
0   300 KM

AUTHOR'S NOTE

Josef, Isabel, and Mahmoud are all fictional characters, but their tales are based on true stories.

JOSEF

The MS *St. Louis* was a real ship that set sail from Nazi Germany in 1939 with 937 passengers on board, almost all of them Jewish refugees trying to escape the Nazis. The Jews expected to be admitted to Cuba—some of them to live there permanently, some to stay only temporarily until they were admitted to the United States or Canada. But when they arrived, the Jews were told they would not be allowed to land. The reason was political: The Cuban official who had issued the refugees' entrance visas had fallen out of favor with Cuba's president at the time, Federico Brú. To embarrass the official, Brú retroactively canceled the Jews' visas. Nazi agents in Havana helped keep the Jews out too, by spreading propaganda that turned the Cuban people against the refugees. The Germans didn't want the Jews in their country, but they also loved seeing the refugees turned away by other countries. To the Nazis, it was proof that everybody else in the world secretly agreed with the way the Germans were treating the Jews.

Captain Gustav Schroeder was real, and he is remembered today for his kindness toward his Jewish passengers, and his efforts to find refuge for them. Otto Schiendick was real too, and was not only the Nazi Party representative on the ship, but also something of a spy, carrying secret messages back and forth between Germany and the Nazi agents working in Havana. Evelyne and Renata were the real names of two sisters whose mother chose to remain in Nazi Germany. Their father, Dr. Max Aber, was able to get them off the *St. Louis* in Havana because he had gone ahead of his family to Cuba and had strong connections with the local authorities. None of the other passengers were so lucky.

Josef's father, Aaron Landau, was inspired by two different men who really sailed on the MS *St. Louis*— Aaron Pozner and Max Loewe. Aaron Pozner, a Hebrew teacher, had been taken from his home in Germany during *Kristallnacht*, the Night of Broken Glass, and sent to Dachau, where he was beaten and humiliated, and where he witnessed incredible atrocities. It was Aaron Pozner who was released from Dachau after six months and told to leave the country within fourteen days, and it was Pozner who was the victim of Otto Schiendick and his firemen while on board. Pozner was also one of the mutineers who tried to take control of the ship when the *St. Louis* was turned away from the United States and Canada.

Max Loewe was a Jewish lawyer who, like my fictional Aaron Landau, had been forbidden by the Nazis to practice law. Loewe had continued to give legal advice to sympathetic German lawyers who paid him "under the table," but the Gestapo eventually caught on and Loewe was forced into hiding. He joined his wife and two children—a boy and a girl—just in time for them to all board the MS *St. Louis* and make their escape. But like Aaron Landau, Max Loewe was a broken man when he rejoined his family. It was Loewe who tried to commit suicide by jumping off the *St. Louis* while it lay at anchor outside Havana Harbor.

The English ship *Orduña* and the French ship *Flandre*, both carrying Jewish refugees bound for Cuba, were initially kept out of Havana Harbor just like the *St. Louis*. But both ships, to the frustration of the passengers on the *St. Louis*, were eventually allowed to dock and disembark their own refugees. But what the passengers on the *St. Louis* didn't know was that the only people allowed off the *Orduña* and the *Flandre* were passengers with Cuban passports. The rest, mostly Jews with now-invalid entry visas like the Jewish passengers on the *St. Louis*, had been turned away to find another country that would take them.

The Jewish refugees from the *St. Louis* who were allowed to enter the United Kingdom were the lucky ones—they escaped the Holocaust. Of the 620 Jewish refugees who returned to continental Europe, the United States Holocaust Memorial Museum estimates that 254 of them were among the six million European Jews who died in the Holocaust. "Most of these people were murdered in the killing centers of Auschwitz and Sobibór," says the museum. "The rest died in internment camps, in hiding, or attempting to evade the Nazis." Ruthie, who survived, would be among the approximately 100,000 Jews who live in Germany today, down from around 500,000 Jewish German citizens before World War II. Many more Jews who survived the Holocaust chose not to return to their European home countries, settling instead in the United States and the newly formed country of Israel.

The tragedy of the MS *St. Louis* is now famous, and has been the subject of many books, plays, films, and even an opera.

ISABEL

In 1994, thanks in large part to the recent collapse of the Soviet Union and the ongoing US embargo against trade with Cuba, hungry citizens of Havana rioted up and down the Malecón. In response, Cuban president Fidel

Castro announced that anyone who wanted to leave Cuba could do so without being thrown in jail, which was the usual punishment for trying to escape. It was a strategy Castro had employed before—when protests threatened to overwhelm his security forces and overthrow his government, Castro would allow people to leave any way they could, usually on homemade boats and rafts. When all the people angry enough to fight him had fled to America, the protests would stop and things would settle back down again. In the five weeks in 1994 when Castro allowed unhappy citizens to leave Cuba, an estimated thirty-five thousand people fled the island for the United States—almost ten times the number of people who had tried to escape to America in all of 1993.

Many Americans objected to the sudden influx of Cuban refugees, particularly because, at the time, Cubans enjoyed a unique path to becoming American citizens that immigrants from other countries did not. Others recognized Castro's ploy for what it was, and argued that the protestors should remain in Cuba in the hope that their riots would finally overthrow the Cuban government. US president Bill Clinton had a big decision to make: Let the Cuban refugees in, or send American warships out to turn them away? While he tried to figure out what to do, Clinton ordered any Cuban refugees caught at sea to be sent to a refugee camp at the US military base at Guantanamo Bay in Cuba. From there, Cuban refugees could choose to return to Cuba, or wait and see if the United States or another country would take them. A few months later in 1995, Clinton announced that the Cuban refugees at Guantanamo would be allowed entry to the United States, but from that point on any Cuban refugees caught at sea would be sent back to Cuba, not taken the rest of the way to Florida or sent to Guantanamo. Any Cuban refugees who made it to America could stay. Isabel and her family refer to this new attitude toward Cuban refugees as "Wet Foot, Dry Foot," though that name wasn't commonly used to describe the situation until the policy was officially made law in 1995. I've also used artistic license to combine the riot that prompts Isabel's family to leave with the US decision to detain Cuban refugees caught at sea. Those two events actually happened a month apart, but I have brought them together here to make my story tighter and more dramatic.

Despite the threat of imprisonment in Cuba and the dangers of sea swells, storms, drowning, sharks, dehydration, and starvation, increasing numbers of Cubans still try to cross the ninety miles of ocean between Havana and Florida each year. According to the Pew Research Center, 43,635 Cuban refugees entered the United States in 2015, and that number was surpassed in 2016 by October. In recent years, many Cuban refugees have skipped America's "Wet Foot, Dry Foot" policy altogether and chosen to fly or sail from Cuba to Mexico or Ecuador, and then walk north into America—an alternate route observers nicknamed "Dusty Foot." But as more and more countries south of the United States close their borders, more Cubans are heading back into the Straits of Florida on homemade boats and rafts. Again, according to the Pew Research Center, 9,999 Cuban refugees entered the United States through the Miami sector in 2015. That same year, the US Coast Guard apprehended 3,505 Cubans at sea. And there is no way of telling how many Cubans die in the attempt each year. In 1994, the year of Isabel's story, an estimated three out of every five Cuban refugees who attempted the journey died at sea.

In 2014, President Barack Obama and Cuban president Raúl Castro, Fidel's brother, announced that Cuba and the United States were reestablishing relations with each other, and in 2015 President Obama announced that formal diplomatic relations between the two countries would resume, including the reopening of their respective embassies in Havana and Washington, DC. As a part of the normalization of relations, the US government relaxed travel restrictions that had barred most Americans from visiting Cuba, and in August 2016 the first commercial flight from America to Cuba since 1962 landed in Havana. On January 12, 2017, in one of his last acts in office, President Obama announced the immediate end of the "Wet Foot, Dry Foot" policy. How these changes to US Cuban relations—and the death of Fidel

Castro on November 25, 2016—will affect the future of Cuba and its people remains to be seen.

MAHMOUD

As I write this, Syria is in its sixth year of one of the most brutal and vicious civil wars in history. The city of Aleppo, Mahmoud's hometown, lies in ruins today because it is home to a large group of rebels who oppose Bashir al-Assad's war on his own people. The city is under siege, pounded daily by Russian air attacks and Syrian army artillery. If they didn't leave by 2015, when Mahmoud and his family went on the run, the remaining citizens of Aleppo are now trapped in a war zone. According to the United Nations, more than 470,000 people have been killed since the conflict began in 2011. That's roughly equal to the entire population of Atlanta, Georgia. And more people are dying every day. In just one week of fighting in September 2016, the United Nations reported the deaths of ninety-six children. That's like an entire grade level of children dying every week. In a major offensive in December 2016, the Syrian army conquered an estimated 95 percent of Aleppo's rebel-held territory, spurring a new humanitarian crisis as hundreds of thousands more civilians were caught in the crossfire. Fighting in Aleppo continues today.

And those who survive often have nowhere to live. The *Guardian* newspaper estimates 40 percent of the city's infrastructure has been damaged or destroyed. Whole neighborhoods lie in ruins. Markets, restaurants, shops, apartment buildings—nothing has been spared. Almost no one goes to work anymore, or to school. Every tree in the city has been cut down for firewood, and when they ran out of trees, the Syrians had to burn school desks and chairs to heat their homes. Hospitals, if they still stand, have no medicine or equipment to treat patients.

It's no wonder then that more than 10 million Syrians have been displaced from their homes. Of those 10 million, the United Nations estimates that 4.8 million Syrians have left their country as refugees. That's more people than live in the entire state of Connecticut, or Kentucky, or Oregon. And more are fleeing every day, leaving behind everything they owned and everything they knew, just to escape the war and bloodshed. Just to survive.

But where do they go? The United Nations reports that Turkey is already home to more than 2.7 million registered Syrian refugees, many of them in refugee camps like the one in Kilis that Mahmoud and his family pass through. Other countries in the region, like Lebanon, Jordan, and Iraq, have all received huge numbers of Syrian refugees, but their resources are stretched to the limit, and public sentiment in many countries has turned against the influx of immigrants. Millions more refugees try to reach Europe, where countries like Germany and Sweden and Hungary have accepted hundreds of thousands of refugees. But getting there is difficult, and often deadly. According to the International Organization for Migration, more than 3,770 refugees died trying to cross the Mediterranean by boat in 2015. And once they reach the European Union, refugees still face persecution and imprisonment from countries that don't want to deal with them or don't have the resources to handle the huge influx of people. Hungary was the first country to build a fence to keep out Middle Eastern refugees walking north, and more and more countries are building walls. Even Austria, which has been incredibly welcoming to refugees, began building a fence in 2016.

According to the Migration Policy Institute, between October 1, 2011, and December 31, 2016, the United States admitted just 18,007 Syrian refugees—less than one half of 1 percent of all Syrian refugees who have resettled in other countries. On January 27, 2017, President Donald Trump signed Executive Order 13769, indefinitely suspending the entry of all Syrian refugees into the United States. The Executive Order was titled, "Protecting the Nation from Foreign Terrorist Entry into the United States," despite a report by the Cato Institute that says that no person accepted to the United States as a refugee, Syrian or otherwise, has been implicated in a major fatal terrorist attack since the Refugee Act of 1980 established the current system for accepting refugees into the United States. The states of Washington and Minnesota have challenged the executive order in court, but as I write this, the outcome—and the future of Syrian refugees in the United States—remains unclear.

The experiences of Mahmoud and his family are based on things that really happened to different Syrian refugees. In 2015, a group of about three hundred refugees who had been detained at a Danish school/refugee camp finally had enough of being held for no reason. As one, they marched up the highway toward Sweden, forming a human chain that stopped traffic. And cheering bystanders really did stand on overpasses and toss down food and water. A similar protest took place in Hungary a week before, when thousands of refugees marched from Budapest to the border of Austria. I have combined the two events in this book.

Mahmoud and his mother and father are composites of different refugees I read about. But Waleed is specifically based on a now-famous photograph of a five-year-old boy from Aleppo named Omran Daqneesh. In the picture, Omran sits alone in the back of an ambulance after surviving an airstrike, his feet bare, his face bloody, his body covered in dirt and gray ash. He's not crying. He's not angry. Maybe he's in shock—or maybe he's just used to this. This is the only life he knows, because his country has been at war as long as he's been alive. He is a member of what the United Nations warns will become a "lost generation" of Syrian children if nothing is done to help them now.

WHAT YOU CAN DO

Beverly Crawford, a professor emerita at the University of California, Berkeley, has written that refugees live three lives. The first is spent escaping the horrors of whatever has driven them from their homes—like the persecution and murder of Jews in Josef's Nazi Germany, the starvation and civil rights abuses of Isabel's Cuba, or the devastating civil war of Mahmoud's Syria. Those who are lucky enough to escape their homes begin a second, equally dangerous life in their search for refuge, trying to survive ocean crossings and border patrols and criminals looking to profit off them. Most migrants *don't* end up in refugee camps, and their days are spent seeking shelter, food, water, and warmth. But even in the camps, refugees are exposed to illness and disease, and often have to exist on less than fifty cents a day.

If refugees manage to escape their home and then survive the journey to freedom, they begin a third life, starting over in a new country, one where they often do not speak the language or practice the same religion as their hosts. Professional degrees granted in one country are often not honored in another, so refugees who were doctors or lawyers or teachers where they came from become store clerks and taxi drivers and janitors. Families that once had comfortable homes and cars and money set aside for college and retirement have to start all over, living with other refugees in government housing or with host families in foreign cities as they rebuild their lives.

You can help refugee families by donating money to one of the many groups who help refugees through every phase of their three lives. Some nonprofit organizations have very specific missions, like rescuing people fleeing the Middle East by boat or battling disease in refugee camps. Two of my favorite organizations work specifically with refugee children around the world. The first is UNICEF, the United Nations International Children's Emergency Fund, which is working to keep Syrian children from becoming a "lost generation" by providing life-saving medical services, food, water, sanitation, and education both within Syria and wherever Syrian refugees have fled. The second is Save the Children, which works with a number of corporate partners and individual donors here in the United States to offer emergency relief to children whenever and wherever it's needed around the world, including a special campaign for Syrian children.

Both UNICEF and Save the Children spend 90 percent of every dollar they raise on services and resources that directly help children. Donations to either of these terrific organizations can be earmarked for specific regions and conflicts, or be used to help refugee children worldwide. Learn more at www.unicefusa.org and www.savethechildren.org.

....

I will be donating a portion of my proceeds from the sale of this book to UNICEF, to support their relief efforts with refugee children around the world.

Alan Gratz
North Carolina, USA
2017

ACKNOWLEDGMENTS

Many thanks to my terrific editor, Aimee Friedman, for all her hard work and devotion to this book, and to editorial director David Levithan for his faith and support. I'm also indebted to the experts who read drafts of *Refugee* and helped me better understand the people, places, and cultures I was writing about, including Sarabrynn Hudgins, José Moya, Hossein Kamaly, Christina Diaz Gonzalez, and Gabriel Rumbaut. Any mistakes that remain are my own. Thank you to copy editor Bonnie Cutler and proofreader Erica Ferguson for making me look good. Thank you to designer Nina Goffi for the stunning cover and interior layout, and to map artist Jim McMahon. And once again I owe a huge debt of gratitude to everyone who works behind the scenes at Scholastic to help make my books a success: president Ellie Berger; Jennifer Abbots and Tracy van Straaten in Publicity; Lori Benton, Michelle Campbell, Hillary Doyle, Rachel Feld, Paul Gagne, Leslie Garych, Antonio Gonzalez, Jana Haussmann, Emily Heddleson, Jazan Higgins, Robin Hoffman, Meghann Lucy, Joanne Mojica, Kerianne Okie, Stephanie Peitz, John Pels, Christine Reedy, Lizette Serrano, Mindy Stockfield, Michael Strouse, Olivia

Valcarce, Ann Marie Wong, and so many others. And to Alan Smagler and the entire Sales team, and all the sales reps and Fairs and Clubs reps across the country who work so hard to tell the world about my books. Special thanks to my friends and fellow writers at Bat Cave for their critiques, and to my great friend Bob who is always so encouraging and supportive. Thank you to my literary agent, Holly Root at Waxman Leavell, and to my publicists and right-hand women Lauren Harr and Caroline Christopoulos at Gold Leaf Literary—I couldn't have done it without you. (Seriously.) Thanks again to all the teachers, librarians, and booksellers out there who continue to share my books with young readers—you're rock stars! And last but not least, much love and thanks to my wife, Wendi, and my daughter, Jo. You are my refuge in the storm.

Don't miss Alan Gratz's next novel: *Grenade*

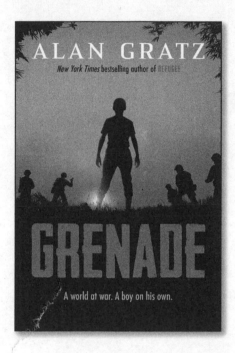

It's 1945, and the world is in the grip of war.

Hideki lives with his family on the island of Okinawa, near Japan. When WWII crashes onto his shores, Hideki is drafted into the Blood and Iron Student Corps to fight for the Japanese army. He is handed a grenade and a set of instructions: *Don't come back until you've killed an American soldier.*

Ray, a young American Marine, has just landed on Okinawa. This is Ray's first-ever battle, and he doesn't know *what* to expect—or if he'll make it out alive. He just knows that the enemy is everywhere.

Hideki and Ray each fight their way across the island, surviving heart-pounding clashes and dangerous attacks. But when the two of them collide in the middle of the battle, the choices they make in that single instant will change *everything*.

Alan Gratz returns with this high-octane story of how fear and war tear us apart—but how hope and redemption tie us together.

ABOUT THE AUTHOR

Alan Gratz is the acclaimed author of several books for young readers, including *Projekt 1065*, which received starred reviews from *Kirkus* and *School Library Journal*; *Prisoner B-3087*, which was named to YALSA's 2014 Best Fiction for Young Adults list; and *Code of Honor*, a YALSA 2016 Quick Pick. Alan lives in North Carolina with his wife and daughter. Look for him online at alangratz.com.